ALIEN ENCOUNTERS

Ashley Ladd
Joy Nash
Dominique Tomas
Jane Toombs

NCP

New Concepts Publishing
5202 Humphreys Rd.
Lake Park, GA 31636

ISBN 1-58608-671-5

NCP books are available at special quantity discounts for bulk purchases for sales promotions, premiums, fund raising, or educational use. For details, write, email, or phone New Concepts Publishing, 5202Humphreys Rd., Lake Park, GA 31636, ncp@newconceptspublishing.com, Ph. 229-257-0367, Fax 229-219-1097.

First NCP Paperback Printing: 2004

Printed in the United States of America

ALIEN ENCOUNTERS

Ashley Ladd
Joy Nash
Dominique Tomas
Jane Toombs

Futuristic Romance

New Concepts Georgia

TABLE OF CONTENTS:

STOLEN BRIDES

by
Ashley Ladd

Chapter One

"Captain! Terrorists!" Lara, the head stewardess shouted over the com, her voice quaking with fear. "They're killing the passengers. Ohmigod! They're disappearing."

Disappearing. Kat Craven, Boeing 747's youngest female pilot, grabbed her weapon and jumped to her feet, blood surging through her veins. She wasn't going down without a fight. How could a terrorist, much less terrorists in the plural, get past their stringent new security measures? No demands been made so the hijackers mustn't want ransom. Just another batch of kooks who thought revenge or religious doctrine justified killing innocents. Her head pounded relentlessly. *Revenge on whom though, and why?*

The door exploded in a flash of blinding light, evaporating in a cloud of dust. A Viking of a man with shoulders almost the width of the doorway filled her vision. Silky, white-blonde hair grazed his shoulders. Intense lavender eyes raked over her, assessing her, as he faced her holding no more than a small iron rod. Brows, which were almost invisible they were so white against his alabaster complexion, pinched together. Deep lines creased his wide forehead.

Behind him the whisper of life faded. When he moved, empty seats met her eyes as far to the back of the plane as she could see. Only a child's tattered teddy bear lay in the aisle, lonely, staring blankly at her.

Rage exploded in her as she fought back tears. Her finger shook on the trigger of her gun. "You bastards! You killed everyone! We're going to crash." Not that it mattered any longer to their passengers or crew but to innocents on the ground....

"Your plane's already crashed. You're already dead."

The oddest accent Kat had ever heard tinged her attacker's words. A globe-trotter, she couldn't begin to guess his nationality. The nonsensical words buzzed in her ears. *Already dead?*

Blood pumped furiously through her veins. "What do you want?" Didn't he want to negotiate? Make demands? They must want something. Then realization struck. They wanted the plane, to crash it into a nuclear power plant or important government building. She couldn't let them.

"Do it!" a second, smaller man urged, scowling at his watch. "We waste precious time."

Survival instinct kicking in, Kat squeezed the trigger aimed at the leader's head. A bright flash of light disintegrated the cabin wall behind where the terrorists stood. The men were there one moment, gone the next, *before* the bullet hit them. She blinked, unable to believe her eyes. "What the he--"

The iron rod pinched her neck, paralyzing her down to her tongue so that she couldn't utter a syllable. Her vision blurred, but she couldn't blink so much as an eyelash. She slumped, unable to catch herself. When she expected to hit the floor, she was sucked into a vortex. Only her lungs vibrated, the pressure against the walls of her chest almost unbearable. How long she zoomed through the psychedelic tunnel of swirling color she couldn't begin to guess. Maybe an eternity. Perhaps only a second. Time buzzed by in the vacuum.

Without warning, she landed. The ground was spongy and soft. Her backside protested as her vertebrae compressed violently.

"No more incoming. Escort the female to processing."

A large hand appeared before her face. Masculine voices devoid of emotion drifted over her. Her muscles twitched, telling her the paralysis had lifted. She squeezed her finger, but her weapon had disappeared. She didn't remember dropping it, but she must have when her muscles went limp. That or her abductors had taken it from her when she was incapacitated. An ex-Air Force fighter pilot who had once before been taken prisoner of war, she wasn't going to be taken captive again without a struggle. She'd kill herself before being tortured again. But she was damned if she wouldn't take a few of the enemy with her. Trained as a lethal weapon herself, she jumped to her feet and swung around in a high karate kick aimed at the aggressor's face.

Her captor caught her leg mid-air lithely, as if she moved in slow motion. Off-balance, she tumbled hard on her ass. Silly as it sounded, she couldn't phrase a better demand. "Take me to your commander. I demand answers," she said as regally as she could considering she lay flat on her back, the animal still encircling her ankle in his iron grip.

"We intend no harm." The man released her leg without warning so that it flopped hard to the ground. Tendons that had never made themselves known before screamed at her. She was in excellent physical shape, but she hadn't tried that drill-team-style, high kick maneuver since her high school days more than a dozen years before.

"Hijacking a plane and kidnapping the pilot is an odd way of showing it." She longed to rub her aching muscles where a charley horse was giving birth, but she was damned if she'd show an ounce of weakness. So she stretched to her full height, rolled her shoulders back and thrust her chest out, facing him squarely. Unfortunately, he towered a good six inches over her 5'9" stature, forcing her to tilt her chin to meet his gaze which put her at a distinct disadvantage.

"Follow me. Processing must commence immediately." The man remained infuriatingly calm, rigid but not noticeably tense.

Her blood boiled and it took every bit of her military training to keep her expressionless mask in place. She stood at parade rest, refusing to move until he answered her questions. "Not until you tell me what this place is and why you brought me here. What type of--thing--was that that transported me here?"

She gulped air into her over-exerted lungs as she took in her surroundings. The air tasted strange, almost like cinnamon, but tarter. Spongy and porous, native plant life was more like an undersea panorama than above ground foliage. The sky she'd always known was gone. One that matched the man's lavender eyes replaced it. It grew deeper in hue as seconds ticked away. Three moons chased each other across the heavens.

She blinked several times. *Three moons. She couldn't be on Earth.* Her abductors weren't terrorists. They were aliens. She was in even more trouble than she'd dreamed only seconds ago. No Green Beret or Navy Seal special operatives would rescue her here. She was on her own. "What planet is this?"

Dear God, she'd never thought she'd ever say anything so trite. If she had to die, she wanted to be buried on home soil, not some alien rock in another galaxy.

"Your questions will all be answered after everyone is processed. Haste is imperative." Irritation slipped into his tones. His formerly lavender eyes darkened to violet. He moved his head and the tips of his pointy ears peeked out.

Pointy ears. She gaped at them, her jaw slack. Her head pounded and it grew increasingly difficult to drag air into her aching lungs. "Holy Star Trek! A blonde Spock."

The word *everyone* registered, if late. "The others aren't dead. What is this *processing*?" Suspicion seeped into her bones. The last time she'd been *processed* she'd been strip-searched way too thoroughly, hosed down, dressed in prison garb, and thrown into a cell with rats larger than her foot.

A prisoner she might be, but not a fool. Her traitorous body wouldn't follow orders, however, and she lapsed into coughing spasms, her lungs seeming to collapse in on themselves. Then her knees buckled and she pitched forward. With each gasp of air, her lungs screamed. Her chest tightened unbearably as if ready to implode.

Her tormentor hoisted her into his arms almost effortlessly as she gasped for breath. "We require emergency healing!"

"Why wasn't this female processed immediately, Davek?" A wizened face lined with deep creases peered into her face. Several tendrils of silvery hair escaped the band that pulled the majority away from his face. He flashed a penlight in her eyes, dilating her eyes, blinding her to further observation. "Why has this female not been processed yet?"

"Healer, this fool warrior resisted processing. She's not been treated to accept our atmosphere as yet." The man's words contradicted the gentle arms that cradled her.

The healer grunted and narrowed his eyes at the younger man as he injected something into her thigh. "You know this atmosphere's poisonous to her kind. We lost the majority of the first travelers before we discovered this. Your father won't be pleased if she expires. Few breeders were harvested this mission and this one is of child bearing years."

"Breeders. Poisonous air?" She thrashed about, trying to lift her head but it swum dizzily. They were trying to poison her. Nothing made sense.

"Take her to the healing ward. She will need intensive care and observation."

* * * *

In ancient reverence, Prince Davek knelt before his father, the King of Antara. Then he pulled himself to his full height and lifted his chin. "The mission was successful, Father. With one exception."

"Give your report." King Sordel nodded, sitting forward in his chair. "How many fertile breeders did you acquire?"

"Only ten that will serve our purposes. Most of the females are beyond their childbearing time or haven't yet come into it. Some have been sterilized. Some who were already mated have their mates in attendance." Davek hesitated, reluctant to reveal the source of his failure. However, it wouldn't surprise him if one of his father's advisors hadn't already informed him one of the breeders hovered on death's precipice. "One resisted processing. She lies in the healing ward under intensive treatment."

Visions of the warrior female popped into his head. A splendid form strained against her uniform, but she was much too militant for his liking. Females on their world were subservient to their mates. This one would never submit to her mate's commands. It was doubtful they could ever remove the obedience collar from her safely.

His father's brows drew together as he tapped his fingers on the arm of his bejeweled throne. "Keep me advised of the female's progress. Meanwhile, make our new citizens welcome and start the assimilation process."

"That has been started already, Father."

"Choose the eight worthiest unmated men in the kingdom and prepare the mating ritual. Hold the celebration on the night of the three full moons. By this time next cycle, I wish to hold the welcome feast for nine new infants."

"Only eight unmated males, Father?" Davek frowned. He had heard nine infants, had he not? "But there are nine healthy breeders."

"You will take first selection. Continuance of the royal line, of our world, must be assured."

"As Prince I had hoped I would be given the freedom to decide when to take a mate, even if I must wait until our next mission, or the one beyond. None of the breeders rescued on this mission are suitable." The warrior female's exquisite face flashed in his mind. Exotically lovely she might be with her rare raven locks and rounded ears, but she would also be disobedient, independent, and willful, not at all the qualities he sought in his mate or the next queen of Antara.

His father drew himself to his feet, his expression thunderous. His voice boomed through the castle. "As monarch, it is your duty to be an example to our people. You cannot expect your subjects to select a mate if you refuse to do so yourself. I will be in attendance at the ceremony to oversee your selection. If necessary, I will choose for you."

Davek bowed to his father, cursing the gods for the millionth time for casting a plague upon their own females that stole their fertility. Formal mating with one of the alien females meant he could no longer indulge in the pleasures of his concubine, a woman who pleased him immensely but who could never produce an heir. "I submit to your will, Father King." He bowed and backed out of the King's throne room cursing the Goddess under his breath.

Chapter Two

Kat awoke from her nightmare, her vision fuzzy, and her ears ringing. Every muscle ached, especially her chest and her backside. Cotton filled her mouth. A blurry figure floated across the room, and Kat blinked to clear her vision and bring it into focus. She elbowed herself off the mattress and tried to swing her legs to the ground but was stopped by IVs and probes hooked up to her. "What the hell?"

"Do not get up. You will hurt yourself." The white-gowned figure scurried to her side and propped her legs back on the hospital bed.

Oh God! It wasn't a nightmare. But maybe she was delusional. She pinched herself, wincing when it stung and her fleshy underarm started bruising. *Damn! She wasn't dreaming and she wasn't delusional.* Either she was in an alien place or someone was playing a very elaborate charade at her expense. Either way, she was in deep trouble.

Horror flickered across the attendant's face. "Don't mutilate yourself! Davek will hold me responsible."

Davek? Who was Davek? The commandant of this facility most likely.

A monitor beeped in alarm, and she noticed she was hooked up to several such instruments, all blinking, flashing, and whirring, presumably assessing some bodily function. She yanked out the offensive IVs, ignoring the blood that spurted from her arm. "Kill me if you must, but you're not going to subject me to your experiments!"

The man blanched, turning ghostly white to the tips of his pointy ears. *Pointy ears.* "So there is a Planet Vulcan?"

"You must remain calm or you will harm yourself. You are being treated, and the only tests we run are to ensure your return to health."

"Return to health?" She lay back down, her ears buzzing. "What did you do to me? What have you done to the others?"

The tall warrior who had stolen her from the plane marched to her side, worry creasing his broad brow. "You will live if you can give Gralek such grief. We were afraid we processed you too late."

Kat sat up, cursing her inferior position. Not only was she confined to a bed, hooked up to test tubes and diodes like some lab specimen, but she was clad in only a hospital-type gown with nothing underneath. "Processed? What is this *processing* you keep talking about?"

"Nothing to worry yourself over. It is merely a medical procedure to assimilate you to this world."

She pictured the Borg, a mindless collective that was more machine than living flesh and recoiled. "I do not want to be *assimilated* to your *world*. What *world* is this?" She looked around the room, obviously a medical clinic of some sort, lined with hospital beds, IV stands, and machinery unlike she'd ever seen.

"This is Antara, fifth planet from the Kas. It is three point seven billion light years from the planet of your origin."

When her jaw slacked, she clamped it shut. "Why are you marauding my planet? Why travel so far from home just to steal people?"

Davek's eyes narrowed. "All will be answered in time. We have need of you. Trust me, the arrangement is of mutual benefit. You will come to accept your new life and home."

"I don't want a new life or home! Take us back now!" She lunged for his throat, her hands ready to commit murder. How could he stand before her so glibly talking about her kidnapping as if it was as mundane as what to have for breakfast?

He pushed a button on the strange device in his hand and searing pain scorched her throat, hurtling her back to the mattress, grasping at her neck. Her fingers found a metal necklace that encircled her like a dog collar. The pain only lasted brief moments, but it left her gasping for air.

She glared up at her assailant, indignant at the atrocities he forced on her. "What is this and why is it around my neck?"

"It is an obedience collar. It will stay in place until you learn to obey--*if you ever learn.*"

"What am I, a slave? An experimental rat?" But if she was a lab rat, why were the other beds empty? Where were the rest of the crew and passengers?

"Nay. You are a most revered guest. Perhaps the last hope for survival of our race."

"Some way to treat a guest," she mumbled, wishing he would stop speaking in riddles. "Where are the rest of my people? I demand you tell me what you have done with them."

"They are safe and adjusting to their new life." Davek rounded her bed, his hands clasped behind his back. He examined the monitors, which she couldn't begin to decipher. The writing resembled hieroglyphs.

She couldn't help raising her brow sarcastically. "They're *happy* here? Why should I believe you? Show me," she said in her most imperative tone of command. Even if she weren't a commissioned Colonel in the United States Air Force any longer, it would serve her well to remember her military training and bearing. As pilot, she was in command and responsible for her people.

"In due time. When our master healer tells me you are fit to leave the healing ward." His imperiousness eclipsed hers, making her feel like a child at play, and she throbbed with resentment.

"What is wrong with me? Your *healer* suggested you tried to poison me. Is that so?" She chafed under her confinement, longing to be free, needing to ensure the safety of the other humans.

He sighed deeply. "That is not so. Our atmosphere is hostile to you. By resisting us upon your arrival, you almost brought your own demise. Your lungs weren't treated in time to make the transition easy. Your lungs rejected our air."

She tried to reason out the puzzle. "So you altered my physiology to allow me to breathe your oxygen?"

"Nay, our atmosphere is carbon based."

"Whatever. Just prove to me my people are alive and well." Her head throbbed under the weight of these games and riddles.

Davek nodded to the man who had been silent at his side. The aide rushed from the room and quickly returned with her head stewardess and friend Lara. But it wasn't the Lara she knew who greeted her weary eyes, but a transformed woman who appeared as alien as the warrior towering over her.

Lara wore a transparent gown that draped one shoulder, exposing one breast. The dusky aureole of the other breast peeked through the translucent material. A long slit that stole up to her navel parted the gown that swished around her as she sashayed across the room. Gold paint shimmered on her flesh. Heavy kohl lined her eyes. She was breathtakingly beautiful. She was absolutely scandalous. Moreover, she seemed to revel in the darkened appreciation lighting all male eyes in the room as she glided forward.

A sunny smile lit Lara's features. "Kat! You made it. We were so scared."

Kat couldn't tear her gaze from Lara's preposterous garb. "Why are you wearing that? You--you're ... exposed."

Lara's laughter tinkled on her ears. "All the Antarian women dress so. I've never felt so liberated! I hated those stuffy, suffocating stewardess uniforms, high collars, and ties."

"You can't be serious."

Lara nodded emphatically. "Oh yes! It took a little getting used to, being ogled, I mean, but it's so erotic."

"Lara! I don't believe this is you. Have they brainwashed you?"

"If treating us like a queen is brainwashing, then yes! I've never been so happy. I didn't know life could be so wonderful!" She flitted around the room, trailing her fingers over the beds, her gown billowing about her slender form. This wasn't the overly-serious professional she'd worked with the past two years.

"And the others? Are they all well? Are they being held prisoner?" She fingered the detested obedience collar around her neck, which she noted was absent from her friend's body.

"Most have been set up in a neighboring village. A few of us have been chosen to receive great honors." Lara's eyes twinkled and her nipples beaded.

"Honors? What type of honors?" Suspicion reared again, almost choking Kat. Her gaze swiveled to Davek's, clashing with it. "What is going on?"

He met her gaze steadily, his chin high, his shoulders square. His bare chest heaved, and she spied the erratic pulse hammering in his neck. "Those human females of breeding age and physique will be mated to our best warriors tomorrow before the King."

Kat gasped, never having heard anything so barbaric. *Breeding.* "Lara will be forced to marry you?"

"What is *marry?* I do not know the term." Davek's brows knitted, and he looked askance to her friend.

"Mated," Lara supplied dreamily, as if she was a love-struck teen mooning over a teen idol. "We will be mated tomorrow."

"Are all the women in agreement?" She couldn't believe every woman would agree to marry men they had just met--if they had even met. They had just arrived!

"All save one." Davek's bold gaze examined her, making her blood boil, sparking her ire.

Exploding, Kat lunged for him again. "I am not a breeder! I will not marry a stranger." Excruciating pain radiated out from her neck again, incapacitating her. Panting, she fell back on the mattress, writhing.

Compassion and worry flooded Lara's eyes as she took Kat's hand in hers, pleading, "Don't do this to yourself, Katrina. Don't resist the wonderful life they can provide. I know you will be happy once you see how much they offer."

"Never! I'd rather die first."

Lara hastily interjected, fear glazing her eyes. "She doesn't mean that. She's still recovering and isn't all herself."

"I do mean it. I'm not for sale. I won't traipse around like some common whore for your satisfaction."

"I grow weary of this childish tirade," Davek said, rubbing his forehead. He turned to Lara. "I pray you can help her adjust. My servant Neala will help you prepare her for the ceremony and teach her our customs. I will send her post haste." With that, he spun on his heal and left the room, oblivious to her curses. His commanding footsteps echoed down the hallway for many moments before fading.

"You'll break a blood vessel if you keep this up." Lara stroked Kat's hair, trying to soothe her. "Your condition is still delicate, and you shouldn't risk your recovery."

Kat laughed bitterly, trying to find a latch to unhook the collar of obedience. "I can't believe you'd go along with these pointy eared beasts. I'm embarrassed for you girlfriend." Her gaze lowered to her friend's nudity again, then flickered away just as quickly, unable to gaze upon such atrocious attire--or lack of it.

"What does it matter if I recover? What then? I'll be used as breeding stock. Like cattle?" Kat snorted and her middle finger twitched irreverently.

Lara sighed deeply and perched on the edge of Kat's bed, depressing the mattress. "No. You will be adored and cherished as men on our planet forgot how to do long ago. You will be deliriously happy--"

"Oh yeah, delirious I'm sure." *If* she succumbed to the same madness that consumed Lara, turning her into a dithering idiot.

The whisper of soft footsteps alerted her to another presence entering the room. Kat looked past Lara to see a gorgeous young woman with a plait of golden blond hair that bounced all the way to her waist. Like Davek and the rest of his race, white-blonde hair framed a heart-shaped face from which lavender eyes shone brilliantly. Spiky ears parted her locks, giving her an elfin appearance. Like Lara, a pert breast was exposed, and like Lara, she didn't seem self-conscious of her lack of covering.

The young woman glided to her bedside gracefully and bowed low. "I'm at your service. Davek has sent me to help you learn our ways."

Kat gazed at the ceiling as she'd often done as a prisoner of war while being questioned, not meaning insult to the woman, but not wishing to learn her customs either. "Please tell your master I'm not interested. I wish to be taken home."

"But that's impossible! You can't go back!" Fear warbled in Neala's voice. Her eyes widened, and her face grew paler.

"Why? Surely if they brought me here they can return me?" Logic dictated that vessels or portals, even ones unlike she'd ever seen before, traveled both directions.

"Please, we must begin our work. I am instructed to inform Davek if you resist. He will be forced to engage the collar again." Neala worked nervously, her hands trembling.

Kat closed her eyes and shook her head. "Resistance is futile," she mumbled, saying good-bye to her soul.

"I promise you, you will find this most pleasant if you cooperate. I dream I could take your place. By the Goddess you have been blessed and do not realize it." Neala's smile turned watery, and she blinked back tears, making Kat feel like a jerk without knowing why.

Neala beckoned the healer. "Remove these instruments. It is time to prepare her for the ceremony." To Kat she asked, "Do you have a name you wish me to call you?"

Kat had been waiting for this, surprised she'd not been questioned before. "I will only give my name, rank, and serial number."

Lara rolled her eyes. "That's so Xena. You're not military any more."

Kat swore under her breath. "I'm not sure I'm even human any more. Katrina Mary Craven, Pilot, 002598734-987987-09," she said proudly.

"We call her Kat." Lara helped Neala open several jars of what looked like gold paint and make-up.

"Kat," Neala rolled the name on her tongue and frowned. "Such a strange, masculine sounding name. I am sure Davek will prefer to call you Katrina. It sounds much more regal than *Kat.*"

"I prefer Davek call me *missing.*" Kat's scowl deepened.

"I can see why he grew weary. I grow tired too, of this verbal sparring. We waste precious time better spent preparing you for the ceremony."

"I will not participate in any ceremony." Kat crossed her arms across her chest, refusing to budge them.

"By the Goddess you will." Davek filled the doorway, the device in his hand. "I feared you might give Neala trouble. I had prayed your intelligence would guide you to conform." He swaggered to their side. "Now undress and submit yourself to Neala's command."

"Undress?" Shock coursed through her, and she pulled the covers up to her chin.

Davek yanked the covers down, lifted her bodily and set her on her feet. He yanked her gown off, ripping it loudly. "You will learn docility, and I suggest you learn it sooner than later."

Kat gasped, covering her breasts with one arm and her vaginal region with the other from his bold, admiring gaze. Completely ineffectual, she was aware that her springy hair curled around her fingers.

"Shave that," Davek ordered, removing her hand and touching her in her most private area, his touch scorching her. He rubbed the course hair between his fingers, his fingertips grazing her flaming flesh. Wildfire coursed through her, mingling with shame.

"Immediately, as you wish," Neala veiled her eyes with her long white lashes.

"I wish. Take care not to injure her. Sedate her if she will not comply."

"I will not!" Kat batted his hand away, prepared to make him a eunuch if he touched her again.

Davek nodded to the other man who'd remained silent in the shadows so that she had forgotten his presence.

Kat felt a slight sting like a bee's on her neck, and everything went fuzzy. She couldn't voice a protest as she slumped and Davek lifted her onto the bed. She was only mildly aware of Neala rubbing the oily gold paint over her entire body, including her eyelids and the crack of her buttocks. No crevice remained unscathed. She knew she should be livid, but she couldn't work up her previous anger. Not even a twinge of indignation.

Lara painted her eyes with the Kohl, and then tinted rouge on her lips. Then she brushed her hair and fashioned it attractively.

Neala's sweet voice droned over her as she explained that she and Lara would be joined to great warriors that very eve in a sacred mating ceremony. She explained the importance of being submissive to their mates, to knowing their place in the kingdom. Then she went into the history of this planet she called *Antara* that she claimed was in the Kalix system.

Kat bristled every time her thoughts turned to Neala's master.

* * * *

Kat knew she should seethe under the indignation and humiliation of being paraded naked in front of the roomful of Antarians like so much merchandise, but she didn't. Covered with shimmering gold oil from head to toe, including every orifice, her skin glistened and she knew she had never looked more radiantly gorgeous.

She trembled when Davek's gaze roamed boldly over her, and she remembered the sizzle of his touch on her womanly core with every fiber of her being. When his gaze darkened on her breasts, her nipples pebbled, and her core tingled. She had never felt such a wanton reaction to a man before, and she could only assume it was due to the bizarre situation of being strutted naked before a roomful of lusting men.

"I shall require a closer look before making a final selection." Davek stood and made his way to the floor. She wondered why only Davek came to inspect the naked women. Was this a marketplace? Was he the merchant? He had *acquired* them. Perhaps he was going to auction them to the highest bidder.

Kat kept her gaze straight ahead as he approached, watching him with the aid of her peripheral vision. He stopped in front of a redhead who must be at least ten years her junior who smiled at him coyly. She licked her lips slowly and gazed at the juncture between his legs. "I know how to please a man like you. Pick me and you won't be sorry."

Her ears pricked to catch the exchange, and she watched through her veiled lashes.

Davek didn't smile as he looked at the redhead clinically. "I think you will be better suited to one closer to your years and maturation, although I am sure you have many productive cycles in which to produce offspring. Your coloring is most attractive, however, and I am sure you will serve one of our warriors well."

"Red haired children will be stunning with your lavender eyes," she crooned, reaching out and tracing a bold fingernail over the rather magnificent bulge in his tights. "You won't be sorry if you pick me."

Davek removed her hand, placing it gingerly but firmly at her side, ignoring her pouty lips. "I think not."

Joy leaped in Kat's heart although she knew not why when he spurned the younger woman. Her nipples tightened when his gaze fell to her, and she grew wet with desire. Then she gasped when a warm hand cupped her breasts and traced her nipples.

"Beautiful." Davek's sultry voice slid over her like silk as his gentle fingers shot wildfire through her. "You are in fine form. I see you have fully recovered from your ordeal."

Sanity tried to escape the haze that entrapped her. Vaguely, she was aware she was not behaving in character, but logic eluded her. "What have you done to me now? Why am I feeling so strange?" She knew he should not take such liberties and backed away a step so that his hand was forced to drop to his side. She fell to her knees as searing pain exploded in her head.

"Stop it Father!" Davek commanded in a regal voice as he reached down and helped her up. "She is unaccustomed to our ways. She will learn. We must observe patience."

"She will learn soon or be relegated to solitary confinement."

The pain stopped as suddenly as it had begun. "It is advisable that you do not anger the King further."

She didn't think she could be shocked more than she had been, but this revelation floored her. "You're the Prince?" Since when did royalty lead dangerous missions and risk their lives? Since before the Renaissance, back in the time of the Crusades. But that was on her world, a million light years away physically, and about a billion emotionally. She hadn't seen enough of this world to know in what century it resided. If this display was anything to judge by, it was more Arabian Nights than any other historical era. And yet, they had mastered space travel and enabled her to breathe an alien atmosphere that was inherently poisonous to her.

"I am." His statement was matter-of-fact, holding neither pride nor shame. "And it is my duty to choose the future queen of my people and mother of my children. She must be obedient and gracious, warm and loving."

"Subservient," she echoed the ghost of Neala's voice in her head as it pounded fiercely. He couldn't be thinking of making her his future queen, could he? "I am a warrior, not wife or mother material. I'm thirty-two, too old to bear children," she stated without conviction.

He tented his eyebrow and his ears twitched. "How do you know what I seek in a wife and mother? You dare question the Prince? That is my decision, not yours. Thirty-two say you. That leaves at least eight good cycles left to you. Yours is the most excellent physical condition. I commend you."

Eight children. She gulped, her eyes widening so far the conditioned air grazed them. Her womb tingled and warmed at the thought of nurturing his children inside her body.

"Aren't the women on your world more appropriate breeders? Our blood will taint your race. Neala would make a fine mate--"

"Neala is incapable of mating. As are our other women. If our race is to continue, new blood must be introduced. We have no choice. We are not the barbarians you seem to think."

Her brow seemed to crook itself, and she couldn't keep the sarcasm out of her voice as she looked down at her nude form pointedly. "You've done such a beautiful job of showing us. On my world, you would be arrested for forcing such indignities on us."

Warning flashed across Davek's eyes. He advanced again so that only a breath separated them. If he leaned a quarter of an inch closer, he would graze her nipples. Did he intend to tease her? Was he trying to arouse her, prove a point? "On our world, you are dangerously close to insurrection. I suggest you watch that loose tongue of yours lest it be the source of much heartache. I will forgive your outspokenness this once as you are new to our ways, but learn to guard your words and choose them with more thought. My father is not as forgiving as I."

"You couldn't possibly wish to saddle your people with a shrew for a princess. Your father would not approve of me."

"I choose my mate, not my father, King though he be. You will produce strong sons and daughters. You will be a strong advocate for your people." He spun on his heel and bowed before the crowd. "I have chosen my queen. I will pair with this female. Let the warriors commence with their selections."

Kat's head reeled and she bit her lip. *Princess. Queen. Wife.* She wasn't made to be wife and mother much less future queen. Although she'd never before applied the word warrior to herself, it was apt. She was a fighter, an independent professional woman. But one thing he had said held her tongue. As queen, she could show favor to the humans. She could protect them as only a member of the royal family, even a member by marriage, could provide.

The flirty redhead was chosen next. Lara was chosen third, joy flooding her face. The whole selection process took under three hours.

Kat sat naked between Davek and his Father, the King who let his gaze roam unabashedly down her length. When he ran his fingertip down the length of her body, from the swell of her breast, over her nipple, to the clean-shaven juncture between her legs, Davek shook his head in silent warning not to protest. "A fine female. I applaud your choice. She should please you in bed and make you keep her womb swollen with child for many long years."

Kat blushed to the roots of her hair, her skin crawling, but she dare not show disrespect to the King. Neala told her that would mean death. At the very least it would mean another painful episode of the collar.

The King squeezed her nipple, then rose regally. "It is time for the ceremony. May each couple proceed to the mating altar."

Davek took her hand in his and led her reverently to the altar. The other couples followed in the order in which the men had chosen the women. She assumed it was by order of rank or royal bloodline. When her soon-to-be husband disrobed, revealing his swollen manhood, Kat's mouth went dry. "It is custom to come to the altar with all revealed. There are no secrets at the beginning of a new life together."

An elderly man in priestly robes appeared before them, smiling on them benignly. He anointed each couple with a red thumbprint on their forehead. "My children. Mating is a sacred ritual that binds the pair together for all eternity. Once the vows have been made, there is no breaking of the bond. Females will be obedient to their mates, unswerving in loyalty and affection. She will provide him with pleasure, many strong sons and daughters, and take care of all his needs. Males will be kind and gentle to their mates. They will protect and cherish them. They will provide sustenance and shelter and ensure their every need is fulfilled. In the name of the Holy Goddess, I pronounce you mated. You shall have no other till death do you part. You may consummate your mating."

She couldn't take her eyes from her new husband's magnificent maleness. It looked ready to start making the first of their eight children.

She throbbed, her juices flowing between her legs, insisting she was shocked that she wasn't aghast at this pairing. Lust twisted her insides, and she couldn't wait to feel his possession.

Each time his penis twitched, she could barely contain the urge to guide him inside her, in front of all and sundry. Her traitorous fingers yearned to touch the silky hardness of him, to guide it to her. She wanted to feel his thickness and his heat. She wanted to feel it pump deep and hard inside her.

She closed her eyes and sucked in a long, deep breath. A little voice in the back of her brain whispered that she was not a randy teenager.

She was a grown woman to be reckoned with. An ex-soldier. A professional pilot.

Who was she kidding? She was a horny bride to be.

Davek slipped a gold bracelet around her wrist that adjusted to a perfect fit. Then he entwined her fingers with his and drew her against him and kissed her deeply, his tongue mating with hers. His tongue was forked, surprisingly much more erotic than that of a human male's tongue. He had much more control of it as well, thrilling her with his mastery of kissing. But it was his engorged penis rubbing against her stomach, and her straining nipples molded to his hard chest that caused her to quiver with desire.

When she thought she could no longer breathe, Davek nibbled his way to her earlobe and bathed it with his tongue. His hands roamed her length, and then he slid a long, thrilling finger inside. He pumped it in and out, lubricating her, driving her insane. He whispered against her lips, his words husky, "The King and our people would consider it a grave insult if we do not allow them to witness the consummation of our mating."

She nodded, unable to formulate a coherent thought as she arched against his hand, grinding her hips wantonly. Taking this sexy man inside her in front of the others was the most erotic thing she'd ever dreamed. At least two of the newly mated couples had succumbed to their baser desires and were already coupling on the floor in the most ancient of dances. She wasn't at all surprised to see one of them was comprised of the young redhead. She *was* surprised to see the other one was Brianna, one of her crew, a stewardess just a year or two younger than herself.

Hungry to know him, she parted her lips for his kiss and drew him down beside her. Feverish, eager to know every inch of him, she opened her legs wide for his entry. She burned for him as she'd never burned for any man before. Her lips ached to taste him, and she licked his hairless chest, delighting in his saltiness. When he slammed into her, she screamed with joy. Meeting him thrust for thrust, she lifted her hips off the ground, loathe that he should slide out when he filled her so exquisitely.

Fireworks exploded in her womb, swiftly consuming her soul. She clutched at him, raking his back with her nails. He pumped wildly, his breathing shallow, his body shuddering against hers, and then he crushed her to him and spewed his seed deep into her womb.

The King smiled and nodded to them. The crowd cheered wildly and leapt to their feet.

"Let's continue in private." Her new husband scooped her into his arms, cradling her against him much like when she'd been dying, but this time, her bare breasts grazed his smooth chest with each step he took. His heart pounded against hers till she couldn't tell where her heartbeat stopped and his began. Fever rose dangerously high as her desire refused to ebb, her new groom's heat stoking her fire again. Is this what it meant to become one, heart, body, and soul?

She didn't feel at all like herself and vaguely realized that she acted out of character, but still she couldn't work up much concern. His ears fascinated her, and she stroked them with a whispery touch, exulting when he sucked in a deep, shuddering breath. "So exotic. So erotic. Yours are the sexiest ears."

"Keep it up wife, and I'll never let you out of bed," he whispered against her hair as he teased her forehead with feather light kisses. Never had such chiseled lips tantalized hers before. As marvelous as the caresses felt on her eyelids, she yearned to feel their wet softness a couple other more sensitive places. She pulled his head down brazenly, eager to feel his lips on her nipples again.

Moans erupted past the lips that sucked her nipples as he carried her down a dimly lit, stone-walled corridor. His loose hair tickled her bare flesh, making her squirm under his ministrations. "A siren as well as a warrior." He paused in front of a heavy oak door then kicked it in, revealing a warm and welcoming room lit by a flickering fireplace. Hundreds of candles cast shadows across the stone castle walls. In the far corner, a Jacuzzi gurgled. Sulfur and melting wax tickled her nostrils, blending pleasingly with but not overpowering Davek's musky scent.

She eyed the largest bed she'd ever seen--at least double a King size back home. Perfect for wild nights.

"You had no other mate on your home planet?" Davek lowered her to the bed and immediately buried his face between her full breasts, licking and nipping expertly.

"Helluva time to see if I'm single or not," she teased breathlessly as she wriggled beneath him. "I was married to my careers. First the military. Then the airline."

Her husband's hands roamed her thoroughly. "It wouldn't prevent our mating. Your contemporaries are long dead and buried."

The fog burned off her brain as his words registered. Fury engulfed her, dissipating her carnal lust. As her husband poised to enter her, she pushed him hard off the bed. "Did you destroy our planet? Was there war? You are murdering bastards."

Davek landed on his back, then rose to a sitting position but didn't climb back on the bed or advance on her. Instead, he rubbed his neck, eyeing her warily. Fire flashed from his formerly lust-filled eyes. "We committed no such atrocity. We did not harm any of your people. To the contrary, we rescued you."

His comments puzzled her as before. "Yet you say my people are dead. How?" She pulled the silky sheet over her nudity, clutching it under her chin, no longer feeling brazen. Judging from his flaccid penis, desire had drained from his body also. Davek rose to his feet, his shadow eclipsing her, no similar shyness making him cover himself.

"We are more than four hundred years into your future. Your plane had crashed. Everybody aboard died."

Her brows knitted together, and she shifted her weight on the mattress. She watched the shifting expressions on his beautifully etched features. "You already said that. But we're not dead. We're here. Alive."

She pinched herself to make sure she wasn't a ghost. It stung, bruising her pale flesh, and she muttered, "Ouch!"

"You're alive because we took you off the plane moments before it was due to explode. We provided you with a second chance. Just as you will give us a second chance."

She rubbed the bridge of her nose and watched him closely. "Whoa! Back up Spock. What do you mean our plane exploded? That we're 400 years into my future. You're time travelers?"

His fascinating ears twitched beneath his silky tresses. "Yes. We studied your history, discovered you were destined to die, and that your people wouldn't miss you."

Logic played hide and seek somewhere in Davek's story but her mind was still trying to wrap itself around this latest revelation. She paced the floor, her hands behind her back, trying to follow his rationalization and poke flaws in his reasoning. "So you thought it okay to kidnap us since we were going to die anyway--according to the history books. You thought we'd be so grateful, we'd give you our bodies and souls?"

"We saved you. We gave you a second chance to live out your lives. There is no one to go back to, no one waiting for you. Everyone you knew died 400 years ago. They are dust."

Her brother and his family gone. They were the only living relatives she had left. Their father, also a soldier, had died before she was born. Her mother had succumbed to cancer three years before. Three years.... Didn't she mean at least 403 years?

Enraged, she attacked the man who had stolen her from Earth. Again, he stilled her arm easily as she attempted to punch him in the eye. "You heartless--"

"Not heartless. Truthful. Antara is your world now. Your destiny lies with us." Davek encircled her wrists in his large hands. "Don't make me control you with the collar. I had hoped you would accept the situation and we'd have no further need of it."

"Earth is still our home." Seething, she cursed her helplessness. She could not sit back and take his word as gospel and yet, she was powerless against the collar. Not that she knew how to get home even if she could ditch the collar and elude his guard.

"Earth's atmosphere is poisonous to you now. So you see, you can never go back. You would expire soon as you breathed its air."

Her hand covered her chest as her lungs pumped in Antara's atmosphere. Memories of her arrival were still cloudy, but wisps teased her brain. The ancient doctor had scolded Davek for not processing her immediately because their air was poisonous to her. *God save us.* She hoped He could hear her in this far point in the universe.

"The aphrodisiac shouldn't have worn off so quickly. You're much stronger than the others."

"You drugged us?" That explained a lot. Deja vu--shades of her previous imprisonment. Flashbacks of experimentation, truth serum, torture, and deceit haunted her. Her fingers twitched for a weapon. "How dare you!"

"It is part of the ceremony, used to enhance the mating night and ensure greater chance of fertility which is so very crucial. If we fail, our race will perish ... *if* the Omagagis don't exterminate us first."

The agony vibrating in his voice thawed the ice from around her heart, and she softened against her will. Compassion for his people, for his positions as leader and protector of his subjects, pushed aside some of her earlier fury. What would she do to save the human race? Or Earth?

"I want to understand *why*. What happened to your females? Why are Neala and your other women unsuitable as mates? But," she looked pointedly at their nudity, "can we cover ourselves first?" She couldn't hold a serious conversation when she was conscious of herself or him.

Davek crossed to a chest at the foot of the bed and withdrew a silk wrap. He draped her with it, leaving one breast exposed, then pulled on a pair of loose pajama-type pants. He lowered himself onto a couch in front of the fire and patted the seat beside him. "Your mind is much too inquisitive for a female, but I will quench your need for understanding. This is merely a reprieve. The mating will continue." As if to underline his words, he reached over and rubbed her tightening nipple hypnotically, inducing shivers. Traces of the aphrodisiac must linger in her system. She fought for mind control over matter, losing. Silently she cursed her mutinous body for thrilling to the enemy's touch.

"What did the Omagagis do to your women?"

Torment pooled in Davek's nearly wine-colored eyes. They glazed over as he leaned forward, staring deeply into the fire. "A plague sterilized our females, so we started searching for other compatible races with which to mate. Our paths crossed that of the Omagagis. Their planet is dying, but their people are strong and many. We offered to share our planet with them, but we discovered too late they were not interested in peaceful coexistence. They wanted our planet to themselves. So we have been at war for the past decade."

"And you found no other compatible races in your time with which to interbreed so that you had to steal people from the past?"

"The plague weakened us so that we cannot wage war with more than one hostile power at a time. I'm afraid the war is not going well. We are losing. We determined that it was safer to find a compatible race with inferior technology. Humans from your time seemed the best match, nor could they retaliate as the Omagagis have done. They won't even know you're missing."

She winced at his final remark, punishing the fleshy meat of her palms with her fingernails. Not one to indulge in feminine wiles, they were short and clipped but still applied enough pressure to prick pain. She wrinkled her nose. The more questions he answered, the more arose. She vocalized her theory, not liking it one bit. "So you tried to take Omagagi females also. Only they didn't appreciate it and retaliated."

He lifted his head so that his hair no longer curtained his finely sculpted cheeks and stared her square in the eyes. "No, we offered a trade for mutual survival. Share our planet, our natural resources, and they would let some of their females breed with us."

"Maybe they didn't like the idea of forced marriage. Some people would rather die than give up their freedom." She didn't think it necessary to add that they might have been made to feel like farm animals whose only value to their owners were as breeding stock. She didn't even want to think about what their other value might be.

"Like you?" Her husband reached for her hand, stroking his thumb across her knuckles hypnotically. He gazed into her eyes so deeply he caressed her soul. "The other females in your group seem quite amenable to their situation. Your friend Lara for instance. Besides, it wasn't like that. There would have been enough females to allow a natural progression of mating. The Omagagis saw our weakness and attacked without honor."

Blood thrummed through her veins. She itched to kick Omagagi butt to the next dimension. It sounded as if her adopted race could use a combat trained warrior. "I'm a fighter pilot. Let me help the cause."

Davek scowled at her and dropped her hand as if burned. He jumped to his feet and circled her. "Out of the question."

"Why? You said you're losing. You need every trained soldier you can get. One man can make a difference." She rose to her full height, still miffed that she lost points because she had to crane her neck to peer up at him. Her exposed breast throbbed under his scrutiny as well, making it obvious she wasn't a *man*.

He stopped pacing, faced her, and crossed his arms in a bluntly annoying male gesture that screamed *no way*.

No man, husband or otherwise, was going to order her around, exposed breast or no.

"You're not a man. Your place is as my mate, queen, and mother of my children." He put his hands on his hips as if to emphasize his lordship over her.

"So my only value on this world is as an incubator." Seething, she itched to show him her combat skill. She could out-maneuver, out-smart, and out-fight most men.

"To the contrary, you hold high, revered positions. Does not propagating life, saving a race, hold value to you?"

If this was the future, why was she re-fighting a battle that had been won in America decades before? She bit back a sigh and rolled her shoulders to get the kinks out. Davek's views were prehistoric, especially for a man of the future. "Those things are important. But there's no reason women can't do both--and then only if it's her choice. There's a lot more to being a good mother than merely being female and fertile. And it took a lot more to be a good soldier than merely being male."

"Your race is quite militant. Perhaps we should fear you." Davek turned his back on her and poured two drinks from a decorated bottle. He took a swig of one and then carried the other to her, swishing the liquid as he rejoined her.

"Some of us can be." Out of the crew, she was the only veteran, but she couldn't speak for the passengers. As they had been set up in a separate village, she hadn't had any contact with them except for the others chosen to be breeders, and none of them struck her as military or ex-military. However, humans could be surprisingly resourceful and resilient which wasn't exclusive to those with military backgrounds. How many Kurt Russell movies had she cheered for when the seemingly mild-mannered man turned into a kick-ass hero? "If you're that concerned, perhaps you should ask them."

She stared at the amber liquid suspiciously as she accepted the glass he held out to her. She swirled it, gazing down into the mini whirlpool that formulated in the center. "What's this?"

"Spirits. I was saving it to toast our union, but I think it is needed to soothe tempers."

She bit back a knowing smile. Ah ... so now he plied her with alcohol to make her compliant. Humans weren't the only resourceful beings in the universe. Of course, Davek's race was extremely intelligent to have mastered time and space travel. But that begged another question. She regarded him through her veiled lashes, heating up when she intercepted his intense gaze. "How is it that you are so advanced that you can travel through time and space and make it safe for me to breathe your atmosphere, but you haven't been able to cure your women? And that you make them dress like this?" Her glance went to her bare breast.

Davek's every muscle froze. He downed the rest of his considerable drink in one gulp and threw the glass in the fire, shattering it. Rage hovered over his face. "How is it that one invention or discovery comes before another? Don't you think we tried to find a cure? That we would allow our females to suffer so?"

"Is that the only lasting effect on your females? And it didn't affect your males?"

"Not as far as we can determine." He leaned over her, his hand on the wall behind her. She could smell the liquor on his breath as he lowered his head to nuzzle her neck. "Of course, the ultimate test of our virility will be whether or not we can impregnate our human wives."

Soft yet firm, his lips trailed fire along the hollow of her neck. He pushed her gown off her shoulder and licked his way down to the mound where the satiny drape teetered on the tip of her breast.

His tongue was more aphrodisiac than any liquor or drugs could ever be, and she squirmed against him. The fire warmed her backside as he leaned closer yet, pushing her against the warm hearth. Mixed thoughts seesawed in her mind. "And if you can't?"

"Can't what?" He worked his way down tantalizingly slow, bathing the rising swell with his tongue, making her want to scream that he hurry up and pull the budding nipple in his mouth.

But she would not give him the satisfaction of begging and tried to focus on getting more answers while his tongue was loosened from the alcohol. "Impregnate us."

"Pray the Goddess we are successful. Failure means death." He slid the offensive material off its ledge so that it pooled around her feet, and then greedily suckled her breast. Hard and throbbing again, he teased her bare stomach, and then slid down to the wet, velvety lips aching for his intimate touch.

Spasms shuddered through her as her legs bowed wider, granting him deeper access. "The plague isn't still here. It won't harm us, too?" Her words came out breathy as her knees refused to hold her weight. She clutched his strong arms for support, her nails digging into his hard flesh.

"That was part of your processing. You have been immunized. It will not harm you. Our healers also ensured your health so that you have nothing that will infect us." He lifted his head and stared deeply into her eyes, passion sparking in their depths. She saw herself reflected in the shiny orbs, naked, eyes filled with passion, silhouetted against the flickering flames of the fire.

He scooped her into his arms and carried her to the bed where he deposited her gently.

A growl rumbled deep in Davek's chest as he latched onto her nipple as if famished.

She moaned, writhing as she clutched his sinewy shoulders, digging her nails into his hard body. His tongue swirled around the excited peak, and then he nibbled lightly, making her gasp from the pleasurable pain.

Wanting to taste him, she swirled her tongue around his male nipple. When he bucked, his throbbing shaft plunged against her, making her gasp and open her legs wide to grant him entry.

Her juices oozed between her legs, slick and ready to take his enormous length inside her. Spasms wracked her at the anticipation, and she couldn't wait to feel the heated rod sink into her softness.

She gasped when he slid a finger inside her and massaged her nub with his thumb. Waves of pleasure rocked her as she thrust her hips hard against his hand.

He released her breast, and she shivered when cool air brushed the wet orb. "I knew we were well mated." Before she could respond, he captured her lips and parted them thirstily. Deeply sensual, his tongue tangoed with hers.

His free hand massaged her breast, squeezing it gently, rolling the excited nipple between his fingers. Then he slid a second finger inside her.

At fever pitch, she sought his penis and wrapped her fingers around its thick girth. His muscles contracted as she ran her thumb over the velvety tip.

She broke the kiss, sucking air greedily, her chest heaving against his. Shudders of delight coursed through her, and she knew she was dangerously close to crescendo. Wanting her husband to climax with her the first time, she pushed his hand away.

He lifted his head, bemusement flickering across his violet eyes. As he opened his mouth, she tugged his penis gently yet provocatively. "Fuck me hard."

He thrust into her gently, hesitantly, and she frowned. She liked it hard and dirty, and she'd expected this hulking he-man of an extra-terrestrial to give it to her better than any of her human lovers. He had certainly mastered the art of kissing and fondling.

Then it struck her, the reason he handled her like fine porcelain. "I'm not a virgin. You won't hurt me." Unable to corral her passion another moment, she thrust upward, grinding her hips against his.

She screamed in ecstasy when he thrust much deeper than she'd been penetrated before. She writhed and bucked, meeting him thrust for thrust.

Dynamite sizzled then exploded in her womb. She molded his firm buttocks with her palms, straining to pull him closer. She raised her lips, parting them in invitation.

Waves of pleasure rocked her as she groaned into his mouth. Her heart pounded furiously against his as he crushed her against him and claimed her one final time, shuddering. Surely their souls intertwined. She didn't know where she stopped and he began. They were as one.

Davek released her lips and dropped feathery kisses on her eyelids. He caressed her ears, staring at them in fascination. "You're the most exquisite creature in the universe. I hope our sons and daughters have your ears and your raven hair. So exotic."

Surprised, she gazed into his eyes. His fingers caressing her ear lobes almost made her purr. No wonder cats loved it. Reaching up, she traced the point of his ear, delighted when he shuddered against her, and he flexed deep inside where he still resided. "You're the one with the sexy ears. They should be x-rated." She'd always harbored a secret crush on Mr. Spock but never dreamed a real being existed sexier than he.

"We can't even agree on our children's ears." He bestowed a loving smile on her, warming her all over.

A grin cracked the corners of her lips. "I don't think either of us will get a say how their ears will be shaped."

"So long as they're as strong, spirited, and beautiful as their mother." He slid out of her centimeter by excruciating centimeter, leaving an emptiness she protested.

She reached for him when he lifted himself off, chilled by his absence. Cool breezes from the ceiling fan wafted over her, and she grasped the blanket to her chin.

Davek took it from her fingers. "I wish to gaze upon my beautiful mate." He passed a lingering look over her and turned on the bed, stretching his long length beside her, his shaft less than six inches from her face. When he buried his face between her legs and stroked her nub with his tongue, she gasped, straining closer.

"You like that, hmmm?" He slid a finger into her vagina and stroked in and out as he lapped her juices.

She tore her gaze from the erotic picture of the blond head burrowing between her legs and allowed it to gaze on the most amazing cock she'd ever seen. A piece of artwork, it must be a foot in length and three inches in diameter. Red satiny flesh adorned it as it flexed to life. Blood pumped through the long, bulging vein.

She couldn't resist touching and traced a fingernail down its length, then cupped his huge balls, which overflowed her palm.

He writhed and moaned, lapping faster, delving his tongue deep into her crevice.

She shifted to her side and bent her head, taking him into her mouth, sliding her lips across the velvety skin. He tasted sweet, and she parted the slit on the tip of his penis with her tongue. He thrust deeper and spewed his seed into her mouth as she felt her own answering release.

Her hips jerked a foot off the bed, the explosion burned so brightly, and she wriggled against him. Finally, so hypersensitive she could stand no more stimulation, she rolled away, gasping in a lungful of air. "I can't take any more."

Passionate glee sparkled in his eyes. "I satisfy you more than your human males?"

She licked her lips and floated back to Earth--no, she meant Antara. She'd have to modify her most basic level of thinking. Smiling coyly at the surprising male, she countered, "Am I better than your Antarian females?"

He climbed up to her and cradled her against his chest, his leg thrown over hers casually as if they were an old married couple. "I think you are my perfect mate."

* * * *

At least in bed. He still had to train the human female to be a good Antarian mate and queen out of bed. The spirit he admired so much when making love wouldn't suit his people well in a ruler. She needed social grace and poise. He had to disavow her of her foolish warrior tendencies of taking a man's place on the combat lines.

Females obeyed their mates on Antara. They knew their place. The queen, even now as princess, had a duty to set the example. His father expected him to control his female and teach her proper Antarian customs.

Chapter Three

Explosions rocked the night sky, obliterating her view of two of the three moons with curtains of white smoke. The ground shook, and buildings trembled on their foundations. Screams rent the formerly still night air.

"The Omagagis!" Davek jumped out of bed, pulling on his trousers as he ran for the door. "How did they get past our detection sensors?"

Kat tugged on her robe, cursing her lack of clothing. If she was going to be blown up, she wanted it to be in her combat boots. "Cloaking devices. You're not aware they had this capability before?"

Davek almost jerked the door from its hinges he yanked so hard. "No."

There was another possibility. "Could you have a traitor in your midst? Someone who disabled or sabotaged the sensors?"

Davek stopped dead in front of her, so that she stumbled against his broad back and bounced off him. "That is more likely, but I can't imagine any of our people betraying us." Anguish tinged his voice as the muscles in his shoulders flexed.

Air raid sirens blared. Electricity blinked off, then backup generators buzzed to life, flooding the hallway with light. "Red alert! Battle stations! This is an all-out attack," a military voice boomed over loud speakers.

Crying women scampered past them. Davek grabbed a particularly stunning one with waist-length curls by her upper arm, halting her flight. "Carlev, take my mate to the women's quarters until it is safe to come out."

When the blonde woman regarded her, disdain and hatred flashed in her mauve eyes. "What is it to me if she dies? Why do I need to be saddled with your human usurpers?"

Kat lifted her chin and glared back at the impertinent Antarian female, assessing her in return. She had to admit surprise that this Carlev didn't bow down and kiss Davek's feet. She didn't fit the meek and unassuming image she'd formulated of her new world's female population.

"She is my mate and as such, Princess of Antara. She will be your queen one day. I suggest you'd do well to remember her place and yours." Fire flashed in Davek's eyes

Carlev merely snorted and tossed her platinum hair over her shoulder, smacking Kat in the face with it. "Only due to the plague. I should be Princess. I was brought up to be queen. You best watch your step. There's a lot of unrest in the kingdom."

Davek's knuckles paled as his fingers clamped tighter around her arm. "Don't threaten me Carlev."

Carlev veiled her eyes with her long lashes, then turned a beguiling smile on Kat's husband. "I'm merely warning you to watch your back for assassination attempts. By the way, does your wife know I'm your concubine?" She tossed him a sweetly false smile, then spun on her heel and flounced away.

Kat's skin crawled. She looked askance at her husband, trying to swallow the bile bubbling in her throat. Neala had told her that Carlev had been Davek's mistress, not that she still was. She didn't want to share anything with that witch and would make it a point to give her wide berth. She didn't need a knife in her back either. "Concubine. You have a lot of secrets you haven't told me, husband." She seethed as she watched the other woman's backside disappear around a corner.

Davek's scowl darkened, his gaze clashing with hers. "This is not the time. We will speak of this later."

Neala passed them at a quick pace, her youth hidden under creases of worry. Her skirts billowed behind her.

"Neala, take the Princess to the underground shelter and see to her safety," Davek growled. Then he turned back to her and in the most domineering voice Kat had heard pass his lips yet, he ordered, "Accompany her and do as she tells you. Do not emerge until ordered to do so."

Neala retraced her steps and bowed before her master. Although she tried to school her features into a calm mask, Kat read the distress and fear pooling in her fuchsia orbs. "Aye, your Highness."

Kat seethed at Davek's impertinence and refused to budge from his side. As Princess, she should have some say in her actions. "If we're under attack, you need your best pilots in the air. I can help."

Disbelief clouded the Prince's eyes, and something else she couldn't quite fathom. Trepidation perhaps. "Nay, I cannot allow a female to take such risks, nor can I expect my men to fight by your side. They would take unnecessary risks protecting your life."

Fury exploded inside her, and she faced off against him, toe to toe. "For such a technologically advanced people, you dwell in the Dark Ages. Gender isn't important!"

Neala's eyes rounded wide as she tugged at Kat's hand. "We must go now and let Prince Davek lead the resistance. We must not distract and delay him further."

"The truth flows from her tongue. She is wise for one so young. She will take good care of you." With that, Davek trotted away without so much as a kiss or salute.

Neala bowed again and didn't arise until his shadow was the only evidence of his recent presence. "Your Highness, we should hurry lest the Omagagis destroy the castle."

Being called *Your Highness* didn't bode well with her. "Call me Kat, please."

Neala paled and shook her head. "Oh no! I would be punished for such impertinence, Your Highness."

"Then I order you to call me Kat in private and Princess Kat or Your Highness in public." Princess Kat tripped off her lips. It did not have a good ring to it and did not flow easily. She envisioned a regal Persian wearing a crown and wielding a scepter and scowled.

"Princess Kat. Forgive me, but it sounds so odd. May I not call you Princess Katrina? It sounds so much more appropriate, befitting your exaltedness."

"That will be fine." Not that anyone had called her Katrina in years. She had been Kat as long as she could remember. The shortened name fit her much better than the feminine version. She'd always been a much more rough and tumble tomboy than frilly female.

Kat craned her neck, looking at the heavens, straining to see the battle high above. Another explosion rocked the walls. Mortar and dust crumbled from the ceiling, misting her face. She felt so helpless being on the ground, so impotent running to hide like a coward. It went against everything she stood for, everything she'd ever worked for.

She fingered the collar around her neck and slipped a finger inside. No one was nearby that could activate the mechanism. She measured the girl before her and decided to take a chance. A patriot and loyal subject, but also a sincere and bright individual. "I can help. I was a fighter pilot on my world. Take me to the space dock."

Neala's complexion paled. "But the Prince commanded--"

A series of explosions almost burst Kat's eardrums and knocked her off her feet. The ceiling caved in a few feet from them in a monstrous roar. Adrenalin pumped furiously through her veins catapulting her to action. "There's no time to waste. Many more attacks like this and we'll all be dead."

Neala nodded silently, then took Kat's hand in hers. "We could both be punished severely if caught."

The hallway where they had just run through caved in behind them. Mushroom clouds exploded, choking her. Coughing spasms wracked her frame. Covering her face with her hand, she squinted to peer through the destruction. "If we're not successful, there might be no one left to punish us." She'd deal with the consequences later, if they survived. It was still preferable to stand and take it on the jaw than to squirrel away in a rabbit hole shivering.

"Let's pray not."

"Pray hard, Sister. I hope your Goddess has good hearing." Kat scrambled over more rubble, wincing when she scraped her bare breast, wishing she wore decent protective covering. She gave Neala a hand over as the younger woman panted from the exertion.

"Do not mock the Goddess. We need her favor." Neala held her chest and climbed. "I hope you're skilled as you claim. I wouldn't want to lose my head over a crazy woman."

Kat shook her head. "Barbaric," she muttered, still trying to come to terms with this contradictory world.

Rays of light lit up the opening ahead and her heart leapt.

A huge space pod landed outside the entrance and a battalion of heavily armed storm troopers emerged from the craft. The ground shook as they marched toward the castle's entrance and Kat pulled Neala back into a shadowy doorway.

Neala whispered in her ear, "They do not take prisoners." She clasped Kat's hand and tugged her into the room behind them and shut the door carefully.

They'd stumbled into another bedroom with an open closet full of clothing. Kat borrowed a soldier's uniform, and although she had to roll up the sleeves and pant legs, it was a huge improvement over the robe.

"I pray you know what you are doing." Neala eyed the masculine garb with disapproval. "Females are not permitted to dress so scandalously."

Kat couldn't help but raise a brow at her new world's perception of what constituted scandalous dress and behavior. Would she ever fully transition to their ways and ideals?

Hysterical feminine screams shook Kat to her core.

"That's Yoki!" Neala ran to the door and yanked it open as Kat grabbed for her and missed.

"No!" she hissed, halting the younger woman. "You can't go out there."

"She's my baby sister. They'll murder her." Pain ravaged Neala's voice, shredding Kat's heart. "We can't just leave her there!"

Kat grit her teeth. "We won't." But they couldn't just rush the soldiers unarmed either. She searched for anything she could use as a weapon and spied a fireplace poker on the mantle. Grabbing it, she clutched it firmly and listened at the door.

"Stay put. I've got more experience in this than you."

"But I want to help! She's my sister."

If Neala accompanied her she'd only slow her down. She might even alert the enemy to their presence. Kat whirled around and grabbed the girl by her shoulders. "Look, this is a covert operation. All I have is the element of surprise. If I can sneak up on one of them alone, I can get his weapon and his uniform and have a prayer of getting your sister back. Her name is Yoki?"

Neala nodded, gulping. Her eyes shimmered with unshed tears. "She's the only family I have left. I promised our mother I wouldn't let anything happen to her. She should have been in the chamber...."

Guilt struck Kat full in the chest. Neala's insinuation that Yoki's life was threatened because Neala had been ordered to baby-sit her instead of attending to her own family first. Fury at her husband for being so insensitive embroiled her, particularly since he'd made such a big show of caring so deeply for his people. It was her fault this girl had fallen into the hands of the invading devils. She would save her or die trying.

"Hide while I'm gone. I'll bring her back here if at all possible." She smiled as reassuringly as she could and sucked in a deep breath. No sound came through the door so she opened it a crack and peeked out. No sign of the soldiers or movement could be seen so she eased her way out and shut the door with a whisper of air.

She spied a lone guard ahead and flattened herself against the stone wall, not daring to breathe. She debated whether to bludgeon him over the head or stab him in the heart. The closer she crept, the more impenetrable his armor appeared. She swung with all her might, whacking him on the back of the neck.

The enemy warrior slumped to the ground with a thud, and she cursed silently. If his comrades spied him down, she'd never be able to surprise them so she dragged him into the nearest chamber, stripped him, tied him to a bedpost, and exchanged her clothes for his. Now she prayed the Antarians wouldn't mistake her for the enemy.

Creeping down the hall, she followed the commotion. She was surprised the girl was still alive since the Omagagis took no prisoners. She'd just be an encumbrance. She hoped they felt the need to keep a hostage as long as they remained on Antarian soil.

She followed the sounds and found Neala's sister--who was still a child. What kind of monsters killed children? She pulled the shield over her face and held the weapon against her stomach, her finger on the trigger. The Omagagi trooper yelled at her in a language she couldn't understand, and beckoned for her to join them. There were only two soldiers with the girl. Not as good of odds as she'd like but better than she'd hoped for.

Nearing the girl, she shoved her down and shot at the closest soldier. The second fired back as she attacked, barely missing her, putting a gaping hole in the wall behind her.

The girl sobbed as she tried to crawl away, but the soldier blocked her exit.

Kat tucked and rolled, landing on her feet and fired back.

The Omagagi monster yanked the girl to her feet and pressed the barrel of his weapon to her temple. "Drop your weapon or she dies now." Sinister hisses punctuated his threat.

The girl whimpered, pleading for her life.

"There's no honor in harming a child." Kat's mind buzzed to find a rescue scenario.

Carlev waltzed up to the warrior, her skirt swishing along the floor. She drew a long fingernail down his cheek seductively. "Why do you hold a worthless commoner when you could take the Princess prisoner. Have you no brains?"

The man's head snapped back around so he could examine Kat. "This warrior is the Princess?"

Carlev treated Kat to a bored glance. "Sad to say, yes. She must have cast a spell over the Prince to make him choose her over me. Beware her black magic. It must be very potent."

"I will bring a much better ransom than the child. Release her and I will go with you." Kat wasn't in the habit of being so noble or self-sacrificing, but it was the only way to save the girl. Once she had safely departed, Kat would stand a chance at overpowering their attacker without the child being hurt.

"So touching," Carlev's voice dripped with disdain. "Release the servant and take the princess."

The girl scurried away.

"You're the traitor." Kat's intense dislike of her husband's mistress escalated to shimmering hatred. Kat snorted. "You're selling out your people because you were scorned? Pathetic."

"Blast her. We don't need this insolent viper." Carlev shook with fury, turning crimson. "How dare this human dung mock me, rightful queen of Antara!"

When the soldier hesitated, Carlev snatched his weapon and spun it around to point at Kat.

But Kat was already lunging on the duo and knocked it from her hands. She landed on the woman, her hands wrapping around her throat, her thumbs pressing on the pressure points.

They rolled, clawed, punched, slapped, and kneed one another. Carlev proved a formidable opponent.

Laser fire erupted. They froze in their struggle, and the alien soldier slumped to the floor, his eyes glazed, lifeless, and a hole in his chest where his heart had resided. Blood oozed from his wound, pooling around his body and soaking into his uniform.

Neala stood three feet distant, Kat's weapon pointed at Carlev's skull. "Move one muscle, and you're dead Carlev."

All color drained from the traitor's face. Her eyes glowed ferociously. "The human female betrayed us, not I. You know well how much she detests our people and mocks our customs. Look at her, masquerading as a warrior. A male. *Sacrilege!* Destroy her."

"Murder the Princess?" Neala frowned. "But I have been commanded to protect her."

"Your first loyalty is to the Prince and Antara. This usurper seeks to destroy all we hold dear, all those we cherish. We will tell the King that the Omagagi scum murdered her. I will back you up. No one will question us."

Neala's eyes narrowed, violet fire flashed from their depths. "And then will you have me killed to silence me?"

Carlev climbed slowly on all four heaving, her hair a tangled hive, her face smeared with perspiration and kohl. "I am hurt you do not trust me."

"I witnessed your treachery as did Yoki. And yes, the King will believe my account of this night. I warn you. Do not move another inch."

Carlev shrieked in rage and leapt for the servant, murder glowing in her eyes.

Kat caught the traitor's foot, felling her as the weapon in her hand discharged. Blinding light drilled a hole in Carlev's forehead. Shock froze in the deceased's eyes.

Male voices and pounding footsteps broke the thick air.

"We must hide." Neala aimed a kick at the dead woman. "That was far more mercy than she deserved."

Kat marveled at Neala's strength. Perhaps there was hope for Antarian women. The younger woman would make a fine soldier.

They merged with the shadows as a troop of Antarian soldiers led by Davek advanced on the fallen Carlev.

Kat watched as her husband was overcome with grief and a strangled cry erupted from deep within his soul, shredding her own in the process. "Find the man who did this, and I will murder him with my bare hands." Reverently, Davek scooped the limp woman into his arms and carried her past the nook where Kat and Neala hid.

Neala trembled so fiercely Kat feared Davek would hear them. She held the young woman, stroking her back, whispering encouragement in her ear.

"The Prince will have my life! What have I done?"

Kat stepped back and put her hands on the girl's shoulders. "You acted in self-defense. You protected your sister, your Prince, and your people. You acted very bravely."

"My liege is distraught. He will not hear the truth. He loved Carlev with his soul."

Kat's heart withered ... and budding love for her new husband with it.

"Surely, he is a fair, honorable man?" she asked, more to calm the terrified girl than from conviction. She barely knew the Prince. They shared little history for her to formulate an accurate assessment of him and how he would react. She had witnessed his heartbreak over his lover's death.

Well, Davek hadn't declared any love for her so she couldn't accuse him of lying. Still, it felt like a lie of omission that he loved another woman enough to want to avenge her. Carlev's ghost would always be between them, for the scene she had just witnessed had burned into her memory.

She prayed that Davek would never learn who Carlev's slayer had been for she wished no harm to come to Neala. On Earth, the young woman would be innocent by laws of self-defense, but customs and justice on this alien world were still unknown to her. Judging by Neala's reaction, they wouldn't be favorable. Still, she wished her husband knew what a treacherous liar his consort had been. Then perhaps he wouldn't worship her memory and would be free to move on. She could tell him the truth of Carlev's death and disloyalty to Antara, but would he believe her. Or would he think her a jealous woman, perhaps making up lies to cover her own duplicity in his lover's death?

No, the risks weren't worth the gain. She would remain silent.

Furious bombing commenced, shaking the castle so that Kat was almost knocked off her feet.

Neala's puffy tear-stained eyes lifted to hers. "They won't stop till they've killed us and erased all trace of our existence."

Kat shed the Omagagi uniform instantly cooling ten degrees. "Go to the safe place with the others. Now!"

"Surely you don't still want to fight them now that you've seen their danger." Neala clutched at Kat's hand, tugging.

Kat sucked in a deep breath, her nerve endings sizzling, her muscles twitching. "That's exactly why I must go. They need every man." She'd rather fight to the death than be slain like cattle.

"I wish you'd stop calling yourself a man." Disapproval gleamed in Neala's eyes. "It is improper, Your Highness, especially for the Princess."

"They need every soldier." She would start the women's liberation movement on this planet later--after she saved it, if it wasn't too late. She gave the servant a gentle nudge. "Go. Now."

When Neala hesitated, her eyes big and round, Kat added sternly in her best colonel's authoritative voice, "That's a command."

Clearly unhappy and indecisive, Neala bowed and backed away. Her step picked up momentum when she turned and neared the hallway junction. Blood and dust stained her gown, and Kat prayed no one would put two and two together. She prayed that Neala's sister knew how to keep secrets.

Chapter Four

Kat made her way outside and found the space dock. She slipped into a ship when the armed sentinel turned his back. She froze mid-action when hieroglyphs confronted her. "Damn damn damn!" She couldn't begin to read the foreign language and kicked the console in frustration.

Kat took a deep breath, and then studied the controls. They seemed similar enough to other aircraft she'd piloted that she could pull this off. If not, well....

Outside the viewport, a ship a dozen feet away disintegrated when a bomb fell on it. She had no more time to waste. "Here goes nothing," she mumbled through gritted teeth, taking her best guess. It was either try to get off the ground or be blown up any moment.

As the craft lifted off, laser fire skimmed past her right wing, blasting a crater the size of her Boeing 747 in the ground where the ship had just sat. She banked hard left and immediately drew enemy attention. Omagagi craft tailed her, shooting laser fire at her. Zigzagging, dipping and flying low, she barely evaded their fire as she adjusted to the controls.

An Antarian ship saw her distress and flew to her backup, blasting the nearest enemy and toying with the second craft.

Coming around, she returned the favor and shot the second ship, thrilled her aim was true as it exploded in a spectacular display of fireworks.

"Identify yourself Dragon Three," her husband's voice commanded regally over the speaker.

She stared at the source of the transmission, groaning. Why did he have to be the one to ride to her rescue? Of course she was assuming her craft was Dragon Three. She couldn't be sure, as she couldn't tell if the name titled the ship or not. She decided to ignore him, hoping he addressed another.

Davek's ship hovered in front of her, refusing to allow her to pass. "This is your last warning. Identify yourself within ten seconds or I will destroy your craft."

Great! She wasn't sure which switch or button to press, as she couldn't read anything. She flicked switches closest to the com, praying she found the correct one. When static hummed, she sighed in relief. "It is I, your mate." Mate almost choked in her throat.

Davek swore harshly. "By the Goddess! Your disobedience will see you dead yet. I ordered you to go to safety with Neala. Return to the shelter at once!"

"No!" She wondered if he intended to kill her in punishment for her defiance or if he meant that her foolishness would cause her demise.

Either way, she didn't have time or desire to debate this with him and flicked off the com, cutting off another string of curses mid-stream.

She darted beneath him, then sought out the center of the combat. Her heart stopped beating when she saw how Omagagi pilots exploded Antarian ships one after another. At this rate, soon there would be no Antarian males left to require her kind. Kat roared with rage, bloodlust flooding her. She shot down the Omagagi fighter that played cat and mouse with Lara's husband Rantel. "You are not going to make a widow out of my best friend!"

When the enemy vessel crashed and burned, she let out a war whoop, smacked the console and leapt for joy. "Yes! One for our side!" Antara was her side now. She desperately wanted Antara to survive, to drive out the hostile force.

An Antarian ship exploded in a furious flash of light. Jerking the helm, she banked to avoid the debris. Kat cursed, wincing as the ship rolled to the side.

She was thrown to the ground and striking her head on something hard and sharp. Pain burst in her temples and something wet trickled down her face, mingling with the heavy perspiration sheening her. Her craft spun dizzily, hurtling toward the palace.

Her vision blurred, and she tried to focus but colors and shapes shifted kaleidoscope-style before her eyes. She struggled to her knees then grabbed on to her seat, the nearest bolted down item she could find and tried to haul herself back into it, fighting G-forces. Every cell in her body screamed, threatening to implode.

What seemed an eternity later, she reached the helm and wrestled to regain control of the ship.

The helm jolted violently, refusing to relinquish its command but she hung on, determined to conquer.

Laser blasts burst beside and in front of her, rocking her ship. Sparks flashed on her control panel.

She spied two enemy ships converging--one in the front, the other from the rear. "Let's see if you can handle 400 year-old Earth maneuvers." She pulled the helm up hard, aiming the craft almost straight up, then barrel rolled across the skies.

The two ships crashed headlong, bursting into a glorious fireball, then evaporated. Sparks shimmered over the castle, the most dazzling sight she'd seen since closing at Earth's largest amusement park on Independence Day. "Woo hoo! It's July 4th baby!"

Renewed vigor energized her. Who needed Zoloft when good old-fashioned adrenalin got the blood pumping? When she emerged from a cloud, she spied an enemy vessel in hot pursuit of Davek. Rage burst through her. "Oh no you don't you Omagagi bastard." Antara needed their warrior prince.

Carlev's glittering eyes haunted her. She wondered if his precious consort had intended for him to die this way. Was she bitter enough to destroy the man she loved? *That black widow.* She didn't deserve any man's love and certainly not Davek's. She wondered if her husband was avenging his lover, or if he didn't care what happened to him now that she was no longer in his world. Both scenarios made her gut wrench.

She swooped down on her prey, targeting him in her sights, careful not to get caught in her own trap and crash into the Prince.

Laser blasts burst beside and in front of her, rocking the ship. The lasers locked on target, and she blasted the enemy in a surprise attack.

Davek banked at the last second, almost into the line of her fire. Her com cracked and her husband yelled, "Remove yourself from the combat before you get me killed, woman!"

She snarled, grumbling, "I'll take that as a *thank you.*" Then she added, 'I saved your sorry ass. You're the stupid jerk who almost botched my rescue attempt. Don't blame me."

"I can't be worried about you. I order you back to safety." He leveled his ship by her side, so that their gazes clashed, his smoldering.

"I am *Princess*, am I not?" Surely the rank couldn't be all fluff. It must come with some perks.

"Even more reason to protect you." Then he narrowed his eyes and glared at her. "And give you lessons in social etiquette."

"*My royal ass*," she mumbled. Louder she added, "If you wanted a true Princess, why didn't you just steal one? I'm a soldier, not a debutante."

Davek sighed as they raced through the sky. "I expect you to act with more finesse befitting your new position."

"I'll think about it--*when I'm not saving our butts.*" She didn't plan to devote much thought or time to his insane suggestion.

He cracked a smile and his haggard appearance softened. "That's *royal* butts."

"Ready to kick ass?"

He lifted a brow and his smile widened. "Is that some human sex game?"

Heat rose up her neck as she tried not to let him see her reaction. "Not precisely. It means are you ready to win?"

He nodded, a wicked glint in his violet eyes.

She led the resistance fighters, until every last enemy had either fled to the safety of the mother ship or been shot down in flames. "This isn't over yet. They may just be regrouping. We have to drive them all the way out."

Adrenalin pumped through her veins, and she wasn't about to stop now with the job halfway accomplished. She'd forgotten how seductive she found battle, how it made her blood hum with excitement.

She pushed the ship to its limits, speeding across space, ecstatic to have made it into space after having been rejected from the space program. If they could only see her now, bearing down on the enemy, strafing them with photons.

She found their weakness in energy generators and fired the shot. Explosions rocked the Omagagi mother ship as the metal hull buckled in a destructive wave. Flames shot out, sucked into the vacuum of space.

The hull cracked, it imploded as fire consumed her, and she blazed brilliantly for several moments, and then disappeared in a cloud of dust. Star-like twinkles sparkled under the moonlight, disappearing into Antara's atmosphere.

* * * *

Davek howled, punching his fist in the air. Joy overflowed in him that the threat to his people had been vanquished. "That should be the end of them." Now he could rest, work on his marriage, and repopulate Antara.

"Now we regroup and prepare for the next invasion." Katrina's lips set in a grim line as they docked their crafts and disembarked. She rolled her shoulders and reached around to massage her neck.

His ears twitched and he blocked her way as she started to ease around him. "What makes you think there'll be another attack?"

His mate crinkled her nose and stared up at him. "Until there is a treaty, it's only wise to prepare a defense."

Haunted, her gaze traveled around the decimated compound. "If they sent reinforcements now, they could wipe us out."

"Do you know something I do not?"

"I know war and strategy. Just because we won this battle doesn't mean we won the war."

"So now you're a general, my little warrior?" He couldn't decide if her superciliousness irked or amused him. He definitely didn't appreciate her manly attire or attitude even if he would be forever grateful that she had helped save his world.

She thrust her chin forward and puffed out her chest. "I'm not your *little warrior*. I was a full-bird Colonel in the United States Air Force. I'm an experienced combat pilot."

"On an archaic world in a long-dead army." Immediate regret for his insensitivity filled him when ghosts flickered across her eyes, even if he spoke truth.

"I didn't notice your side winning until I entered the combat. Or was I imagining the castle walls caving in and enemy ships shooting us down?"

"It is inappropriate for females to enter combat, especially a Princess, especially now when every fertile female is needed for procreation." She could be carrying their child this minute and if so, had taken extreme risks with not only herself but with the heir to the throne. Additionally, her incessant need to disobey his edicts and argue every word out of his mouth fatigued him, especially now after his muscles already ached from extended battle.

Furious heat infused the apples of her cheeks and smoke smoldered in her green eyes, making them sparkle like rare emeralds. She seethed, her body rigid, her nipples taut even through the offensive fabric of her borrowed uniform. "Is that all I'm good for? Breeding stock? If not *pour moi*, the Omagagis would still be massacring us and there'd be nobody left to breed!"

Her beauty stole his breath and if not for the fact she clenched her fists at her side as if ready to do battle with him, he'd smother her lips with kisses and teach her who the master was. In fact, maybe that wasn't such a bad idea. He stepped toward her, closing the gap between them. He put his finger under her chin and tipped her face, forcing her to gaze into his eyes. "What if you're already carrying our child? You should take better care of the next prince or princess."

He bent his head to capture her lips but was halted by a brusque clearing of the throat. Circumspectly, he stepped back releasing his mate, but sending her a glance full of possession and passion of what to expect in future. When color suffused her neck, disappearing under the V of her top, his groin responded by tensing painfully.

General Vidak, a pompous, blasé man that he didn't much care for, but who had his father's ear, marched to his side, clicked his heels, and saluted sharply. Polished and sleek, not a speck of grime or dust on him, he didn't appear to have partaken of battle. "Your highness. May I have your ear?" Vidak waited to be acknowledged, his gaze sizzling on Katrina in a most disturbing fashion.

"Speak your mind, General." Annoyed that his vassal had interrupted them before he could put his mate back in her place, he willed the man to expedite his business and be gone. The sooner he put Katrina back in her place, in female attire, in his bed where he would prove once again who was master, the better. And he would insist she answer to Katrina, not such a masculine, aberration of her beautiful name. He wondered if the other human females were giving their mates such headaches and heartache, if they were all so headstrong, hard willed, and aggressive. Perhaps the race was more warrior-like than the history annals had led them to deduce.

"A witness stepped forward to Carlev's assassination."

Katrina paled and her whole frame stiffened, her tension seeping into his bones. He wondered if she had been told of his former concubine and cursed himself for not telling her himself and assuring her the relationship had been severed upon his mating vows to herself. But in his defense, they had barely had time to get acquainted, and Katrina had filled his senses, mind, and heart driving all thought of Carlev away.

"Assassin. An Antarian, not the Omagagis?" Rage erupted, boiling in his blood. How dare one of his people commit such an atrocity against the Goddess, and against the throne! "The guilty one will pay with his life! Is the witness able to name the assassin?"

The general's gaze slithered to Katrina disdainfully. "It is not an Antarian, Your Highness. It is one of the human females."

Fear strangled Davek's heart, but he struggled to rein it in and maintain a regal stance. "What proof does your witness have?"

"Absolute proof, Sire. There were two witnesses in agreement. And we have the murder weapon with finger prints." Vidak snarled and snapped his fingers high in the air.

Several armed guards surrounded them.

"What is the meaning of this?" Davek's protective instincts screamed to remove Katrina from this place but of course he couldn't. He surmised what his general was about to accuse but he had to hear it, needed to see the proof for himself. He wished he could cut out his tongue for pronouncing the punishment to the crime.

"The *Princess, her Royal Highness*, was the assassin, Sire. I am most distressed to be the one to inform you of this unforgivable insult to the throne, to our people, and most of all to yourself." Whereas the man's voice had been highly supercilious when pronouncing Katrina's titles, it had slickened to honey over his profession of regret.

Katrina's eyes winded, sparking with indignation. Her muscles bunched, her spine stiffening to the breaking point. "I did not murder my husband's *consort*."

Derision dripped from the word consort, making Davek sigh and peer closely at her, wishing he could read her mind. How much did she know?

A sly smile snaked across Vikak's thin lips. He cocked his head and tsk-tsked. "So she knew of your relationship with Carlev and was filled with insane jealousy. Prime motive for murder."

Davek felt as if he'd been punched in the stomach, even more than at the sight of Carlev's lifeless body. Although Katrina hadn't been thrilled about being taken from her home world, even though she was stubborn and defied his authority, she had proven her loyalty by saving them from the Omagagis. Moreover, she had come alive in his arms, unable to deny the need they shared for one another. Dare he presume love had blossomed between them? He had hoped so, now he feared not. "It can't be."

The General nodded to one of his assistants.

A young soldier garbed in the uniform of the palace guard stepped forward carrying a glass case. He bowed low and held the case out to Davek. "Your Highness."

A laser gun rested inside, scorched and twisted, splattered with blood, attesting to fierce battle. "What is this?"

"The evidence Your Royal Highness." Vidak snapped his fingers again. "Arrest this enemy of the throne."

Bile rose in his throat as his heart was ripped from his chest. He pinned his gaze to his mate, praying she was not already mother to his child and heir. *What then?* "How could you?"

* * * *

Kat sucked in a deep breath, shuddering. This nightmare was never ending! "I didn't kill Carlev. It was ... it was self defense." She couldn't exhale and had never been so close to hyperventilating, even in the hot scorching sands of the Sahara desert. Not only had her husband had a mistress, now he believed her capable of murder. But she couldn't reveal Neala either. If not for Davek ordering the young servant to guard her at the expense of her own family, none of this would have happened.

"Your orders, Sire?" Glee danced in the vile liar's eyes. Why would these supposed witnesses bear false witness against her? It didn't make sense, unless they just hated the humans who had been brought forcibly here to save their necks.

Davek turned his back on her, sticking a virtual knife in her gut. "Take her."

The General activated her collar, sending her to her knees in excruciating pain. "That's for Carlev."

Davek grabbed the General's wrist and wrestled the device from him, deactivated and confiscated it. He snarled, growling. "That's unnecessary. Do it again and you'll answer to me."

Kat dropped to all fours, gasping for air, weak, barely any energy to breathe much less stand.

Vidak's nostrils flared as he got up in Davek's face. "And you will answer to the King. Why do you hesitate to assert obedience and punishment to your *mate?* Perhaps she is not the only traitor?"

"I am not a traitor!" Kat pushed out through gritted teeth as she held her lurching stomach and rose unsteadily. "Carlev was the traitor. She was conspiring with the Omagagis. She was angry that Davek married me and not her."

"Pathetic lies. Now she's casting wicked aspersions on the dead. Treason *and* sacrilege!"

Vidak's scathing glance would make the most stalwart soul squirm, but Kat refused to give him the satisfaction of letting him see the reaction he had on her. He was good, but she knew he was a filthy liar. *Why?*

What disturbed her more than the snake trying to swallow its prey was the lack of due process on her new world. "Don't I get a trial and a chance to prove my innocence? Do I get an attorney and a phone call? Haven't you heard of innocent until proven guilty?"

All gazes turned on her as if she was daft and hope died in her chest. Déjà vu. She was back in the prisoner of war camp, a non-person with no rights, no hope, no future.

"Attorney?" Davek's brows pinched together. He massaged his creased forehead.

"Lawyer. Counsel. Representation." Frustrated, she wracked her brain for terms they could understand. Shouldn't the universal translator translate? Unless they had no justice system. There might be three full moons bathing her from above and violet vegetation all around, but she felt as if she was back in the African desert in a sweat box trying to force her to confess to crimes she had never committed. Perhaps three full moons meant thrice the insanity of merely one full moon back on Earth. Her neck burned and itched under the repulsive collar, and she was going to be sick to her stomach all over Vidak's superbly polished boots.

"You shall be granted an audience with the king. His decree will be final." Regency vibrated in her husband's voice that sounded more alien than ever.

"I tire of this. Lock the prisoner up." Vidak sighed and rolled his shoulders one by one.

Kat decided she had no choice but to tell the whole truth. She wrestled herself away from the brute confining her and ran up to Davek, blocking his path. "Don't I have a right to defense? I have witnesses, too. Neal--"

Vidak grabbed his guard's obedience device and aimed it at her, and mashed the button.

Immediately the collar blazed unbearable pain through her, making her clench her teeth so hard they should crack. She shook uncontrollably.

"Enemies of the throne don't deserve consideration."

"I *saved* your sorry ass! And your people. I protected the throne!" She let her glance slide over his spotless appearance. "I'd like to know what you were doing during the battle."

Davek rounded on his general. "She speaks the truth. She fired the shot that destroyed the Omagagi mother ship. She led the final resistance."

"More treason! A female engaging in battle, wearing a stolen uniform, a misbegotten craft, and trying to assassinate the prince! Very devious. Yes, very devious, this one." Vidak circled her, looking her up and down. "She was going to kill you and make it look like an accident. In disguise, no one would have suspected a female. They would have been searching for a male." Vidak tapped his chin and treated her to his narrow-eyed glare.

"Consider yourself on report for defying my orders." Davek bristled but did not attempt to comfort her. He barely looked at her, as if the sight of her sickened him.

"Take her." Davek pivoted on his regal heel and marched off without a backward glance.

She was escorted to a dungeon below the palace, which contained a moth eaten bunk bed, a rusty sink and toilet facilities in full view of anyone gazing through the iron bar door. "What, no matching towels and bidet?" Shouldn't royalty, even by marriage, get thrown in the A-prison? Even crooked senators and white collar criminals back home got sentenced to the country-club prisons with the golf courses, tennis courts, and gourmet food.

"Your wit doesn't amuse me, female," the prison warden said drolly. "Be quiet and we'll get along. I won't have to activate your obedience device."

Like she wanted to hold a conversation with that pointy-eared Mensa. Pointy eared this race might be, but they weren't all geniuses like Mr. Spock. Nor was she the type to play a harmonica or sing forlorn love-gone-bad songs. She doubted harmonicas existed on this world. In fact, she hadn't heard a note of music, which she sorely missed. Music would probably soften their souls and give them more humanity.

He tossed a one-shouldered gown at her. "Here, change into this and give me that uniform. Females are not permitted to dress like men."

She gazed at the detested Antarian gown with distaste. Why should she do his bidding if she was already being punished? Would compliance lessen her penalty?

The warden lifted the device and aimed it at her, a wicked smile playing about his lips. The devil obviously enjoyed inflicting pain.

"Oh, all right. Turn your back while I dress."

The man didn't budge, his beady fuchsia gaze ever watchful. "You dare give *me* orders?" His thumb hovered over the button that would inflict horrible pain.

Kat undressed and dressed simultaneously, pulling the gown around her neck and removing the clothing underneath, shimmying out of it. Not that it provided a great deal of modesty as the material was practically transparent and one breast stood out in full view of his lascivious male gaze once the uniform had been discarded. She tossed the soldier's garb at his face, wishing it was a rock she threw instead.

"Your impertinence will not gain my favor, wench." The wrinkled, unkempt warden scowled at her.

"That's *Your Highness*," she said, lifting her chin, glaring at him. For the moment anyway, she supposed. "And why would I want *your* favor?"

The warden stomped off grumbling. He slammed things around his desk, then gulped down a tankard of Antarian liquor and belched loudly.

She thought she'd go stark raving mad without so much as a cockroach to watch scuttle across the floor, the only sound the warden's gross intestinal noises. She tried to recall the mind games she'd practiced during her former incarceration to keep from going mad. At least there, she'd had other prisoners to talk to. Here she was in solitary confinement save for her guard who scowled at her if she so much as made a squeak.

The musty, urine soaked mattress almost gagged her for the first hour. They hadn't put so much as a sheet on the lumpy bed. She preferred the pitted, dusty floor to that flea trap, despite her protesting backbone. She tried to get comfortable, shifting from crossing her legs Indian style, to laying prone on her back, to resting on her stomach and pillowing her head on her arms.

Hours, or perhaps only minutes later--she couldn't tell as there was no way to decipher time--the general strutted to her cell. "Pity you human usurpers had to invade our world and try to mess up carefully laid plans."

She refused to look the bastard in the eye or acknowledge his presence, although he had piqued her curiosity. She crossed her arms over her chest in a show of chastity. She'd already surmised he was in league with the late Carlev. Proving it was a different matter. Obviously no one was going to listen to her, especially not her beloved husband.

She had been wise to shun marriage. She cursed Davek for forcing her into a sacred union, stealing her heart, then breaking it in the cruelest way. She prayed she didn't carry his child. How would this ungrateful world treat the offspring of a *traitor*?

"No need to cover yourself from my eyes. I do not find you humans in the least compelling." Vidak stroked his white goatee as his dispassionate gaze dissected her. "No, you are not an attractive race with that mud-colored hair and moldy eyes. We should have kept searching for a more compatible race with which to mate."

Sticks and stones.... Who cared what the imbecile turncoat thought? His opinion meant nothing to her. He didn't rate a response.

"Do you not hear me female?" Obviously the general didn't appreciate being ignored. He raised his arm and pointed the device at her. "Admit your guilt or suffer the consequences."

She refused to admit guilt to a crime she hadn't committed. She'd endure torture and death instead, but never incriminate herself unjustly. By now, she was old friends with the first. She enjoyed the anger she evoked through her passive resistance. It might be the last bit of pleasure she knew in this lifetime.

Davek strode purposefully toward the general, his eyes sparking violet fire. The wizened healer followed him closely. "I warned you Vidak. If you don't want to join her in the neighboring cell, you best back off and let me see to this."

"Your impartiality in this matter is questionable, Prince Davek. Your loyalty is not assured." Vidak stroked his mustache.

"Remove yourself and do not show your face in this cell again as long as Princess Katrina remains. Do not insult me again." Davek pulled himself up imperially, his jaw thrust forward. He towered over the military man.

"I must object to your reference to her as *Princess*. She does not deserve such an exalted title. I also must warn you to tread carefully. I have many loyal followers. Many Antarians are unhappy with your decision to mix human blood with ours. Their violence and treachery is legendary."

"Be gone with you and still your tongue lest I have it cut out."

"You have been warned Davek." Vidak flared his cape behind him and flounced away. Dust motes danced in his wake. The stench in the room seemed to lessen.

Kat turned her head and stared at her husband, lifting a brow. But she did not rise and refused to bow to him. "To what do I owe this royal audience?"

Davek extracted a key and unlocked her cell. He opened the door wide and held it. "Come with us."

She hung back. "To where?"

"Do you have to question every order woman?" Davek roared, wrath contorting his handsome features. "Come now or do I have to carry you?"

"Why resort to brute strength when you can just push a button and bring me to my knees?"

"Contrary to your low opinion of me, I do not enjoy inflicting pain and do so sparingly. And if you are expecting a child, I do not want him or her injured." He advanced on her, then stood before her with his hands on his lean hips.

Hope flared momentarily, then fizzled when he made it clear it was only the possibility of a baby for which he cared. His concern had nothing to do with any tender feelings he might harbor for her.

"Come with us, Dear," the kindly healer said, taking her elbow in his hand. "We need to run some tests on you."

Clarity dawned on her. "You want to see if the rabbit dies?"

"What is a *rabbit*?" Davek frowned as he led the way out of the dungeon past the bowing jailor.

Homesickness for her world assailed Kat. "A small Earth animal. Cute. Floppy eared. Fuzzy tailed. Likes to hop around. Big teeth. They eat carrots." She made a rabbit face behind her husband's back. "Never mind." Another thing she missed here were fuzzy little creatures like cats, dogs, and the aforementioned bunnies. Not that she would be here much longer to enjoy them anyway at this rate. If only she could cuddle a cat again. She was unaware of any similar animals on this alien world.

"It is of no consequence." Davek waved his hand in the air as if he was bored and set a fast pace. His princely robes floated behind him, nearly smacking her in the face. The reached a room with a bed, a table of shining medical tools, and a chair. The healer gestured them inside.

Kat felt ill looking inside but went in reluctantly. What choice did she have?

"Lay down on the bed." To Davek he turned and said, "You do not need to stay. I will inform you of the test results as soon as I have them." The old healer readied his medical instruments across the room, his back to them.

Davek pulled up a chair and lowered his frame into it, crossing his arms over his heaving chest. "I shall remain." He sat forward, lacing and unlacing his fingers, his gaze never leaving Kat's face.

"So what happens now?" Bitterness tinged her voice. "If I carry your child, I will be spared? At least till he or she is born. Then what? And if I don't, I'll be executed now? Will you hear my side now that we are in private?"

"What have you to say that can alleviate your guilt?"

"That I didn't murder Carlev."

"But you admitted to taking her life...." Davek jumped to his feet and paced, his hands linked behind his back. "General Vidak and his guards were privy to your admission. They will testify that you admitted guilt."

Kat bolted up in the bed and flung her legs over the side of the mattress. "I didn't commit murder, and I admitted no such thing! I said it was self-defense. I did not say I was the one who committed self-defense. I wasn't permitted to speak another word on my behalf."

"But the witnesses. They are above reproach." Davek's frown deepened, the crinkles in his face making him look much older.

"And my word means nothing? Because I'm a female? Or because I'm a human?" She fingered her raven hair, then touched her eyelid. "Is our coloring so offensive to you like Vidak claimed? If so, why did you bring us here? Why did you choose me?"

Davek strode to her side and hauled her against him, her nude breast crushed to his chest. Before she could judge his next move, he crushed her lips beneath his in a searing kiss. "Because Vidak speaks on his own behalf. You are not abhorrent to me. My blood boils for you and my loin lunges at the site of you. Cannot you feel it now?"

He was indeed engorged, straining against the fabric of his tights. He rubbed his pelvis against her stomach. "It is my shame that my body still yearns for yours."

"Why is it a shame? I told you I'm innocent." Her body burned, too, much to her chagrin. Her nipples pebbled, and she wished he could order the healer to leave the room and let them have some privacy. It could be their last. Why not? He was prince. He could order anything. Against his lips, her breaths coming out raspy and shallow, she suggested, "Tell the healer to leave us alone for awhile."

Davek nodded, as if her thoughts filled his mind. He lifted her onto the bed and growled. "Leave us to talk."

She hoped he wanted to do more than just talk, although she did need him to listen to truth and common sense, even if her body was on fire.

"Aha! Did I not tell you how the Prince acts foolishly, with his loins instead of his head?" Vidak practically purred.

Davek released her as if burned, removing his hands to his sides.

"What is the meaning of this?" King Sorel strolled into the room, his bearded face a study in shadows, his lips thinned. His muscles bunched and his gaze drifted from his son to her and back. "I did not believe Vidak when he informed me that you were protecting the traitor to the throne, but my own eyes do not deceive me. What have you to say for yourself my son?"

Davek bent on one knee and bowed before his father. "My mate declares her innocence, and claims she has been falsely accused. I also need to discover if my child is in her womb so I brought her here for the healer to test."

"But the evidence against her.... The witnesses?" The King motioned for Davek to rise and face him as an equal. "Have you an explanation?"

Kat slid off the bed and joined her husband in front of the King. She bowed as she had seen him do and ignored Vidak as he snickered at her obvious ignorance of the ways of their people. "I have, Your Highness."

"Did I address you?" The King looked down his patrician nose at her. His intense gaze seemed to burn through her, and she had the oddest sensation he had the ability to read her mind and look into her soul. She wished he did, then he would see the truth of her assertions.

"No Sire, but I wish to speak in my defense and hope it is permissible. I still do not know your ways." Kat cursed her ignorance of the customs and mores, wishing she had been a more willing student. She wasn't sure how long to keep her head bowed, so she tilted it to look at her husband, pleading him with her eyes for instruction. It wouldn't do to offend the King more than she already had. When Davek nodded almost imperceptibly, she rose to her full height.

"It is highly irregular. Do you feel she has a case?"

Color rose in Davek's neck and then infused his cheeks. "I have not heard the entire story."

"See. She bewitches him with her magic." An evil smile cracked Vidak's thin face. "He believes her innocent before she states her case. She has *no* case."

Kat rushed in, fearing she wouldn't be permitted chance to speak over Vidak's hatred of her and all that was human. "I was not the one who killed Carlev, Your Highness, although I was present and saw the whole thing."

Vidak's smile transposed into a sneer. He lunged and pointed a laser pistol at her. "Do not listen to her lies. She conspired with our enemies to annihilate us. She took Carlev's life in cold blood, and then disguised herself to enter battle so she could murder the Prince without detection. She took us for fools, thinking us too ignorant to unveil her treachery."

"And when exactly did I have time to do all this?" she asked Vidak sarcastically.

"Hold your tongue, traitor."

The king looked thoughtful, stroking his chin.

"What harm can it do to hear her out, Father?" Davek placed himself between her and the general.

"Put your weapon down, Vidak." The King gave his vassal a stern glare and pantomimed replacing it in his holster. "The request is not without reason. I am capable of deciding the truth."

"But she weaves demonic spells over us. See how the Prince behaves out of character? Earth history is rife with magicians and wizards who wield great powers to be feared and avoided. As you recall, I advised you not to bring her kind here, that they would be our downfall." Vidak didn't lower his weapon, and his hand started to shake.

"You are out of line!" Sorel bellowed, his face flush with rage. "Now put down your weapon and depart."

"No." Pouty, contemptuous, Vidak turned his weapon on the King. "I tire of you old man. And your progeny is no better. You have destroyed our world and it is time new blood reigns."

"Yourself Vidak?" Davek stiffened, his back ramrod straight.

"Guards! Apprehend this traitor!" The King roared, the deep timbre of his voice rattling the glass in the windows.

The guards drew their weapons on the King, Prince, and Kat instead, surrounding them in a semi-circle, backing them up against the bed. Their faces devoid of expression, they resembled robots.

"What is the meaning of this?" The King's great chest rose and fell rapidly. The hair on the back of his nape stood on end.

"Isn't it obvious? The guard is loyal to me. They have lost faith in such weak leaders who cannot even control a mere woman, who bring dangerous species to our world and threaten our existence." Vidak strode forward and plucked the King's crown from his head and put it on his own.

"This is blasphemy! May the Goddess strike you down!" The King slid a glance to Kat. "If you know magic, this is the time to use it, and you will be pardoned."

How she wished she possessed such power! She wouldn't be here if that was the case. "I have no such powers. Magic is merely a bedtime fairytale to entertain little children."

"The people won't stand for this! They will rise up against you and seek vengeance." The King backed up against the edge of the bed, his hands in the air above his head.

Kat couldn't stand here and let Vidak win. She shoved the rolling bed with all her might, sending it reeling across the floor. The King lost his balance, falling out of the line of Vidak's laser fire and it gave Davek and herself room to lunge an attack.

Ducking and rolling out of the way of the guard's fire, she tripped on her long gown and landed on the floor. Rolling, hiking her skirts up, she kicked the feet out from under two of the guards. They dropped their weapons, the guns skidding across the floor with a rattling scrape. She grabbed for the closest weapon, her fingertips grazing it when Vidak stepped on her hand, laughing maniacally. "I think you've caused enough trouble. It's time to say goodbye. Too bad your God won't hear you out here."

Bones broke in her right hand, severe pain catapulting through her. Dizziness overcoming her, she swallowed the whimpers that strangled her throat as the general dug his boot heel in and smashed the bones. Her vision dimmed, and she blinked rapidly to keep from passing out.

The general's finger twitched on the trigger as he gloated above her, distracted. Seeing his one chance, Davek roared and tackled him. The weapon caught between them, and the men fell heavily to the floor beside her. They rolled and grappled, growling and grunting, struggling for dominance.

Kat limped out of the way on her knees, cradling her useless limp hand. She ripped a strip from the fragile gown and wrapped her hand quickly, then made a makeshift sling over her shoulder to keep it out of the way as best she could. Light glinted on a metal object half hidden under a bed, and she recognized it as one of the weapons. She made her way to it, picked it up with her uninjured hand, and aimed it at the men in the life and death struggle. She couldn't get a clear shot of the general without risking hitting her husband instead.

Movement on her peripheral caught her eye, and Kat spun around and shot a guard that was creeping up on her.

Amazement flickered across his face before life seeped from his eyes and he sunk to the floor.

There were more of them. She dropped quickly to the ground, using the bed as a shield and scoped out another guard. When she had a clear shot, she pulled the trigger and the shot hit him square in the forehead. He too looked amazed, and then fell backwards across a medical tray, which slammed to the floor, spilling its contents.

Davek and Vidak continued their battle, straining her nerves with each hit, each grapple. She was powerless to help Davek. She swore under her breath and willed them to separate so she could get a clear shot.

Vidak knocked Davek back with a meaty thud. Davek staggered as Vidak raised his arm to deliver another blow. Kat responded instantly to the opening.

A laser buzzed and then two men stilled, looking at each other. Shock flooded Vidak's eyes, and he clutched his heart and fell hard, smacking his head on the floor. The neck snapped and his lifeless eyes stared at the ceiling.

Two ragtag guards still stood. They turned and fled from the healing center. Davek turned his weapon on them and felled one. The other escaped down the hall. Her husband swore loudly and gave chase.

"No Davek! Don't risk it." She knew his chances weren't good as the other man could round the corner then stand in wait. She'd seen it happen too many times in hand-to-hand combat.

But her stubborn husband ignored her and rushed into the hall, his blonde hair flying loose behind him, his laser rifle held closely to his chest.

She shimmied out from under the bed, wincing when pain flared through her hand, up her arm to her heart. Awkwardly, she used the bed as a crutch, using the elbow of her good arm to help her rise to her feet. She followed, but by the time she rounded the door, Davek had shot the remaining guard.

Relief shuddered through her, and she braced herself against the doorframe, trying to suck in air.

Davek, bloodied, scratched, and bruised, limped toward her. One eye was swelling shut, a nasty cut above the lid. He stopped and held open his arms. "Come here Katrina."

She hesitated for only a fraction of a second, and then fled into his arms, wrapping the uninjured one around his waist.

His heart pounded against her ear, racing. His raspy breath warmed her neck. He lowered his lips and she tiptoed up. They drank deeply of each other. His lips tasted salty and then she realized it was blood.

Alarmed, she pulled back and studied his face, bruised and battered, but still beloved. "You need medical attention."

He touched her arm gingerly. "As do you, my love."

"*My love?*" Had she heard right. Did she dare believe her ears?

"Yes, my love. I love you, Katrina." On his lips, Katrina sounded exotic and so sinfully sexy. He examined what he could see of her fingers that the material didn't cover. He bent his head and kissed the tips gently. "The healer must see to this immediately. I wish I could kill that traitor again for doing this to you. And for what he did to Carlev."

Mention of her husband's mistress brought her back to reality, burning the fog off her brain. She stepped back, retrieving her hand. "Vidak didn't murder Carlev. It was Neala." She added hastily, "Don't punish her. She saved her sister's life. And mine. Carlev was working with the Omagagis and she tried to kill me."

Clouds rolled across Davek's eyes, muting them. He looked to be in shock. "Carlev was loyal. She would never do that."

Kat's heart dropped to her knees. "So you did love her. You can't believe she could do anything bad." She turned away, unable to look at her husband another second.

Heavy hands fell to her shoulders, holding her hostage. "I thought I loved her at one time, but no longer. Another fills my heart now. I was just shocked she was obsessed with me."

Obsessed ... that was an apt description. "So much so she'd rather see you dead than have you marry me and make me your Princess."

"She could be childish at times, but I never dreamed she would betray our people, or myself. She would not have made Princess material even if the plague had not stolen her fertility. I would not have made her my mate."

"And I do? A warrior who dares wear masculine clothing and lead battles? A human with green eyes and black hair?"

Warm, firm lips nuzzled her neck. Then a wet, erotic tongue dipped in her ear, making her squirm. Her husband's warm breath made her shudder. In her ear, he whispered huskily, "A most amazing, exotic beauty who is a rare find, who saved our world, who saved her Prince, and who drives him mad with desire." He rubbed his swollen groin against her back at the top of her buttocks.

"I must agree--a most amazing female. One who deserves to be awarded with our highest honors for saving her new King, Prince, and world. We are most pleased with our new human Princess. I can only hope my grandchildren have your spirit, intelligence, and beauty."

The King walked up, startling them apart. He bent and kissed her on both cheeks. "I am proud to call you my daughter, and to know you will serve well beside my only son. Please accept my apologies. Can you forgive me, my dear Katrina?"

Kat smiled, feeling daring. "If you call me Kat."

"Kat," her father-in-law amended, chuckling. Mirth danced in his eyes, so like his son's except for the many lines fanning out from his eyes and the graying brows tenting his eyes. If this is how Davek aged, she would be blessed with such a handsome husband.

Davek turned her around gently and lowered a soft kiss to the tip of her nose. She had never felt so adored. He brushed the back of his hand against her exposed nipple, flaming the fire smoldering in her womb. As he led her to the clinic, he murmured against her ear, "I reserve the right to call you Katrina."

The End

DREAM GUARDIAN

by

Joy Nash

Chapter One

The music sounded like something from outer space.

Julia Maria Borelli crammed her head under the pillow, but the howling barely dimmed. Root canal would have been less painful.

Jewel lifted one corner of the pillowcase and peered at the clock. *Great. Just great.* Six a.m., and the tenant in the upstairs apartment was blasting Yoko Ono loud enough to produce permanent hearing damage.

If there were a place for Jewel in hell, it would sound like this.

Yoko's voice careened up an octave, heedless of innocent bystanders. Jewel sucked in a breath. She hadn't seen her new neighbor, but a rusty U-haul had been blocking the alley when she'd left for work last night. Just her luck, she now shared her South Philly row house with a tone-deaf jerk.

She rolled out of bed and staggered into her miniature kitchen. If anything, the screeching was louder there, and the high-pitched accompaniment did nothing to improve Jewel's mood. She grabbed a broom, climbed on top of the breakfast bar and pounded on the ceiling with the blunt end.

The effort was futile, given the volume of the so-called music, but it felt good. She slammed the broom into the ceiling again. This time it stuck.

"Oh, shit." She tugged it out, releasing a shower of plaster. Apparently, the one-hundred-year-old ceiling was no match for an angry woman wielding janitorial equipment. Now she'd end up paying for repairs.

Out of her travel fund.

A blinding surge of anger propelled her into the hallway and up the stairs. She pummeled the door to the cretin's apartment.

It opened while her fist was in mid-swing. Unable to stop her forward motion, she fell over the threshold, into something--no, make that somebody--hard.

A strong hand grasped her arm and held her steady. Jewel regained her balance and looked up, into the darkest eyes she'd ever seen.

They were so black that she couldn't tell where the pupil and iris met. They were the sky in the hour before dawn: clear, brilliant, and lit with the sparkle of a thousand stars. Black diamonds set in a face of harsh angles.

High cheekbones and a long, patrician nose. A jutting chin touched with about three days' worth of stubble. Long, dark hair falling over a proud forehead and brushing ever so slightly against a firm jaw. Her gaze traveled lower.

Jewel caught her breath. Despite the fact that last night's frost had put a damper on spring, her new neighbor wasn't wearing much at all.

And he was *ripped.* The man must have been working out forever. His incredible pecs and washboard abs were dusted with the most interesting sprinkle of black, curly hair, which disappeared into the low-slung waistband of his Sponge Bob boxers. Jewel swallowed hard and tried not to stare at the bulge rounding out Mr. Squarepants.

My God. Andrea Bocelli and Fabio rolled into one incredible, heart-stopping package.

That would be one heart-stopping package with hideous taste in music, she reminded herself.

"Yes?" His voice was deep and husky, a welcome contrast to Yoko's latest attack on C flat.

Jewel peeked around the hottie's massive shoulders. His apartment was even smaller than hers. His head came dangerously close to the ceiling, giving Jewel the impression of a giant crammed into a playhouse. She'd interrupted his cooking--the heady aromas of coffee and bacon wafted from the doll-sized stove.

She stabbed a finger at the source of her audio agony--a half-built computer wired to a portable CD player. "Do you think you could turn that thing down?"

"Sorry." Mr. Hunk strode to the offending instrument and bent over. While he adjusted a knob, Jewel ogled his tight butt and long, hard thighs.

Blessed silence filled the air. *Thank heaven.* Now was the time to lay down the law about blasting alternative music.

"I'm Jewel. From downstairs." Mentally, she winced. Not an auspicious start for a dressing-down.

He stood up and turned around. "Hello, Jewel."

She detected a hint of an accent. Dare she hope it was Italian?

Long seconds ticked by while she stared at her neighbor's pecs. Maybe he wasn't a total wash. She could try introducing him to classical music.

He cleared his throat.

She looked up into his sinful eyes.

Then he smiled.

Wow.

A few stuttering heartbeats passed before Jewel gathered her wits. “And you are....”

“I am Darius.”

“Darius,” she said. His name swept over her tongue like chocolate mocha cappuccino, and for once in her life, Jewel couldn’t think of what to say next. God, she was an idiot. What was wrong with her? She didn’t normally fall apart over a great ass and a smile like a Greek god. At least, she didn’t think she did.

“Please, call me Dar. Would you like to come in? I am preparing breakfast, and your company would be most welcome.”

Definitely an Old World accent. “Okay.” She trailed him into the kitchenette, ignoring the open sofa bed as she picked her way past an assortment of half-unpacked moving boxes.

He shoved a pile of computer guts off a chair. She sat down at the breakfast bar and eyed a stack of programming magazines, the only neat element in the chaos he called home. Who’d have thought? It looked like her newfound Apollo was a geek.

He rummaged through one of the boxes on the floor by the refrigerator and took out two chipped ceramic mugs. “Coffee?”

“Sure.”

He moved to the stove, where a real coffee pot, battered but serviceable, was perking merrily. She could see the brown liquid bubbling in the little glass doohickey on top. Dar poured two cups of steaming java. Jewel wrapped her hands around her mug and sniffed appreciatively.

Dar transferred several slices of crisp bacon onto a plate lined with paper towels, then cracked half a dozen eggs into a bowl. Within moments, it seemed, he presented Jewel with a cheese omelet so light it barely touched the plate.

He sat his buns of steel down in the chair opposite hers and took a swig from his mug, then bent his head to his meal. Jewel took a bite of omelet and tried to remember when a man had last cooked for her.

Nothing came to mind, unless she counted the time her older brother, Joey, had boiled the spaghetti water, but even then, she’d had to open the jar of sauce.

She took another bite, then realized that Dar had already finished and was staring at her breasts. Admittedly, she didn’t have much up top, but....

Jewel caught her breath, suddenly aware of her attire--the soft, snug T-shirt and silky boxers she slept in. The outfit didn’t leave much to the imagination.

A weird flash of hunger ripped through her. Not her own--the emotion was Dar’s, though how she knew that, she couldn’t say. She gripped her cup and gulped a mouthful of java.

She waved her fork at her plate, trying to distract him. “This is great.

Thanks."

He caught her gaze. "Any time."

He might have been talking about breakfast, but somehow Jewel doubted it. She cleared her throat, which had suddenly gone dry. Maybe if she just pretended she was fully clothed, he'd get the hint. "So, where'd you move from?"

"New Jersey. Just across the river."

"Did you live there long?"

"No."

"Where'd you come from originally?"

He hesitated, then replied, "I'm an alien."

"Illegal, I bet." Anything that looked as good as Dar did had to be illegal.

"You could say that."

"Where were you born?"

"Tar'ana."

"Is that in Italy?" She held her breath.

"No."

"Then where is it?"

His expression darkened. Jewel ran over the question in her mind. It was harmless enough. So why did Dar suddenly look like he was going to explode?

"My home is a planet in the Tarnassa System," he said tightly. "Fifteen light years from Earth."

Jewel hid a spurt of annoyance. Typical geek humor, badly in need of an overhaul. Of course, he couldn't know she was the very last woman he should be baiting with alien jokes. Joey and his best friend Ronnie had seen to that, back in tenth grade when she'd still been naïve enough to believe the X-files were real cases from the FBI. The incident known as "Spacey Jewel's Alien Abduction" was a permanent part of Borelli family lore.

"Okay, Mr. Alien," she said, trying her best to look amused. "I'll bite. Why'd you come to Earth? Research? Invasion? Or are you just slumming it on the wrong side of the Milky Way?"

Dar's serious expression didn't flicker. "None of those things. I am a fugitive."

"From justice?"

"No." He nearly spat out the word. "Not from justice."

A slap of raw anger hit Jewel so hard she nearly fell off the chair. As before, instinct told her the emotion came from Dar, even though she felt it in her own gut.

What the hell was going on?

She closed her eyes and counted to ten. The anger receded. Then she opened her eyes. Dar was staring at her as if she'd suddenly sprouted two heads.

"What?" she said.

He shook his head, as if trying to clear his brain. "Jewel, do you sing?" He held himself very still, waiting for her answer.

"How did you know that?" she said, stunned. Then she remembered. "Oh. You must have heard me running scales yesterday. Yes, I sing--opera." She watched for his reaction through half-closed eyelids. No one ever expected a young, skinny diva.

"Opera." Dar's eyes turned thoughtful for a moment as he searched some internal database. A startled expression flitted across his face.

"You are a singer of stories," he whispered, and Jewel felt his surge of elation. She gripped the edge of the table. This was too weird.

"It suits you," he said.

She looked at him in surprise. "No one's ever told me *that* before. Usually they think I'm nuts. My father does."

"Why?"

She jabbed her fork into the last of her eggs. "I don't know, maybe because he thinks I'm a flake and I need a husband and six kids to keep me busy? Oh, and then he's of the opinion that hell will freeze over before someone pays me to stand on a stage." Those miserable words still echoed in Jewel's head. "When I left home, he told me I'd be back in a week. But you know what?"

Dar raised his eyebrows.

"That was two years ago. I came to the city on my own and won a scholarship at the Academy of Vocal Arts. Plus, at night I'm a singing waitress at Victor's."

He shot her a baffled look. "Who is Victor?"

"Victor's isn't a person, it's a restaurant. The Victor Café. The wait staff sings arias between courses. The tips are fantas--"

A low, vibrant hum interrupted her words. Dar was on the computer-slash-CD player in a flash, bending low, turning dials and tapping on a small keyboard Jewel hadn't noticed before.

She blinked. "I thought you turned that thing off."

Dar didn't answer, and she had the distinct impression he hadn't heard her. She sensed his tension, his soul-consuming hope. He spiked his fingers through his thick black hair. A moment later, the noise stopped.

Dar dropped back on his heels and uttered one short, sharp word Jewel didn't recognize. No doubt its English equivalent had four letters.

She scooted her chair around to face him. "Is something wrong?"

He pushed to his feet and shook his head. "I'm hoping for a message from...." He paused. "My brother."

"On that? What is it, some kind of ham radio?"

He stared down at the thing. "Not exactly, but similar."

"Wouldn't email be easier?"

He hesitated again, then shook his head. "Your Internet isn't capable of transmitting a message through the rift in space-time."

Jewel gave him a half-smile, but truthfully, Dar's geek humor was *not* amusing. She couldn't complain about his cooking though. She contemplated her empty plate and wondered what he had planned for dinner.

Before she had a chance to ask, Dar, who had been heading back to the kitchen, froze in mid-step. His body went rigid. Beads of sweat appeared on his forehead. A low, inhuman cry vibrated in his throat.

Jewel's heart lurched. Maybe he was epileptic or something. "Are you okay--"

The words died on her lips as Dar took two jerky steps toward her and gripped her shoulders. His fingers dug into her flesh and pinned her to the back of the chair, but the pain she felt from his touch was nothing compared to the agony pouring from his soul.

She closed her eyes against it, but it did no good. She felt her soul reach for him, touch him in a place she was sure no other had before.

A landscape of ice invaded her mind. Miles and miles of ice, harsh wind and rocky peaks. A wilderness so desolate Jewel found herself fighting back tears.

"Jewel--"

She opened her eyes and gasped at the emptiness she saw in Dar's eyes. Something cold and dark lurked there. A feral demon, wrapped in black power. She sensed it reaching, circling, heard its soul-shattering cry. It hungered, and it wouldn't hesitate to take what it needed.

Then, suddenly, it vanished.

Dar blinked, then looked down at his hands. He jerked them off Jewel's shoulders as if he'd been stung.

He straightened and attempted a smile, but his hands were shaking. "I'm sorry, Jewel. I didn't mean to frighten you."

Jewel's chest tightened. She could feel the cold swell of Dar's fear, and she sure as hell wasn't too calm herself. What had happened?

She wasn't sure she wanted to know, so she didn't ask.

"Well, I better be going. I have class in an hour." She pushed her plate back and stood. Dar's gaze tracked her movements, but he made no move to stop her as she inched to the door.

"Thanks for the breakfast." Jewel jerked the door open and nearly fell into the hallway.

* * * *

Dar'ii Uus, son of Larn, watched the delicate Earth female scurry from his dwelling like a shorthaired *kornos* pursued by a wild *gorna*.

A Singer of Stories.

May the Ancestors have mercy.

He battled the urge to pursue her. The effort nearly brought him to his knees. Dar had walked on Earth for more sun rotations than he cared to count, searching for a Singer. Now, at last, the woman he sought had come knocking--nay, pounding--at his door.

And how had he greeted the unexpected arrival of his salvation? Like a slavering demon on the hunt.

He closed his eyes and began a Prayer. The intricate chant emerged from his heart, steadying him. The Voice, always with him now, faded into the shadows, but he did not allow himself to hope it had gone completely. Soon enough it would be back with double the force.

But for the first time since his shuttle had crashed on Earth, he did not fear the call to the Dream Journey.

He had found his Singer--his Dream Guardian--the woman who would tame the dark demons of his soul.

Had Goreth been as lucky? Dar crouched by his makeshift Rift probe and coaxed the controls to a higher frequency. He'd sent his message into the Rift for one full Earth year, yet no answer had come from his twin. Was his brother dead?

No. Dar would know if he were, as he had felt the loss of his sister during the massacre. The mindlink that Dar shared with Goreth was silent, not broken. Dar rose and paced the length of his new dwelling, which he had chosen because of its location on one of the slender threads vibrating from the Rift.

A shaft of sunlight streamed through his open window. The golden ribbon spilled onto the floor's soft covering, illuminating swirls of dust. Dar smiled. The day would be bathed with heat.

He stepped into the light and turned his face to the sky. The yellow sun kissed his skin with a mother's love, and like a new babe, he craved the caress. He could almost believe that if he stood long enough in the sun's embrace, it would melt the winter ice of his heart.

His body welcomed the warmth, but his mind spun in cold circles. Goreth had made the most of the diversion Dar's shuttle had provided--Dar had seen his brother's ship disappear into the Rift an instant before his own smaller craft was hit by the Mardulan spiker in pursuit.

There was every chance that Goreth and the others had reached Tar'ana rather than being forced, like Dar, to put down on the nearest inhabitable planet. But though he prayed Goreth had reached their homeworld, Dar could not be sure of his brother's fate. He could only look into the eyes of his own destiny.

Those eyes were deep and brown, set wide and framed by dark curls. Their owner was small and lithe--beautiful, and brimming with passion. Her scent was of spice and freedom. Her skin was fine, and softer than the *rallah* cloth his mother had loved to weave. The memory of it lingered on his fingers.

In her presence, the long years of ice and captivity seemed no longer than a heartbeat. Jewel's goodness had touched Dar's soul. Could she tame his demons? His life depended on the answer.

She had instinctively tried to do just that when the Voice had called to him. He'd pulled back from her protection, but not before she'd been badly frightened. She'd bolted out the door as if running for her life.

Which, a nagging voice whispered in his head, she was.

Dar pushed back a flare of guilt. His circumstance was dire, and

Jewel was his last hope. He considered the dilemma. He could not pretend to be a man of Earth--a Dreamer did not dishonor his Guardian with lies. Yet if Jewel knew the whole truth, she would run as far and as fast as her slender legs would carry her, leaving Dar to face his Journey alone. The ravenous demons hidden in his soul would devour his mind, leaving him insane.

A chill wind swept through his heart. Dar had wished himself dead many times since he'd set his feet on Earth's soil. He could endure physical bondage, pain, humiliation--even death. But to travel the Dream Path without a Guardian....

That prospect truly terrified him.

Never before--even on those nights when he lay in chains awaiting Shata's pleasure--had he felt such despair as he had when he contemplated facing his Dream Journey alone. At least during his years as a slave, he had shared the mind link with Goreth.

Here, on Earth, unending loneliness iced his soul. Dar had contemplated taking his own life, but the lust for survival that had sustained him for so long would not allow him to choose a coward's path. He had prayed instead, pleading for the Ancestors' mercy, though the Old Ones rarely saw fit to dispense such a commodity.

Now, it seemed, they had.

The chill vanished, leaving Dar's soul to flare as hot and bright as the brilliant orb floating in the Earth's blue sky.

He had little choice. His survival depended on Jewel taking the role of his Dream Guardian. He would need to set the snare with infinite care.

He did not flatter himself that she would be happy when he succeeded.

Chapter Two

"You're home. At last."

Jewel closed her eyes and resisted the urge to throw the cordless phone against the wall. "Hi, Mamma."

"I've been trying to reach you all morning. Where have you been?"

"Out." She glanced at the steady red light on the answering machine. "Why didn't you leave a message?"

"You know I don't talk to machines, Jullina."

Jewel winced at the pet name. "I was in class, Mamma, and I have just enough time to go jogging before I have to get ready for work. Why are you calling?"

"Do I need a reason to call my baby?"

"No, but you usually have one."

Jewel could almost smell her mother's disapproval wafting through the phone line. "Well. I called to tell you that Christina Torre is getting married."

"That's nice."

"Nice? How can you say that? She's three years younger than you."

"What is she, pregnant?"

Jewel almost smiled at her mother's strangled cry. "It doesn't matter what Christina is. She's marrying a very nice insurance salesman in June, and he's building her a new house. She isn't wasting her time waiting tables, let me tell you. I do hope you'll come for the wedding."

"I'll be in Italy, Mamma. You know that. I'm leaving the day after graduation."

Jewel's mother uttered a prayer to the Madonna. "Julia Maria, give up this Italy nonsense and come home. I miss you. And you haven't even seen your sister's new baby."

Jewel swallowed past the sudden lump in her throat. "I know, Mamma, but I have to live my own life. If I go back to Hershey, I'll end up staying and hating myself. I want to sing. In Italy. I've got three auditions lined up in Rome." Okay, so maybe that was a bald-faced lie, but Jewel was sure something would come up once she got to the Eternal City.

"How can you turn your back on us Julia? How? You haven't been home in two years. Your father misses you. I remember when you were a little girl, how you'd tell him Hershey was your favorite place in the world. Now you won't even put foot in your hometown. Pop's not getting any younger, you know. One day you'll come back, and he'll be gone."

Ouch, that hurt. "If you remember, Mamma, the night I left, Pop specifically told me not to come back unless I came to my senses. I haven't. Besides, I've asked you enough times to come to Philly for a visit, and you never have." Two could play the guilt game, she thought grimly.

"Your father and I worked our fingers to the bone to get out of that city. Why would we want to go back?"

Jewel rubbed her forehead. Time to hang up, before she said something she regretted. "Well, when you see Christina, tell her I hope she'll be happy married to an insurance company, and I'll look forward to seeing the baby's picture on the Internet. Bye."

Jewel dropped the receiver onto the cradle and headed into the bedroom. A few minutes later she was dressed in running shorts and a T-shirt, ready for a stress-relieving run. She slammed out the door and walked the two blocks to Broad Street, then caught a bus. Sure, some people jogged in the narrow streets of South Philly, but she preferred to tone her butt in scenic Fairmont Park.

She got off at the Art Museum. Her regular route was three miles, past the university boathouses and along the east bank of the Schuylkill River.

She had just settled into an easy rhythm when someone fell into step beside her. She glanced sideways and nearly stumbled. *Holy hot tamales.* Her new neighbor. The sexy geek with questionable taste in music.

He probably thought she was a ditz for running from his apartment the way she had. At the time, she'd have sworn some sort of ill wind had blasted her out, but afterward, in the familiar surroundings of her own kitchen, she wondered if she hadn't been imagining the whole thing.

He flashed her a smile. "Hi."

"Hi." She dared another peek in his direction. His running shorts looked like he'd picked them out of a bag Goodwill had left for the Salvation Army. But who cared about clothes? His bulging muscles, shining with sweat, blazed in naked glory. He'd pulled his long hair into a tight ponytail, accentuating the hard angles of his face.

My God, he looked good enough to eat.

"Do you run much?" Well, that was lame. She might as well have asked him his sign. Leo, if she had to make a guess. He was way too hot for a Capricorn or a Taurus. Though with all that simmering sensuality, Scorpio was a definite possibility.

"Every day, between shifts."

It took her a second to focus. "Shifts? Where do you work?"

"A second-hand computer shop just off Vine Street, near the bridge. Take a bite."

She blinked. "Of what?"

He flashed her a grin. "That's the name of the shop. Take a B-Y-T-E."

Jewel flushed. "Oh. What do you do?"

"I rebuild old computers."

"Did you go to school for that?"

He hesitated, then said, "It is not difficult."

"If you say so."

"Hi, Gorgeous." A leggy blonde jogged up on Dar's opposite side, brushing her bouncing forty-four double D's against his arm. The hussy glanced sideways and batted her false eyelashes.

Dar's head swiveled and dipped, his gaze falling somewhat further south of Miss Clairol's dark roots and simpering smile. It was pretty clear he wasn't admiring her intellect.

Men.

She gritted her teeth and kicked into a sprint.

A few seconds later, Dar caught up to her. "Jewel. Where are you going?" He leaned close and touched her arm.

It was only the briefest caress, but Jewel felt as though she'd suddenly gone into slow motion. The world around her contracted. Dar filled it with his body, his scent, his unwavering attention. A tingling feeling began in the pit of her stomach, and she felt her nipples contract against the thin cotton of her T-shirt. A stab of desire pierced her, so heady and potent that it left her gasping. And somehow, she knew Dar was feeling it, too.

A shiver of apprehension overtook her but, perversely, instead of moving away, she stepped closer, unable to resist the pull of Dar's need. He smiled, and his eyes were so dark and beautiful she forgot to be afraid.

"How far will you go?" he asked.

Jewel blinked her confusion. "What?" Surely he didn't mean....

"How far are you running?"

It took her a moment to realize her feet were still carrying her down the jogging path. Her cheeks reddened, and she prayed that he hadn't noticed. "Oh! Just ... up to the stone arch and back."

He nodded, and turned to watch the trail ahead. A group of joggers approached, making it difficult to run side by side, so Jewel dropped back and let Dar take the lead.

She matched his easy rhythm, her gaze traveling a slow path up his body. He moved with sensual grace, like a large, sleek cat. His legs were long and lean, his butt firm, his back and shoulders....

Jewel started. Dar's ponytail had fallen over one shoulder, giving her an unobstructed view of his upper back. Two deep, puckered scars marred his skin at the base of his neck, one on either side of his spine.

An image of Dar's magnificent body, prone on a narrow white table, sprang into her mind. His arms and legs hung over the edges, shackled to cuffs on the table's supporting frame. His head was unsupported, and as Jewel watched, a gloved hand grabbed his hair and yanked upward. A second shadowy figure bent a white metal rod around his neck and plunged the pointed ends into the vulnerable flesh at the nape of his neck. The rod flashed, then settled into a steady glow.

Pain came, in waves that crested higher and higher. He broke into a sob of pure agony. Then all sensation faded, until nothing was left but a whisper.

My God, how had he endured it?

Jewel stumbled and would have fallen if Dar hadn't caught her arm. She looked up, half-expecting to see his face twisted in pain, but the vision had faded. His expression was concerned, not tortured, but his eyes held a spark of--what?

She tried to identify the emotion as she braced herself with one hand on his shoulder.

Vulnerability. But why? Did he know she'd seen into his past, or was he just....

Jewel gave herself a mental shake. Damn. She was losing it. The next thing she knew, she'd be opening a tarot shop on South Street.

"I'm sorry," she muttered. "I guess I ... tripped or something. I'm okay now." She released his arm and took a step back.

Pain shot through her ankle. Her leg crumpled. Once again, Dar's hands steadied her. With calm precision, as if he performed such services every day, he scooped her up in his arms, pivoted, and started back up the path.

He threaded his way through the joggers, ignoring Jewel's protests. Heads turned, people pointed, and a group of teenage boys hurled crude comments. Jewel buried her flaming face in Dar's chest.

His scent overwhelmed her. She'd never considered a man's sweat to be an aphrodisiac, but the musk of Dar's exertion combined with his unconscious display of strength stirred her in a way she'd never have thought possible.

With every step, his body stroked her.

Erotic images rose and fell in Jewel's mind.

She raised her head and tried to gain some distance. Which, considering her position in his arms, was ridiculous.

"Put me down. We're almost at the bus stop."

He carried her to the three-sided shelter and set her on the bench. Jewel's heartbeat slowed, but not to anything approaching a normal rhythm.

"You don't have to stay," she said. "I can make it from here."

He didn't answer, but his assessing look told her that hell would freeze over before he'd let her go home on her own. A moment later, a city bus rolled to a stop with a squeal of hydraulics. Jewel sighed and braced herself for his touch.

He carried her up the steps, twisting to negotiate the narrow space. Somehow, he produced two tokens and dropped them in the slot.

Jewel looked over her shoulder. Great. Standing room only, and no one was offering her a seat. Dar opened his stance and shifted her in his arms, prompting a hoot of laughter from two punks in the back row. Jewel closed her eyes, hot with embarrassment. Dar tightened his grip.

Every jolt of the bus sent a tingle through her body, and the walk to her apartment wasn't much better. Finally, she was standing on one foot at her apartment door, fishing her key out of the tiny pocket hidden in the waistband of her shorts. When the door opened, Dar's arms came around her again.

He deposited her on the sofa.

"I guess I'll have to call work," she said. She reached for the phone on the side table, but stopped when she saw the red light blinking on the answering machine. Three messages. *Damn.* It sure hadn't taken long.

She pressed the "play" button.

Beep. "Jewel, it's Claudia. Why'd you have to go and get Mamma all upset? Just drop the singing thing and come home. You know, Johnny Devlin isn't married yet, and he asks about you all the time. Do you want me to--"

"No. Definitely not." She hit the skip button.

"Hi, Jewel, Joey. Guess what? There's a job opening in my

department that you'd be perfect for. So call me and--"

"Forget it, Joey," she muttered. "I'm not going hawk chocolate bars." She skipped to the last message.

"Jewel, don't you think it's time you came home? You've proved you can live on your own, now it's time to grow up. Mamma is worrying herself sick with you in Philly. If you go to Italy, it'll be that much worse. And Pop hasn't been feeling well lately. Geez, girl, get a grip. How selfish can you be?"

"Not nearly as selfish as you, Marissa." Jewel blinked back tears that she was sure weren't worth crying. Two years ago, she'd been written off as a bizarre aberration in her otherwise perfect family. She would prove them wrong. She would live her dream of singing on the stage, in Italy, where Opera divas rivaled rock stars in popularity.

She would not give in to their narrow plans for her life.

And she ... would ... not ... cry. She *never* cried. It was her number one rule.

A single, disobedient tear trickled down her cheek.

* * * *

Tears.

Dar could endure anything in the universe except a woman in tears. Instinctively, he reached out to Jewel with his mind and offered what comfort he could.

She jumped at his mental contact, and he pulled back quickly. Her wet lashes fluttered open and she turned her face to him, confusion evident in her eyes. No doubt she thought she'd imagined his psychic embrace.

"Do not cry, Jewel," he said, unable to endure the sight a moment longer.

"I'm not crying." She sat up, blinking rapidly. "I *never* cry." She attempted a smile. "It's my family. They can't understand why I left an idyllic small town and the prospect of marrying a doctor's son to study voice in Philly."

"Your family does not approve of your singing?"

Jewel shook her head. "No. They approve of a rich husband, two-point-six children, and a big house. You see, I'm from Hershey."

"Hershey?"

She nodded vigorously. "Hershey, Pennsylvania. You know, where they make the chocolate bars? The Sweetest Place on Earth. A perfect town full of perfect people living perfect lives." She punched a throw pillow hard enough to raise a small cloud of dust. "I am *not* going to be one of them."

"I do not doubt you."

She tried to stand, then winced and fell back on the cushions. "Damn. I can't afford to take the night off."

He picked up the phone and handed it to her. "I do not think you have a choice."

She snatched the phone out of his hand and dialed. While she talked, he wandered into the kitchen and rummaged through the cabinets and refrigerator. He opened the freezer, loaded some ice into a Ziploc bag, and went back to the sofa.

Jewel sat among the bright throw pillows, looking pale and drained. He could feel her pain thudding in his own mind--her ankle was hurting more than she cared to admit. He smiled. His Jewel was brave, a fine quality for a Guardian to have. He eased the phone from her hands and hung it up, then propped up her leg on the coffee table and draped the bag of ice over her ankle.

"It will be better in the morning," he said.

"I hope so." Jewel dropped her head back and shut her eyes.

Dar moved around to the back of the couch and placed his hands on her shoulder. His thumbs massaged her neck, soothing the tense muscles, urging her to relax. He brushed her mind with his--just a gentle touch, so that she would not be alarmed.

She let out a contented sigh. "That feels wonderful."

He continued his ministrations, reveling in the simple pleasure of touching a woman while at the same time holding her in his mind, a completely new sensation. After a few minutes, his fingers ached to touch her in a more intimate place.

He suspected a typical Earthman would not have hesitated. But Dar was Tar'an, and Jewel was the woman he sought as Guardian. She was required to initiate their first intimate joining.

No. Even though his rod clamored for immediate attention, he could not claim her outright. He needed to entice her into the role of seducer.

Reluctantly, he drew back. Her dark eyes blinked up at him.

"Stay here," he said. "I will prepare a meal."

"There's not much in there," she called after him as he strode toward the kitchen.

"I know. I have already looked. But do not worry, Jewel. I am very creative."

* * * *

It was truly pitiful what a person would do for money.

Jewel ducked out the back door of Victor's. When she added her take of the evening's tips to the balance in her travel fund she could almost convince herself that the five hours of agony had been worth it. Her ankle hurt like hell, but she hadn't wanted to miss a second night of work. Graduation was only three weeks away. She had to have as much money as possible stashed away by then.

She put her foot down and winced. She really shouldn't have gone to class today either, but with so little time to go before the commencement concert, she hadn't dared to skip rehearsal. That aria from "Aida" was a bitch.

And after graduation--Italy.

She came to a halt at the end of the alley and shut her eyes. For one shining moment, she pictured herself on the stage at La Scala. Wrapped in silk and jewels, she sank into a graceful curtsey amid shouts of "Brava!"

Not that she had a clear idea of what the inside of La Scala might look like, but in her fantasy it resembled Philadelphia's Academy of Music, with tiers of gilded balconies and a giant crystal chandelier. Although, truthfully, only a major miracle would place a young, unknown, American singer anywhere but in the audience at the world's most famous Opera House.

Oh, well, even a seat in the back row would be nice.

Jewel turned onto Twelfth Street, into the wind, and started the half-mile trudge to Queen's Village. This section of South Philly wasn't a bad neighborhood, but she never quite relaxed until she caught sight of her row house.

She'd limped about two steps when someone stepped out of the shadow of a doorway and touched her on the arm. She lunged to one side, but not fast enough. A grip like steel closed on her wrist.

A surge of utter terror choked her. She screamed, hitting a high F sharp with a force that could have shattered glass.

"Jewel!" The mugger hauled her into the aura of a street lamp and released her.

"Dar?" She eyed his T-shirt, baggy shorts, and sneakers without socks. She hardly recognized him with so many clothes on.

He offered a sheepish grin. "I am sorry. I did not mean to frighten you."

"Yeah, well, could have fooled me," she said, rubbing her wrist. "What are you doing lurking in doorways at one a.m.?"

"Waiting for you." He frowned. "You should not walk the streets at night without an escort."

She snorted. Her father would have said the same thing. And he would have been right. But Jewel wasn't about to admit it. "I've been walking home from Victor's for months. Nothing's ever happened."

He shrugged. "Even so, I will walk you home."

"I'm not helpless, you know. I took a self-defense class, and at the Academy we studied Stage Combat for a whole semester. Plus," she added, "I ran track in high school."

Dar raised his eyebrows. "You can barely walk on that ankle," he pointed out. "How fast do you think you can run on it?"

Rather than answer, Jewel turned her back on him and started up the street. Unfortunately, her ankle gave way, ruining the effect. Dar was beside her in a heartbeat.

"No," she said before he could pick her up again. "I can walk. Just let me lean on your arm."

They walked, mostly in silence, to the row house. Dar stopped at the bottom of the stairs and waited for Jewel to unlock her door.

She thought for a moment he would ask to come in. He wanted to, she could tell, but some other, stronger emotion held him back. Finally, he said goodnight and gave her a friendly nod.

Jewel prepared for bed. For the first time in nearly two years, she'd walked home from work feeling safe, but she didn't like thinking she needed a man to protect her. She toyed with the idea of using some of her hard-earned money on cab fare.

No. She needed the money for Italy. As long as she was careful, she'd be fine.

But Dar and his incredible bod was waiting at Victor's back door the next night, and the night after that. He walked her home, and though she was sure he was interested, he didn't once angle for an invitation to her bedroom. Or even her living room, for that matter, no matter how much she flirted.

He seemed to be waiting, but for what, Jewel couldn't begin to imagine.

Chapter Three

Dar had thought, at first, that the sky was falling.

The lavender clouds shimmered. A shrill whine pierced the air. The fine hairs on his forearm lifted and tingled. A firestorm? If so, it was unlike any he'd ever experienced.

From his vantage point in the entry court of his parents' home, Dar watched as a fleet of Mardulan spikers dropped from the sky and swept over the Tar'an grasslands.

"By the Ancestors! What's happening?" Goreth sprinted from the doorway and skidded to a halt at Dar's side. Dar felt his brother's fear mingle with his own as they watched the silver birds streak toward the city.

"Mardulans," he replied, his throat tight.

"They will not prevail. Their hoarfrost torpedoes are no match for the mind web of the Elders."

"I pray you are right, brother." As the words left Dar's lips, an explosion rocked the ground. He met his twin's horrified gaze.

They tore out of the forecourt and down the dusty road toward the city. All around them, Tar'ans darted from their houses, moving with one purpose. The mob surged through the narrow streets and spilled into the assembly circle. There, twelve spikers had landed. They stood like silent raptors surveying their prey.

Goreth caught Dar's arm and gasped. "The Elder House! Father...."

Dar steadied himself with one hand on his twin's shoulder. A thick sheath of ice encased the domed palace that housed the Council. Inside, he knew, his father and the rest of the High Elders sat in the gilded throne room of the ancient kings.

Dar caught sight of his sister at the edge of the market stalls. He tugged Goreth toward her, but the press of bodies refused to yield. He stopped when the stones beneath his feet started to tremble. A high-pitched whine screamed from one of the spikers.

The Palace of the Ancestors shattered.

Dar watched as the building crumpled, falling outward under the weight of the heavy dome. A sound like fire-thunder filled his ears, but instead of flames rolling across the sky, ice sprayed overhead.

Needle-sharp shards struck his face and chest, and he covered his head with his arms, leaning into Goreth for protection.

His brother's panicked voice hissed in his ear. "I can't feel him, Dar. I can't feel Father."

Tears scalded Dar's eyelids. He gripped his brother's shoulders, not wanting to believe what he knew to be true. Their father--and all the High Elders--were dead.

A white light flashed about the perimeter of the assembly circle, then shot over the crowd in a low arc and dropped like a net over the crowd. With it came a curious numbness in Dar's limbs. He fought against it, but like quicksand, his struggles only deepened his peril. Finally, he stood motionless, trapped like a *kornos* in a snare.

The entry hatch of the nearest spiker slid open. A woman emerged, her long, yellow hair bound tight around her head. She wore the one-piece white suit of a Mardulan warrior--an obscene creation that molded her body but left her breasts bare. She uttered a word Dar did not understand.

The hatches of the remaining spikers lifted. A hundred women or more, identical in dress as the leader, poured from the ships and streamed among the Tar'ans. Shining weapons nestled in their hands.

They attacked with swift precision, blasting ice right and left. Each victim froze, encased by ice, then shattered. Dar watched in horror, struggling against his unseen bonds.

A blast hit his sister. Pain seared his mind as their link severed.

"By the Ancestors," Goreth whispered, his grief choking his words.

Dar's anger blazed like a tempest, but the Mardulan ice proved stronger than the hottest firestorm. He could do nothing but wait for his own death.

It never came. The younger men and the boys were spared. Goreth's presence at his side was Dar's only consolation as an ice-tipped spike prodded him toward one of the spikers.

Dar's last glimpse of his homeworld was bathed in fury.

* * * *

He woke in chains.

He lay supine, the weight of the iron cold on his limbs and neck. Darkness crowded his vision; he could see nothing of his prison, but the chill of the air on his bare skin told him he was naked.

His bonds were more than adequate.

"Goreth?"

No answer. Panic flared. Dar drew a deep breath and reached for his brother with his mind. The response came at once. Goreth was afraid, but unhurt.

Dar waited in the darkness, his heart pounding in fear, until he thought he would go mad. The Mardulan assault played over and over behind his eyes. The Elders' mind web--forged with the power each wise man had gained during his Dream Journey--had repulsed previous attacks with ease. Yet the defense had fallen within minutes under the Mardulans' newest weapon: a numbing cold that rendered every Tar'an helpless.

May the Ancestors have mercy.

A portal slid open, casting a sharp slice of light across Dar's face. He shut his eyes against the glare.

"I envy you, Shata," a woman's voice said. "This young one will give you a good ride."

Laughter, like shattering glass. "There was another just like him. Did you not see?"

"Yes." The first woman's voice held a note of annoyance. "Mora got to him first."

"Well. Perhaps I'll share."

One set of footsteps retreated. The other drew close. Dar opened his eyes, but the portal had closed and he could see nothing beyond his enemy's dark outline.

Her cold hands floated over his bare skin, branding him with ice. Her fingers stroked his belly, his thighs, teasing, then stroked the length of his sex.

"So large." A chuckle escaped her. "And not even at its full length."

She took him in her hands. Dar's body clenched, and his mind filled with revulsion.

His cock, however, had other ideas.

His flesh grew hard under her coaxing. "Are you virgin?" she asked.

At Dar's sharp intake of breath, her laughter began anew. "Of course you are. The men of your race don't take their pleasures lightly, do they? They save themselves for one woman, and mate for life." A wet tongue scraped the swollen tip of his rod. "Such a waste."

She came over him then, a dark shape straddling his hips. He strained against his bonds, hurling curses into the blackness, bucking his hips. His resistance served only to aid her as she captured him within her body.

"Oh, yes. *Yes.*" Her hips rose and fell with fevered urgency, faster and faster. Desperate to deny her what she sought, Dar willed his cock to shrivel. His traitorous flesh grew harder, until his own groans joined the Mardulan's triumphant climax.

Shame and pleasure burst from his rod.

"Oh, yes, my pet." The woman's voice held a soft, dreamlike quality.

"You were well worth the price I paid." She rose, her movements slow and languid, and left the room.

Dar lay alone in the darkness, his chains no longer the worst part of his humiliation.

* * * *

Suffocating despair hurtled Jewel across her bedroom, toward the window. She grabbed the sill and struggled to catch her breath.

The cool morning air snaked into her lungs, and the pounding beat of her heart slowed just enough for her to gather her wits. A dream. Just a dream.

She struggled to remember, but the images scattered. Only snatches of emotion remained. Anger, despair.

Desire.

Ohmigod. An erotic maelstrom, dark and shameful, battered her senses. Her body thrummed with arousal. Her breasts ached. Heat pooled in her belly, and lower. Her hands were shaking.

That had been one hell of a dream. Too bad she couldn't remember it.

"Shit." Jewel stumbled into the bathroom. She plunged into the shower, but it wasn't until she was in class, running warm-up exercises with her voice coach, that she felt like herself again.

A few hours later, when she stepped through the Academy's front door, she saw Dar standing by the curb. A rush of pleasure overtook her. He'd shown up at Victor's for the past few nights, but this was the first time he'd sought her out during the day.

He stood with his back to her, watching the traffic stutter along Broad Street. Jewel paused a moment to drink him in. As she watched, he lifted his arms over head and laced his fingers together in a lazy stretch. The muscles of his back and shoulders rippled beneath his T-shirt. Jewel's belly quivered in response.

No doubt about it, the man was hotter than sin.

A thin woman wearing black lipstick and a diamond nose stud emerged from the Academy and came to a dead halt at Jewel's side.

"Girlfriend, that is one *fine* looking piece of real estate. And I'm in the market to buy."

"Don't even think about it, Cass."

Cass glanced at Jewel over the top of her wrap-around sunglasses. "You know him?"

"He's my neighbor."

"No shit."

Jewel nodded.

"Is he as good as he looks?"

"I wouldn't know."

Cass regarded Jewel with patent disbelief. "Wake up and smell the salsa, girl. You live next to *that*, and you haven't thrown yourself at it? What're you waiting for? His butt is--" She sucked in her breath and lowered her voice. "He's not gay, is he?"

"No!" Jewel's cheeks flamed red. The thought had never occurred to her. "At least, I don't think he is."

Her friend uttered a sound of exasperation. "Damn it, Jewel, you're the only woman I know who still blushes. That small town upbringing just doesn't wash off, does it?"

Dar chose that moment to turn around. A smile sprung to his lips as he made his way across the crowded sidewalk to Jewel's side. "Hello."

"Hi, Dar."

Cass cleared her throat.

"Oh! This ... this is my friend, Cass. Cass, this is Dar."

Dar nodded, then turned his attention back to Jewel.

Jewel's friend snorted. "Well. I guess I'm on my own, then." She tapped Jewel on the arm. "Remember what I said."

"What did your friend say?" Dar asked when Cass had gone.

"What? Oh! Nothing." Jewel squinted up at him. "Why?"

"I have come to take you to lunch."

"Lunch? Really?" Damn. She seemed to be unable to manage anything more than one-word sentences. She took a deep breath. "That would be nice."

They walked to Reading Terminal Market and bought cheesesteaks from one of the vendors. That night Dar appeared at Victor's, and the next day he showed up again at the Academy. Cass rolled her eyes and made kissing noises when she saw him.

By the next week, Jewel was spending all her free time with Dar, and things were progressing nicely. He didn't play Yoko in her presence. He *was* somewhat vague about his background, but at least he hadn't tried the alien joke on her again. He was sexy and sweet, and a damn good cook. But though he looked at her with unmistakable heat in his eyes, he didn't so much as venture a kiss.

It was as if he were waiting for Jewel to make the first move.

Well. She was a woman of the new millennium. She could handle that.

Maybe.

Okay, so what if she didn't have much experience in seduction? She wasn't a virgin, for crying out loud. And just because her previous boyfriends were so much chopped liver compared to Dar was no excuse not to jump his bones.

Just do it, Borelli.

The next day, Jewel and Dar visited the Rodin Museum. There, surrounded by the brilliant sculptor's magnificent naked bodies, Jewel invited Dar to an intimate midnight dinner at her place.

"I found a new recipe," she lied. "I'd like you to try it." She swallowed. "And maybe a few other things." Then, before she could change her mind, she rose up on her toes and kissed him full on the mouth.

He caught her about the waist. His lips parted hers. His tongue traced the full contour of her lower lip, then trailed a hot, wet line to her ear.

The undercurrent of heat in his voice was unmistakable. "I would be honored, Jewel."

"Good," she breathed.

A thrill of anticipation shot through her.

So she didn't know how to cook--big deal. She'd order take-out and offer herself as dessert.

* * * *

"Here you go, my pet."

Dar held himself very still as the cold metal touched his neck. There was a shock when the ends of the collar slipped into place, then a tingling as the signal pulsed along his spine. He struggled to keep his muscles taut, but the effort only succeeded in drawing an amused chuckle from his mistress. His limbs relaxed, his mind numbed, and he accepted another day of defeat.

Shata inserted the key into the lock and released the chains, clucking softly as she inspected the raw sores on his wrists and ankles. "Why do you struggle? You cannot break free."

Dar knew she spoke the truth, but yet, each night when the collar came off, he tried to break his chains. The pathetic act of defiance was the only source of pride left to him. His wounds were the only proof he had that he hadn't yet completely broken. That, and the fierce hope he felt when mindlinked with Goreth.

He rose to his feet at Shata's soft command, his body responding automatically to the collar's instructions, bypassing the input of Dar's own will. By the Ancestors! He would sell his soul to the darkness to be free for one heartbeat.

He would need no more time than that to kill her.

Shata placed the key on the platform and sighed, as if resigning herself to the folly of a small child. "No matter. Once you complete the Journey, you will no longer be so eager to escape."

She must have seen the surprise in his eyes, for she continued, "Yes. I know of the Dream Journey you Tar'an males endure as a bridge to your full power. It was one reason my sisters and I were so eager to harvest the young men of your planet. You see, here on Mardula, there will be no Guardian to protect you when the call comes." She stroked one finger along his collar. "Once you have lost your mind to darkness, I will no longer need this device to control you. You will truly belong to me then."

Leaning close, she continued speaking, false intimacy edging her words like hoarfrost. "Have you seen the men of Mardula, my pet? They cannot compare to you. They are small, pitiful creatures, and their rods never harden. This was not always the case, you see. Some time ago, a contaminant found its way into our water supply, causing our males to wither. Now Mardulan women have no choice but to take to the stars in search of men."

She splayed her icy fingers across Dar's chest. She was tall, almost as tall as Dar, and her breath mingled with his as she spoke. "Your planet was an incredible discovery. Well worth the effort it took to develop a weapon that could breach the mindweb of your Elders." She kissed him tenderly. "You pleased me last night," she whispered, "and my sister was satisfied as well."

A contented smirk curved her lips. She moved against him, rubbing like a darkcat in heat. Her gown, ice blue and transparent, slid across his naked rod, and for the first time, Dar was glad of the sense-deadening collar. While he wore it, his flesh could not respond to her teasing. He stood very still while she fingered him.

When she finally met his gaze, he made no effort to hide his contempt.

Her smile disappeared. "Come," she said.

He could do nothing but obey. Later, lying naked on his cold bed, Dar closed his eyes and dreamed of heat, but even the hottest firestorm would not be enough to melt the carapace of ice that Shata's touch had left on his soul.

Only a Guardian could work such a miracle.

* * * *

Truly, the female's howling was hideous.

Dar let his memories fade. He fiddled with the controls on the Rift probe, adjusting the volume and tone of his transmission to the changing frequency of the Rift. The woman's shrill voice struck a high note, matching the current vibratory rate of the subspace fissure with uncanny accuracy, then undulated wildly. Dar could not have asked for a more perfect surge with which to enhance the range of his mindlink with Goreth.

A sudden, strident squeal caused him to wince. Thank the Ancestors, it was morning and Jewel was in class, or she would be beating down his door with all the fury of a firestorm. Still, finding this recording had been an incredible stroke of luck. Earth's scientists may be ignorant of the Rift, but the gaunt, hollow-eyed female composer of this melody could not have created a Rift probe by chance.

It was obvious the singer was alien to the planet.

He switched off the transmission and listened intently, hoping as he always did for any hint of Goreth's reply, but for the first time, the edge had dulled on Dar's urgency. Even the ever-present murmuring of the Voice could not chill the warmth spreading throughout his body.

After endless days of waiting, Jewel had kissed him. Not only had she kissed him, but she had all but requested his presence in her bed. It was not an offer he intended to refuse.

And if his conscience whispered that Jewel didn't understand the consequences of her invitation, he chose not to listen.

Chapter Four

Whoa, baby. She was seriously set for seduction.

Jewel stood on the stoop and shifted her grocery bag to one hand. The other hand rummaged in her fanny pack for her key. A quick stop at the Whole Foods Market on South Street had provided a mouth-watering selection of upscale, ready-to-eat delicacies. After that, she'd hit the state store and splurged on a bottle of Secco Montepulciano, before snagging a box of chocolate-flavored prophylactics from a jungle display at the funky Condom Palace.

Tonight was the night. After she got off work, Dar would be hers from midnight until dawn.

Anticipation set off sparks in her stomach, and lower. None of her old boyfriends had excited her half this much. Dar was so different, and yet at the same time so familiar. Sometimes it seemed like she could even read his mind.

Maybe she could convince him to go to Italy with her.

"Excuse me, Miss."

Jewel turned, key in hand, and found herself staring up at a stunning blonde woman. Which was a surprise, since Jewel was on the stoop, and the Swedish Amazon was standing on the sidewalk.

"What?" Jewel's gaze leveled off and was assaulted by the woman's incredible breasts. Even encased in a dark business suit, they were impressive. She jerked her head up again. "I mean, can I help you?"

"I am looking for this man." She held up a photograph. "Do you know him?"

Jewel squinted at the picture. Dar's face, hard and unsmiling, stared back at her. A field of ice stretched into the distance behind him. Despite the chill of his surroundings, his torso was bare. Jewel's gaze lingered on a thin white bar encircling his neck.

My God. Dar must have escaped from some Siberian prison camp. No wonder he avoided talking about where he came from. Well, Jewel couldn't imagine the Dar she knew could have done anything horrible--other than playing really bad music, but she hardly thought that was a crime deserving of incarceration. He must have been a political prisoner, like on those spam emails she got sometimes. There was no way Jewel was going to let this Immigration officer get her manicured hooks into him.

She drew her brows together and pretended to think. "No." Amazing, really, how steady her voice sounded. "I've never seen this man."

"Are you sure?"

Jewel sent the woman a smirk. "Definitely. I would, you know, *remember* a guy like this."

She turned and jabbed her key into the lock. She didn't look back, and she felt, rather than saw, the woman move on down the street.

* * * *

Dar was more than ready.

He waited for Jewel in his usual spot by Victor's back entrance, resisting the urge to rip open the door and haul her out of the restaurant's kitchen.

She emerged at last, her gaze searching the shadows. His heart picked up a beat, and his whole body lightened, as it did whenever he was in her presence. This beautiful Earth woman was everything he'd ever hoped his Guardian would be.

She smiled, her excitement rippling in waves around her. His cock responded instantly.

"Sorry I'm late," she said, falling into step beside him and linking her arm through his. "One of the new waiters dropped a tray. What a mess!"

Dar attempted a light-hearted comment, but when he opened his mouth, the words stuck in his throat. He had pursued Jewel because he needed a lover to Sing his passage through the dark twists of the Dream Journey. But in the weeks he'd spent wooing her, he'd come to want her for so many other reasons: her pure heart, her shining humor, her undaunted determination. He loved her strong, slender body, and the way her smile found its way to her eyes a moment before it reached her lips.

But perhaps most of all, he loved the way he felt when he was with her--free. Truly free, in spirit as well as mind, as though the years of his captivity had never occurred. When he looked into Jewel's eyes, the memory of his captivity vanished, like a nightmare shattered by daybreak.

Jewel waved her fingers in front of his eyes. "Hello?"

He stopped walking and looked down at Jewel's anxious expression.

"Dar, is something wrong? Because if you'd rather not have dinner...."

"No," he said quickly, grazing her cheek with the back of his fingers. "Nothing is wrong. Why do you ask?"

She uttered a sound of exasperation. "Maybe because you just walked right past our row house?"

Dar looked up, surprised to see that they indeed had arrived at their dwelling. He gave an embarrassed shrug.

Jewel led the way into her apartment and disappeared behind her bedroom door. When she emerged a few minutes later, the narrow black skirt and white blouse she wore while working had been discarded in favor of a soft, sleeveless dress swirled with color. Her feet were bare.

Dar swallowed hard as she spun around only an arms length in front of him.

"Tie-dye. I got it on the boardwalk last summer. Do you like it?"

He nodded, following her with his gaze as she moved about the kitchen, pulling out dishes and thrusting various foods into the microwave.

"I thought you were experimenting with a new recipe," he said.

"I am. I'm improvising on how long to set the timer on the microwave." She grinned. "There's a real art to it."

He laughed and opened the bottle of wine she gave him. He filled two long-stemmed glasses and set them on the table on either side of a three-wick candle. He ate slowly, watching the expressions flit across her beautiful face as she spoke.

She looked up and blushed, suddenly tongue-tied. She'd felt his desire, he knew, just as he sensed hers, and the bond confused her.

She hesitated a moment, then leaned close. "Dar, do you ever feel like ... well, like we're *connected?* Like sometimes we can read each other's mind?" When he didn't answer immediately, she blushed and looked away. "Okay, I know that sounds weird, but--"

"No," he said quickly. "It does not." He paused, searching for words that wouldn't frighten her. "I too, feel close to you."

She leaned across the table and kissed him. His groin tightened, and for a brief moment, the lust he kept under tight control threatened to break free. She broke the kiss and returned to her meal.

Dar forced himself to take a deep breath and take a forkful of his own dinner. Jewel took a sip of wine and resumed her friendly banter.

"I'm going to Rome. Do you know that in the ruins of the Baths of Caracalla, they perform the opera "Aida"? Radames--he's an Egyptian prince, and the man Aida loves, though she's only a slave--returns from war in the Sudan. There's a triumphal procession, and real elephants and camels march across the stage." She closed her eyes briefly, then continued the story. "But Radames doesn't know that one of his prisoners is Aida's father, the King of Sudan. The King wants Aida to spy on Radames. She doesn't know what to do--she loves them both."

Dar took a deep sip of his wine and let himself bask in the sparkle of Jewel's beautiful eyes. "And then?" he asked.

"When Radames is found talking with the Sudanese king, his own father--the Pharaoh--sentences him to be buried alive for treason. Can you imagine? But he doesn't die alone. Aida joins him in the tomb and they die together."

She sighed. "It's sooo romantic. I just love it. That's why I decided to sing Aida's death song for the graduation concert." She picked up her wineglass and took another sip. The pink tip of her tongue darted out to catch an errant drop of wine. Dar's entire body clenched at the sight.

"Will you Sing for me, Jewel?"

The words slipped out before he realized he had spoken. It was the ritual question asked of a Guardian at the start of a Dream Journey. Dar knew Jewel didn't understand the full import of his words, but at that moment he needed to hear her answer more than he needed to take his next breath.

Jewel put down her glass. "You ... want me to sing for you? Now?"

"Yes. Please."

For a moment he thought she would refuse, but at last she offered him a half-smile. "All right."

He turned his chair away from the table. Jewel rose and moved a few steps away, toward the open window, then turned back to him and fluffed her hair with a nervous flip of her fingers.

"I've been practicing, but it's not perfect yet, so no laughing."

Jewel closed her eyes and went very still. Dar sensed her gather the story and drop it into the peace of her soul. When she drew one long breath and began to sing, laughter was the farthest thought from Dar's mind.

The melody washed over him like the breath of spring, melting the frozen wasteland of his past and touching the fertile soil of his soul. Her voice was strong and sure, her tone pure and untouched by winter. Dar's spirit leapt into the song. Sheltered in its arms, the Voice in his head faded, then vanished completely.

Dar had guessed Jewel's Song would be strong, as she was, but he could not have imagined the extent of its potency. Her sweet voice lifted in exquisite sadness, and he felt the words in his soul.

O terra, addio, addio.... O Earth, farewell, farewell....

Sogno di gaudio che in dolor svani.... My dream of joy vanishes in sorrow.

A noi si schiude il ciel e l'alme erranti volano.... The sky opens to us and our wandering souls fly....

Jewel's pure voice wove its way into Dar's heart, melting the shell of ice that had held him prisoner for so long. His hope soared free. He would surely survive his Dream Journey with Jewel as his Protector.

Then, in the midst of his elation, a wave of guilt crashed over him. Yes, he would be safe, but would Jewel? If she were a woman of his own race, she would be well trained as a Guardian, ready to confront the demons that lived in the darkest corners of every man's mind. But Jewel was not Tar'an. No matter her instinctive strength, if she Sang as his Guardian, she would be in the gravest danger.

The Dream Journey could well destroy her mind.

The last, haunting strains of Jewel's song faded into the flickering candlelight. Dar sat unmoving, barely breathing, caught in the heat of her gaze.

Jewel's desire seared him. His own lust flared in response.

He wanted her so badly he was sure he would go mad if she did not come closer. She obeyed his silent plea, drawing close and kneeling between his knees in one graceful motion.

Her fingers danced along the hem of his T-shirt, then slipped beneath the cotton to tease the muscles of his stomach. Her hands moved higher, brushing his chest, her thumbs flicking over his nipples.

He shut his eyes and stifled a groan. She tugged his shirt up.

Wordlessly, he raised his arms over his head.

She threw the shirt on the floor, then continued her exploration of his torso. Her lips followed her fingers, blazing a hot trail from his navel to his neck.

Her arms encircled his neck, pulling him close. Her breath mingled with his. He drew back, trying to regain power over his body. He would not destroy his chance for salvation by losing his self-control at the last moment.

She gazed up at him. Her eyes were warm and brown, like the life-giving soil of her world, and his memories of barren ice began to fade.

With the wonder of a child, he realized that he loved her.

"Kiss me," she whispered.

He had no choice but to obey. His lips brushed hers, and he trembled for an instant before surrendering to their sweetness. He dove deep, stroking the velvet softness of her mouth with his tongue. He filled his hands with her body, cupping her breasts, groaning when she pressed the hardened peaks into his palms.

He teased her nipples, rolling them between his thumbs and forefingers, his satisfaction flaring when he heard Jewel's strangled cry of pleasure.

Her arms unwound themselves from his neck. Her fingers stroked his collarbone, his chest, his stomach, his....

He caught her hands in his. His need had reached its pinnacle. One touch and he would surely disgrace himself. He closed his eyes and chanted a silent Prayer. The verses steadied him.

He rose, pulling Jewel to her feet and guiding her to the couch. He lowered himself beside her on the cushions and kissed her again, with all the reverence a Guardian deserved.

But Jewel was fire in his arms, burning away his most ardent resolve.

"No. Don't be gentle," she breathed. She straddled his thighs, pressing her heat against his groin. Her tongue darted into his ear, her fingers tugged at the button on his shorts.

The closure resisted her efforts. She shifted backward, a frown of concentration marring her brow as she worked the button through the hole. Dar watched, mesmerized by the sight of her slim fingers.

At last the fastening came free. Jewel pulled down the zipper, freeing his swollen flesh. He heard her sudden, shocked intake of breath as her gaze took in his full length.

She looked up at him and gave him a dazzling smile.

At that precise instant, the full import of what Jewel was about to do slammed into him. She was offering herself. Though she did not know it, once she joined her body with his, she would be his Guardian. When he called her to the Dream Journey, she would not be able to refuse. If she could not control the slavering beasts that lurked in the corners of his unconscious, they would devour her.

Jewel's hand closed on his rigid flesh and stroked upward. Stars exploded behind Dar's eyes. He uttered a sound more animal than human. He longed to tear away the thin fabric of her dress, part her legs and bury his shaft in her body.

No. He needed to make her understand the truth. She deserved to know what she risked by making love to him.

Jewel licked her lips and lowered her head. *By the Ancestors....*

With the last measure of his control, Dar gripped Jewel's wrists and yanked them upward. Cool air slipped between their bodies.

"Stop," he commanded.

Jewel's head jerked up, her dark curls falling forward over her eyes. Her lips parted. "Did I do something wrong?"

"We cannot do this." The words came out harsher than he had intended.

"But I thought you--" Her eyes widened. "Oh my God! Was Cass right? Are you gay?" She peered down at his erection and frowned. "Or bi, maybe? I didn't think you were--you don't look like a gay guy. Not," she added hastily, "that there's a *look*, you know, or anything, but--"

Dar frowned. "What is 'gay'?"

Jewel reddened. "You know, gay. Homosexual. A man who likes guys instead of women."

"By the Ancestors! You believe that I would be intimate with a man?"

Jewel bit her lip. "Well, would you?"

"No!" The thought sickened him. "I assure you, Jewel. I am not gay."

"Oh." She thought a moment, then smiled. "I didn't think so. But why did you want to stop?"

"Before we make love, you must know where I come from."

"You don't need to tell me that," she said quickly. "I know you're an illegal alien. I don't care what you did before I met you."

"You believe I am from another country on your planet, but I come from a place much more distant. I was born on a planet called Tar'ana. Fifteen light years from Earth."

Jewel slid off his lap and paced a few steps away. "Don't start with that outer space joke again, Dar. It's not the least bit funny."

"It is no joke," he said quietly. "It is the truth."

She turned to face him. "Do you really expect me to believe that? You are so out of your mind."

"I have never lied to you, Jewel."

"Right. Let me see. You're an alien. In another minute, your spaceship will hover outside that window. Then a beam of white light will pick me up and float me to your laboratory, where I'll be used for science experiments."

Dar jerked to his feet and advanced on her. "Jewel. Hear me out. Please. I beg you." He reached for her with his mind, but a shell of anger had closed around her, blocking him out.

She backed away, putting the coffee table between them. "No. You listen to me. I am *not* going to be made a fool of again."

"Jewel--"

"It was bad enough when my brother Joey and his nerdy friend dressed up like aliens and staged my abduction. Of course I thought it was real! I had just watched the entire first season of the X-Files on DVD, for crying out loud! *Anyone* would have been too freaked to notice Joey's costume had been pieced together from metal shop scraps!"

"Jewel, I--"

"But at least they could have let me in on the joke before I told the whole school about it! Oh. No." An expression of absolute horror crossed her face. "Did Joey put you up to this? Is this some sort of twisted attempt to get me to go back to Hershey?"

Dar caught her by the shoulders and gave her a shake. "Jewel! I swear it to you by all that is holy--this is no joke. My planet was attacked by hostile forces. I was captured and sold as a slave on another planet. I was held there for about three of your Earth years before I managed to escape, but my ship did not reach my homeworld. It crashed here, on Earth."

Jewel twisted out of his grasp. "Oh, please. You are so full of it!"

Dar gritted his teeth. He could have joined with her and been done with it by now. Except--by the Ancestors! He owed her his complete honesty, even though he risked his own survival to give it to her.

Yet the stubborn woman refused to believe the truth.

Jewel's eyes snapped with the red fire of the Tar'an sun. "Get out."

"Jewel, I--"

"I don't know why you think I'm an idiot, Dar, but I can see it's true. I will *not* stand here and take it. Get out." She yanked the door open and glowered at him. Then her gaze traveled downward, to his groin, where his shriveled rod hung over the waistband of his boxers.

"Don't forget to zip," she said.

Chapter Five

The box of chocolate condoms hit the wall with a thud.

A primal scream rose in Jewel's throat, but she gritted her teeth and forced it down. No sense damaging her vocal chords just because Dar had made her the punch line of his stupid joke.

She plunged the dinner dishes into a sink full of soapy water and scrubbed them until they sparkled. After the kitchen was spotless, she put away her clean laundry before hauling the vacuum cleaner out of the closet and attacking the carpets. She was one step away from alphabetizing her spice rack before her anger finally fizzled. She sank down on the couch and surveyed the Good Housekeeping cover shot that used to be her apartment.

Holy shit. She'd turned into her mother.

She hurled a pillow across the room. Why couldn't she drown her sorrows in Double Chocolate Haagen-Dazs like a normal woman?

She pulled on her pajamas and got into bed--hurt, disappointed--and horny. After about two minutes, she kicked off the covers. Damn. Two minutes in Dar's arms had gotten her hotter than she'd ever been in her life.

A flush warmed her skin at the memory of his lips capturing her, of his tongue stroking the slick lining of her lower lip, of his fingers tugging on her....

Stop.

Her cheeks burned. How could she have read him so wrong? For the past week, she'd been so sure that they were soul mates, and she'd been ready to tear off the few articles of clothing he wore. But the humiliating fact remained that when they'd gotten right down to the nitty-gritty, he'd managed to back off quite easily and start joking.

She blinked back the tears that threatened to spill. She would *not* cry over this.

Still, Dar's rejection stung. Jewel ran through that part of the scene a few more times, just to make sure she wouldn't focus on what his hands had been doing just a few moments before he'd stopped her from going down on him.

Damn. Now she was angry again.

She lay back on the pillow, emotionally exhausted, but still unable to sleep. It was past three and she had rehearsal in the morning. She really needed to get some rest, or her voice would sound like roadkill.

She flopped over onto her stomach, but the fierce emotions raging through her body refused to abate.

Anger. Frustration. Hurt.

Fear.

Jewel lunged for the light, panic squeezing her lungs, her body suddenly chilled. The terror wasn't hers, but she felt it just the same. It burrowed deep, driving shards of ice into her heart. She squeezed her eyes shut and tried to escape it.

A snowy landscape floated before her eyes. An unforgiving winter wind swept through her. She drew the blankets tight around her, but she shivered beneath them.

It was Dar's soul she felt. She did not know how that could be, but she knew it was true. And somehow, she knew she had turned him away when he'd needed her most.

Could he truly be from another planet?

Jewel squeezed her eyes shut, fighting the tears. She sensed she could reach out to him, but she held back, because within his ache she felt a warning.

Loving him could cost her everything. Was she willing to pay the price?

* * * *

Dar. Are you there?

Dar rose to the surface of his dream and reached out to Goreth with his mind. Normally, Tar'ans shared only emotions, never thoughts, unless they were lifemates. But the bond Dar shared with his twin was exceptionally close, and three years of captivity had honed it to a perfection never imagined by the Elders.

I am here, Goreth.

Dar felt his brother's excitement even before Goreth's next thought seeped into his mind. *I have a plan to get us out of here.*

He tensed, not daring to breath. *How?*

We fly away, brother. On a spiker.

Dar digested this bit of information. If not for the absolute seriousness he sensed behind Goreth's words, he would have dismissed it as nothing more than a pleasant dream.

First we must get free of our collars. How do you propose we do that?

The sunflare, Goreth answered.

What?

All the collars are linked to a single control. The bitch that owns me designed the system herself. The sunflare interferes with the transmission.

The sunflare was a yearly event, greatly feared by the Mardulans. For one long day, the planet's small sun blazed, setting off a storm of sparks that lasted several days. The Mardulans spent that time in prayer to their Goddess, begging deliverance.

How do you know this?

I've accessed the city's central computer. The data is all there.

Dar's mind raced. His brother was a genius with computers, but how in the name of the Ancestors had he thrown off his collar's control long enough to access his owner's terminal?

Goreth, how...?

His twin's mind grew tight with shame. *Unlike you, brother, I have learned to play the slave.*

By the Ancestors, Goreth, what did you...?

Do not ask me that, Dar. He paused, then forged on grimly. *Just believe me when I tell you that Mora trusts me to run her household. I have access to her computer. It was a simple matter to hack into the program that controls our restraints. When I cross-referenced it with the data flow from last cycle's sunflare, I discovered that during the main surge of the sunflare the collars were non-operational for precisely three minutes. It will happen again Dar, while the Mardulan females are in the Temple.*

Dar nearly laughed out loud. *My only guard will be a Mardulan male.*

You think my plan will work, then?

Goreth, don't your plans always work?

They do when you put them into action.

Indeed. It had been like that since they were boys. Goreth planned, Dar acted. They'd been in and out of more adventures than Dar cared to count. None, however, had been as deadly as the one they faced now.

I'll need to act quickly, Dar told his twin. *I'll free as many Tar'ans as possible. You have only to get to Mora's spiker. Do you know the route to Tar'ana?*

Yes. I've studied the stellar maps and found that the Mardulans know nothing of the Rift. If we can reach the rim, we can make it home.

Dar's elation surged, then just as quickly dimmed. *Tar'ana will not be as we remember it.*

That I know, brother.

* * * *

"Jewel. It's me. Marissa. Pick up the phone."

Jewel's hand faltered on the doorknob. She was already late for class, but something in her sister's voice told her this wasn't a routine when-are-you-going-to-grow-up call. Still, she stared down at the receiver for a few seconds before lifting it from the cradle.

"Hello?"

"Damn it, Jewel, what took you so long?"

"I'm late for class, Marissa. If you have something to tell me, make it quick. Or better yet, I'll hang up and you can call back and leave a message."

"Geez, Jewel. Lighten up." Marissa drew a quick breath. "I'm calling for Mamma. She--"

"Oh, God--is something wrong with Mamma?"

"No, nothing like that. It's just...."

"Just what?"

"She wants to come to your graduation."

Jewel's knees gave way and she found herself sitting on the couch. "You want to say that again, Mar?"

Marissa sighed. "Mamma wants to come hear you sing. We all do. We love you, even if we think you're nuts. Tell us when the concert is and we'll be there."

Jewel blinked back a rush of tears. "Pop, too?"

Marissa's eloquent silence gave Jewel her answer.

"Well, I guess I can't expect miracles," Jewel said quietly.

"Jewel, you of all people should know how Pop is. I mean, you inherited his stubborn gene." When Jewel didn't answer, Marissa gave a sigh and forged on. "Anyway, when's the concert?"

"Next week."

"Well, email me the directions and whatever else I need to know.

Mamma and I will be there. Joey and Claudia, too, okay?"

Jewel swallowed past the lump in her throat. "Okay."

"Great. Oh shoot, the baby's crying again. See ya."

The line went dead. Jewel pictured her Martha Stewart wannabe sister, hurrying through a perfect house to a pastel nursery and scooping a beautiful baby out of a designer crib.

She hung up the phone and burst into tears.

* * * *

Dar could no longer ignore the Voice.

It haunted his waking hours and dominated his dreams. It whispered behind every thought and wove its way into each breath he took. It stole his strength, his resolve, his hope.

He would find no Guardian on Earth. Even if by some miracle Jewel came to believe the truth and offered herself as Protector, he would turn her away. He valued her too much to risk her life for something so trivial as his sanity.

By the Ancestors, he loved her. She deserved so much more than his cowardice.

He kept vigil by the Rift probe, binding his mental plea to the undulating squeal, raising the volume of the device to its maximum level. No doubt Jewel thought he was deliberately seeking to disturb her, but he had little choice. Only a message from Tar'ana could save him now.

Through it all the Voice whispered and seduced, tempting him with the promise of paradise. Dar listened.

Listened, and waited for the hour when he would no longer be able to resist its call.

Chapter Six

"You know, Cass, the whole sorry story just goes to prove that vibrators are better than men."

Cass looked up from the soft pretzel she was slathering with mustard. "Sound like you're still hot for the guy."

"No way." Jewel took a savage bite of her extra long, extra thick bratwurst.

"Ouch," her friend commented.

The streetcart vendor--a guy who looked like his last job had been picking up roadside trash in an orange jumpsuit--didn't bother to disguise his amusement. Jewel glared at him. She grabbed Cass' arm and pulled her away from the cart.

Jewel slumped against the Academy's distinguished façade and let out a groan. "I shouldn't have been so mean to him. I think he really believed what he was telling me." She took another bite of her lunch.

"Let's face it. I made a total fool of myself."

Cass shook her head. "You made a fool of yourself in front of a guy who thinks he's an alien? Get real. Dar's whacked, Jewel. You did the right thing, throwing him out." She laughed. "Shit. I wish I could have been there."

"No you don't. It was awful."

"Yeah, well, it's over now, and who cares, anyway? You'll be on a plane to Italy next week."

"Yeah." For the first time, the thought held little appeal. No longer hungry, Jewel took a long look at her bratwurst before tossing it in the trash. "Guess I'll head home and start packing."

"Do it, girlfriend."

Walking home alone felt stranger than it should have, given the fact that she'd been doing it for almost two years. How the hell had Dar gotten so completely under her skin in such a short amount of time? She was truly pathetic.

One of the Lost Lennon Tapes--featuring Yoko's truly incomparable soprano--was blaring from Dar's apartment when Jewel got home. Damn. Whoever had found that ungodly recording should have lost it again right away.

What idiocy had made her fall in love with a guy who liked music like that, anyway?

She jerked her suitcase out from under her bed and began throwing things in it. *Love.* Was she really in love with the guy?

No. She was in lust with him, that's all. And what was so bad about that? A woman could fall for a sexy body just as easily as a man could. In a few weeks, she wouldn't even remember Dar's name.

Yeah, right. And the Pope wasn't Catholic.

That night, she worked a double shift at Victor's, but even the sharp pain in her calves couldn't get her mind off Dar. She knew she'd hurt him, but hell, what did he expect? That she would believe he was from another planet?

Maybe he is, a small voice in the back of her head whispered. But Dar didn't look like an alien. At least, he didn't look like what Jewel thought an alien should look like. Maybe he....

Stop it. Just stop it. Jewel took a deep breath. She was *so* not going to go there.

The night had been slow, and the maitre'd let her leave a few minutes early. Jewel yanked open Victor's back door with a bit more force than was necessary and stepped out into the warm May night. A hint of summer tinged the air. A bright full moon flooded the alley, making the shadows seem even darker than usual.

God, she missed Dar.

She pushed the thought away and hurried to the end of the alley, gripping a can of pepper spray in her right hand. Once she turned onto Twelfth Street, her breathing steadied. Just a few blocks and she'd be home.

A solitary car with one headlight cruised by, but otherwise, the street was deserted. Despite the warm weather, Jewel shivered and picked up her pace.

"Hey, babe." A man stepped into her path.

Shit. Where had he come from?

Jewel stepped off the curb to avoid plowing into him.

The guy wasn't tall, but when Jewel dropped the six inches into the gutter, he seemed to grow. Jewel squared her shoulders and kept walking. Muggers didn't attack confident women, right?

He kept pace with her, walking backward. She angled across the street to the opposite sidewalk. She could see cars rolling through the intersection up ahead. If she made it that far, the guy would probably back off.

The man followed, skirting the bumper of a parked car and hopping up on the sidewalk beside her. She assessed him out of the corner of her eye as her fingers curled around the pepper spray. He was young, with a shaved head and some kind of a tattoo on his cheek. Oh shit, a swastika? Just what she needed.

"What'za matter? Too good to talk to me?"

It probably wasn't a good idea to get Nazi-boy pissed.

"No," she said.

He grinned. "She's nice, ain't she?"

"What--"

"Yeah, real nice," a voice answered.

Jewel spun around, heart pounding. A second thug, considerably taller than the first, stood about ten feet away. This one wore his hair long and greasy. He grinned and started toward her. Jewel raised the pepper spray and blasted him.

Too soon. The stream hit the lapel of Greaseball's leather jacket.

She turned and ran, into the arms of Nazi-boy. Twisting, she jammed her knee into his groin. A glancing blow, but it succeeded in buying her about a half-second of opportunity.

She sprinted for the corner, praying they wouldn't follow.

Greaseball tackled her. The sidewalk slammed into her knees. Jewel screamed, kicking against her assailant, but damn, he was strong. He wrapped one arm around her torso and clamped his other hand over her mouth. She bit his finger. He swore.

He yanked her into a narrow cleft between two buildings and threw her onto the ground. Nazi-boy ducked in behind him.

Jewel scrambled backward. Her spine hit iron bars. Frantically, she clawed at the latch on the gate. Maybe she could make it into the courtyard and wake the owners of the house.

Nazi-boy dragged her from the gate and backed her up against the brick wall, grinding his erection against her. She pummeled him with her fists, but he just laughed and grabbed her wrists with one hand.

With the other, he hiked up the hem of her black waitress skirt.

He leaned close, his breath rotten in her nostrils. "I love fucking a woman in a dress."

Pure terror flooded Jewel's brain. This could not be happening.

"Hurry up." Greaseball was standing at the mouth of the alley, peering into the street.

Nazi-boy rubbed his hand between her legs, then tore through her pantyhose. Her struggles were only exciting him, Jewel realized. What the hell had the self-defense instructor told her? *Wait.* Wait for the right moment to attack.

She forced her mind to blank and went very still, sagging, letting gravity draw him down with her. His hold on her wrists loosened.

"Yeah, that's it, baby. Relax and enjoy the ride."

He fumbled with the zipper on his jeans. Jewel forced every muscle in her body to soften, waiting, waiting....

At the last possible instant, just as he began his upward thrust, she slammed her knee into his balls with every ounce of her strength.

Nazi-boy's voice hit high C. He staggered backwards and crashed into the opposite wall of the alley, his head hitting the bricks with a satisfying smack. He dropped to the ground in a tight ball, clutching his groin and moaning.

She sprinted for the street, but Greaseball caught her around the waist and threw her back. She landed on the cobblestones. He came down on her, his hand covering her mouth as his knee parted her legs.

She gasped for breath and braced for his violation.

An inhuman growl and primal wave of anger surged through the alley. Greaseball's neck snapped back. His body rose, dangling in the air like a marionette for a brief second before flying over her head and hitting the gate.

Jewel shoved herself to a sitting position, shoving her hair out of her eyes with a shaking hand. A dark figure loomed over her, shaking with fury.

Dar.

She launched herself at him, flinging her arms around his waist. He clutched her shoulders and eased her back. "Did they...."

"No," Jewel replied quickly. "They were going to, but--"

Dar set her aside and stepped toward her assailants. Nazi-boy had recovered his voice. "Hey, man, you heard her. We didn't do nothing."

"Scum." Dar bent and picked the man up. He pinned Nazi-boy's neck to the wall with one hand. Jewel's attacker clawed at Dar's fingers, gurgling.

Dar gave the thug a shake. Nazi-boy's head hit the bricks and the gurgling stopped. Dar's finger's loosened, allowing the limp body to slither to the ground.

Greaseball was huddled against the gate, sobbing.

Dar looked at Jewel. "Shall I kill him for you?"

My God. He was serious.

"No," she stammered. "Just get me out of here."

Without another word, Dar turned his back on Jewel's assailants and scooped her into his arms.

He cradled her head with one large hand, pressing her into his chest and whispering soothing words first in a language she couldn't understand, then in English. Jewel wrapped her arms around his neck and let the tears come.

"I am sorry I did not arrive sooner." Jewel felt the wave of guilt that overtook him.

She sobbed harder. He carried her home. She'd lost her fanny pack in the struggle, so he simply broke the lock on her apartment door. He strode across the living room and lowered her onto the couch.

A few seconds later, a box of tissues and a glass of water were in Jewel's hands. Dar stood by the window, silent, as she pulled herself together, but she could feel his emotions burning, and she knew the attack had shaken him.

She drew a deep breath, fighting the urge to vomit at the memory of it. "I ... I'm going to take a shower," she whispered. "Please, don't go until I'm done."

Dar gave a brief nod, his expression inscrutable.

Jewel turned up the water as hard and hot as possible. She scrubbed, trying to remove her memories along with the dirt and sweat of her ordeal. But when she stepped into her bedroom a few minutes later, she still felt dirty. Used. Her mind ran on fast forward, envisioning what would have happened if Dar hadn't appeared like some avenging angel.

Her hands shook as she tied the belt of her white terry cloth robe.

She stood for a long moment, staring at her closed door. Dar waited on the other side, his anger and self-hatred simmering. He'd saved her life, but he thought he'd failed her.

Before she could second-guess her motives, she backtracked to her nightstand and yanked open the drawer. Her fingers shook slightly as she slipped the foil packet out of the box and placed it in the pocket of her robe.

When she returned to the living room, Dar was standing with his back to her, palms flat on the windowsill. His head was bowed. Her gaze skimmed over the bulging muscles in his shoulders. They were so tense she thought they might burst from his T-shirt.

His emotions coiled in darkness, drawing her in.

When he didn't turn, she went to him and wrapped her arms around his waist. Her cheek rested on his upper back, her stomach pressed against his buttocks. She closed her eyes and let her body melt into his. He stiffened but didn't move away.

"What's so interesting out there in the street?" she asked.

"Your world. Have you any idea how amazing it is?"

She didn't answer at first. Instead, she slipped her hands under his shirt and began kneading his lower back.

"You came to Victor's, even after last night," Jewel said.

"I tried to stay away. I could not do it. But when I reached the restaurant I was told you had already left."

Her hands moved higher, stroking, exploring the hard planes of his torso.

"Stay with me," she said.

Dar's breath left in a rush. "Jewel--"

"Just for tonight. I won't ask for more. If you go, I won't be able to forget--" Her stomach lurched. When she closed her eyes, she saw Greaseball's cold, flat eyes. He stepped toward her and....

"Please, Dar. I need you."

She loosened her belt and let her robe fall open. The night air brushed her bare skin. She lifted his shirt and pressed her bare torso against him. Then she moved, slowly, seductively.

Dar's body went rigid. Jewel shoved his shirt over his head and down his arms, until it lay at his wrists like shackles. Head bent, she trailed kisses over his back, running her tongue just above the waistband of his shorts.

Her hands trembled as she reached around to unsnap his shorts.

He turned then, flinging his shirt to the ground and covering her hands with his. "You don't truly want this."

She leaned forward and covered his chest with kisses, scraping his nipple with her teeth. "Are you crazy? I've wanted this since the day I met you."

"You don't know what you're offering."

She gave a low, dark laugh. "Oh, believe me, I know." Her fingers found the pull on his zipper and tugged downward. "So do you. You're fighting it--I can't quite tell why--but you want this." She slipped her hand into his boxers. "You want it as much as I do."

His hot, rigid flesh felt incredible against her palm. "Try to tell me you don't."

"You do not know me, Jewel."

"Then I guess it's time to learn."

She dipped her hand into her pocket, then sent the robe to the floor with a shrug.

Dar sucked in a breath. "By the Ancestors. You are exquisite."

His tone held a reverence that sent heat flooding her face. "I'm nothing special Dar, but I--" *I love you.* Thankfully, she stopped herself before she said the words. Drawing a deep breath, she raised her arms over her head and did a slow, full turn.

His hungry gaze raked her, sending a stab of lust through her gut. Her thighs dampened.

She closed the distance between them. She knelt and tugged his shorts down to his ankles, then ripped open the condom wrapper. She placed a wet kiss on his navel, plunging and circling with her tongue. Dar groaned and gripped her head.

She drifted lower and caught his glorious cock in her hands. She positioned the condom on its tip and rolled it into place with her lips.

The taste of chocolate mingled with the musky scent of his arousal as his shaft slid into her mouth. His fingers tightened in her hair, almost painfully. She drew him in as deep as she could, then released him, savoring his shudder as she drew back inch by excruciating inch.

She sensed his turmoil, his need. Felt the precise moment that he lost control.

He caught her under the shoulders and hauled her into his arms. "Jewel...."

She threw her arms around his neck and met the full force of his passion. He kissed her, drinking deep, claiming her mouth with his tongue. She moaned and rubbed against him. His mouth left hers and moved lower. His teeth scraped her jaw and left a series of stinging bites along her neck.

The sensation drove her wild. She wrapped her legs around his waist, desperate to relieve the throbbing ache between her thighs. His hand gripped her buttocks, his legs flexed as he moved across her living room.

"I want you inside me, Dar. It's all I can think about."

His reply was unintelligible, a low growl. He propped her on the breakfast counter and drove into her.

Jewel writhed on his shaft. It reached deeper inside her than she would have thought possible, and was so thick that Dar's slightest movement sparked rippling currents.

He moved again, drawing back and thrusting forward with a smooth motion and she couldn't stop the moan that welled up in her throat. She was going to die. It was that good.

But the physical sensation paled beside another, more intimate joining. Dar was inside Jewel's body, but she was inside his mind, feeling his emotions as he made love to her. The realization knocked the breath from her lungs.

Dar braced his hands on either side of her, quickening his pace. The pleasure coiled unbearably. But even as Jewel's passion rode higher, straining for release, her mind descended into a place of suffocating darkness. She gasped for air, clutching at his shoulders, fear licking at the edges of her pleasure.

She looked into Dar eyes and her fear intensified. And then it shattered in ecstasy, and Jewel was falling, falling, and Dar's hoarse cry was mingling with hers. She landed in the shelter of Dar's arms, utterly spent.

"Jewel," he whispered.

She opened her eyes and lost herself in his gaze. She saw satisfaction there, mingled with reverence. Lurking behind it was a touch of guilt.

Dar slid from Jewel's body, and for a moment she thought he would move away. She wrapped her arms around his neck and drew him down for a kiss.

He lifted her from the counter and sank to the floor. He settled her on her back and came up on his elbow beside her. She lifted her hand and traced his jaw with her finger. "That was...." She shook her head. "I don't know *what* it was."

"It's not over yet," he murmured. He caught her hand and pressed it against his groin.

Jewel's eyes widened. He was still hard as a rock. She felt his amusement even before she heard him laugh.

He came over her and slipped inside, once again filling her so completely that every thought in her brain was displaced by the wonder of him. He loved her again, more slowly this time, drawing out her pleasure until she begged him to make her come. He did, and the sensation washed over her in endless, endless, waves.

She was only dimly aware of him carrying her into the bedroom and lowering her onto the bed. Jewel looked up at him, dazed.

He stroked her cheek. "Ah, my Jewel. You are so beautiful." His hands wandered lower, cupping her breasts. His head bent. He caught one nipple then the other in his mouth, suckling gently.

Several minutes passed before Jewel realized he intended to make love to her again. Was that even possible? She watched as he reached for the box on her nightstand.

She managed to come up on her elbows, though her bones seemed to have turned to jelly. Dar covered himself, then rolled her onto her stomach. As he entered her, her only coherent thought was that she would be dead of pleasure by morning.

But three hours and seven orgasms later, Jewel was very much alive. She sank into the pillows, wrung out but still conscious enough to feel a thrill when Dar pulled her back into his chest and tucked her head under his chin. Her bottom nestled against his groin, and to her utter amazement, she felt him grow hard again. *My God.*

The man *had* to be from another planet.

No Earth guy was this good.

Chapter Seven

Jewel's bedroom looked like a hurricane had hit it.

No doubt about it, even from her limited vantage point on the floor, it was one hell of a mess. Her sheets had parted company with her mattress, which was now listing over the edge of the boxsprings. A chair was overturned and the pictures on the wall were crooked. Her hairbrush, a silk scarf, an empty jar of fudge sauce, several banana peels and a Dustbuster were strewn across the carpet.

Her dresser top was bare. She'd lain on it last night while Dar had done things to her that....

Well. She now had firsthand experience with the term "hot monkey sex."

Dar, still asleep, sprawled on his back beside her, gloriously naked, one arm flung over his head. She eased up to a sitting position and looked down at him.

A troubled expression flitted across his face. Under his lids, his eyes fluttered briefly, then stilled.

His torso jerked, his lips drawing back in a snarl. A low, inhuman moan sounded in his throat.

"Dar!" Jewel caught his flailing arm before it struck her. Shifting, she grasped his shoulders and shook them. "Dar! Wake up!"

Longing sliced through her, hard and hopeless. A voice called, just far enough away that she couldn't make out the words. But God, she wanted to. She wanted to move closer....

Dar shot bolt upright, knocking her backwards. He blinked rapidly several times before his eyes focused. The brief flair of desperation in them frightened her.

She touched his arm. "Dar."

He swung his gaze at her and stared for several seconds, as if trying to remember where he was and why. Then his expression cleared, and his eyes raked her bare breasts.

"Good morning, Jewel."

She blushed. Damn, when would she learn to stop doing that? "Good morning."

He leaned forward and kissed her. His hands stroked her back, urging her closer.

Jewel melted into his arms.

He made love to her again, there on the floor, then left her in the shower while he went to cook breakfast. Jewel emerged from the bedroom into the aroma of coffee. Dar, standing in front of the stove, deftly flipped two thick slice of French toast onto a plate. Smiling, he handed it to her.

She could get really, really used to this.

She started for the breakfast bar, then, remembering last night, made an abrupt turn and sat at the table instead. Dar joined her, bringing his own plate and her coffee.

Gripping the mug tighter than necessary, she tried to keep her voice nonchalant. "Have you ever been to Italy?"

Dar froze for an instant, then continued cutting his French toast. "No."

Jewel took a swig of her coffee. "So, do you think you'd want to go?"

A muscle in Dar's jaw clenched. Several seconds of complete silence ticked by.

Maybe he hadn't quite understood. "To Italy. With me. I'm leaving next week, and if you wanted, you could, you know, come along."

"I am sorry, Jewel. I cannot."

"Oh." It was the only word she could manage to get out. Damn, she was pitiful.

"It is not that I do not want to go," he continued quietly, "it is that I cannot. I am not--" He paused. "I am not free."

"Not free?" Jewel regarded him with something akin to horror. "Are you telling me you're married?"

His head jerked up. "By the Ancestors! No. Do you think if I were lifemated that I would have--" He took a deep breath. "No. I am not married."

"Then what's stopping you? Is it the money? I've got enough to last a few months, while I'm auditioning. I'm sure you can find some kind of job. Everyone needs a computer guy. Unless...." She frowned. "Unless it's because you can't risk leaving the country, with Immigration looking for you. Are you afraid they'll send you back to Siberia?"

"Siberia? What--"

"You don't have to tell me about it. It... it must have been awful. When that Immigration woman showed me your picture, I...."

He leaned across the table and grabbed her arm. "What Immigration woman?"

"The one that was hanging around here the other day, looking for you. I didn't tell her anything," she added quickly, "I said I'd never seen you."

Dar's expression hardened. "This woman. What did she look like?"

"Blonde. Tall." Jewel winced. "Mean."

A blast of pure hate struck her. Dar's hand on her wrist tightened.

"Ow!" She tugged at her arm. "You're hurting me."

He swore an oath in his native language and released her. "When was she here?"

"Two days ago."

He started for the door, but halfway there, he turned and strode back to the table. Bending low, he caught Jewel's mouth in a searing kiss.

Then he was gone.

Jewel brooded over the scene as she washed the breakfast dishes. It had a sense of finality that she just didn't want to face, but it wouldn't do her much good to obsess about it. Either Dar came back before she left for Italy or he didn't. Period.

She walked into the living room and pulled out her sheet music. The graduation concert was only days away, and her family would be sitting in the audience. If she gave them her best performance, maybe they would understand why she wasn't going home. If only Pop....

No. She wouldn't think of that, either. She sang a quick scale in A major, then an arpeggio in G. From there she launched into Aida's death song.

She ran over the more difficult passages six or seven times, until she was satisfied she would nail them on Friday night. Then she sang the easier sections again, because God only knew that during performances she always messed up on the most basic stuff.

She was just leaving for class when the phone rang. She backtracked into the room to answer.

"It's Joey." Her brother's voice was close to panic.

Jewel gripped the arm of the couch. "Joey? What is it? What's happened?"

"It's Pop."

"Pop?" Oh God. "Is he--"

"No," Joey answered quickly. "He's not. But he's had a heart attack and he's pretty bad off. The doctor's not sure if--" He swallowed, then tried again. "He might not last, Jewel."

"How's Mamma?"

"A wreck. Jewel, will you come?"

"Yes. Yes, of course I will. I'll be on the next bus. Tell Mamma, okay?"

"Okay."

She hung up the phone and sprinted into the bedroom. Three minutes later, she was packed and grabbing for the door. She swung it open and nearly choked.

The Amazon was back.

"What the hell are *you* doing here?"

"You lied about the man I'm looking for."

"I don't know what you're talking about," Jewel said. "Look, I'm in a rush, so if you'll excuse me--"

Jewel tried to push into the hall, but the woman caught her arm. "Miss, the man you're protecting is a dangerous man. He's prone to violent seizures."

Jewel stilled. "Seizures?" Dar had had some kind of seizure the first day they'd met.

"Seizures and delusions. He believes he's from outer space." The woman leaned closer. "He's also a murderer. He stalks his victims, gets close to them--intimately. Then, he kills them."

Dar--a murderer? "I don't believe it. I--"

"Where is he?"

"Get out of here." She tugged on her arm.

The woman let go and slid a photo from the inside pocket of her suit coat. She held it before Jewel eyes.

A woman. Hacked to pieces. Jewel thought she was going to be sick.

"I have reason to believe you could be his next victim," the woman said.

Jewel regained her wits. Even if Dar did believe he was an alien--hell, even if he *were* from outer space--she couldn't believe he was a serial killer. He was just too sweet and gentle. "Look," she said. "I can't help you, and right now I'm in a hurry."

The woman drew a small object from her pocket and pointed it at Jewel. "I had hoped you'd be more cooperative."

Jewel blinked. Shit, she had a--an egg? What the hell was the bitch going to do, make her an omelet?

A white beam of light burst from the orb. Jewel staggered back, momentarily blinded. A second blast hit her, knocking her to the carpet. When she tried to get up, nothing happened. Her limbs were frozen.

And then she knew.

This was a real, live alien abduction.

* * * *

Size really did matter.

Neither of the Mardulan males had stood higher than Dar's navel, and they had fallen without a struggle. He'd trussed them with the spare coil of cable he'd found stowed in the rear of the ship.

He hoped they would enjoy living on Tar'ana.

Once Jewel had alerted him of Shata's arrival, it had taken Dar only a few moments to construct a tracer from various items he'd had stored in his apartment. The device had led him to Shata's spiker, hidden between the city and the ocean, in the heart of a pristine pine forest.

Dar leaned over the spiker's instrument panel, scanning the readout on the stellar map. Though the Rift wasn't marked, he knew the approximate location of the nearest rim. Less than two Earth days after he entered it, he would be on his homeworld.

Would it be soon enough?

A skilled Priestess could protect his Dream Journey, though ideally a man's lifemate performed the role. Dar would have given anything to have Jewel protect him on the Journey, but he knew now that he would never ask her to take on the dangerous task.

The Voice called inside his head, deeper and more resonant than ever before, reminding him that his time was short. He should depart immediately, and leave Shata stranded on Earth. But the knowledge that his former mistress knew of Jewel stopped him cold. He couldn't leave Earth before dealing with Shata.

He searched the bulkhead compartments until he found the ship's weapons storage: freezers, hoarfrost lasers, ice blasters. If he wanted to kill, the latter would be extremely effective.

Dar gripped a blaster and imagined the deadly beam striking Shata. It didn't matter what part of her body the ice touched--he knew that only too well from what he'd seen during the attack on Tar'ana. One hit and there would be very little left of his former owner.

A fitting end, indeed.

Yet Dar hesitated. Tar'ana was a peaceful planet, employing weapons solely for defense. As a boy, he'd been taught to revere all life. Had Shata succeeded in turning him from all that his people held sacred?

He closed his eyes and chanted a Prayer, asking the Ancestors for wisdom. When the verse ended, he replaced the blaster with a hoarfrost laser. It could inflict excruciating pain, and minor injury, but not death. He cradled it in the crook of his arm as he headed for the door.

He had to find Shata before she got to Jewel.

* * * *

Alien sex was great. Alien abduction sucked.

The blond Amazon--who definitely wasn't an Immigration agent--was striding through the woods at a brisk pace with Jewel flung over one shoulder. The swaying pines, dense and upside down, made Jewel's head spin.

They were nowhere near Philadelphia. The bitch must have brought her into the New Jersey Pine Barrens.

Jewel pummeled the woman's back with her fists. "Put me down!"

The woman's only response was to tighten her grip across the back of Jewel's thighs.

Jewel let out a sigh of frustration. She'd tried screaming when she first woke, but had only managed to hurt her voice. Apparently, they were too deep in the woods for anyone to hear.

It seemed like the woman had been walking for hours, though in reality it had probably been less than twenty minutes. Finally, the world shifted, and Jewel was deposited on her feet.

"It's about time," she muttered. "Just what the hell do you think you're doing?"

The woman curled her lips in what Jewel guessed was a smile. "You were in need of protection."

"Protection! This is your idea of protection?"

The woman nodded. "You'll be safe enough here, until I recapture the man."

"Here? Why here?" Jewel swept her hand to one side and began a slow pivot. "What's so--oh, shit."

About fifty feet away, nestled among the ferns and blueberry bushes, sat something that looked like a small airplane with the wings and tail cut off. No windows were visible, but a short ramp led to a narrow slash that could only be a door.

Well, what do you know? A spaceship.

Now she was *really* screwed.

Jewel shifted, trying to gain a bit of distance from her abductor. The woman put her hand in her pocket and pulled out the egg.

Okay, time for Plan B. Stall. "You're not, um, thinking of taking me to another planet, are you?"

The woman opened her mouth to answer, but the words never came. At that moment the door to the spaceship slid open. Dar emerged, holding a very scary-looking weapon in his arms.

And boy, did he look pissed.

Chapter Eight

"Step away, Shata." Dar eased the catch on the laser and held it loosely, ready to fire. Shata held a freezer in one hand, trained on Jewel.

Jewel's eyes were wide and terror poured from her in waves. The thought of his former owner abducting the woman he loved caused blotches of red to swirl into Dar's vision. If Shata harmed Jewel, no power in the universe would stop him from enacting revenge.

"Step away," he repeated. "Now."

Shata seemed genuinely amused by his order. "I know you have many talents, pet, but is shooting one of them? I thought your race prided themselves on non-violence."

He answered her with a blast from the laser.

It scattered the sand at her feet. Shata darted behind Jewel and wrapped one arm around her torso. "Try that again. Perhaps your aim will improve."

Jewel elbowed Shata in the stomach. "Let me go!"

Jewel struggled against the larger woman. Shata held her in place with one hand while the other reached into her suit pocket. Dar ran toward Jewel, then stopped cold. Shata had exchanged the freezer for an ice blaster.

"That's right," she said, pointing the deadly weapon at Jewel's head. "I won't hesitate to kill her, pet."

Dar dropped the laser.

Shata smiled. "Let's go back to the ship, shall we?"

Once inside, the Mardulan woman took one look at her trussed crewmen and shook her head. "Useless. I can't imagine why I even brought them along."

She jabbed the ice blaster into Jewel's side, then met Dar's gaze and nodded toward the helm. "There's a compartment near the pilot's station. Open it and retrieve the contents."

Dar pressed the latch. A single object lay in the niche, and he drew it out slowly. His slave collar. He had sworn he would die rather than wear it again.

"Put it on."

Shata's finger stroked the ice blaster's trigger. Jewel's corresponding surge of fear buffeted him.

"When I do, will you release her?" he asked.

Shata inclined her head.

A lie, most likely, but Dar knew Shata would not hesitate to pull the trigger if he disobeyed. Grimly, he looped the collar about his neck.

The ends sunk into the receptors. A pulse of electricity shot along his spine. His muscles softened, relaxed. His mental link with Jewel dimmed.

He sank into a crouch on the deck of the spiker and waited for his mistress to give her next command.

To his great relief, Shata released Jewel. "Thank you for your help, my dear. He won't be able to hurt you now."

Help? What in the name of the Ancestors-?

Jewel avoided his gaze. "He seemed so gentle," she told Shata.

The Mardulan shook her head. "That is the reason he was able to kill so many. He's desperate, you know."

"Why?"

"His species is capable of mind-linking. Surely you felt it."

Jewel's gaze slid toward him, then away. "Yes. Yes, I did."

"He is close to a developmental stage that his people call the Dream Journey. If he can complete it, his psychic power will be great. If not, he will go insane. It's an arduous path however, and impossible to journey alone."

Shata paced toward Dar and placed her hand on his head. "He was searching for a Singer to guide him."

Jewel drew in a sharp breath. "A Singer?"

Shata nodded. "A woman's song can tame the demons that lurk in his mind. But not just any woman will do--she must share his mind and invite him to her bed before the journey begins."

Even through the deadening shield of the collar, Dar felt Jewel's shock.

"You would most likely not have survived the journey with your own sanity intact. The demons of his mind are ferocious."

Jewel turned to him, eyes wide. "Is that true?"

"Speak the truth," Shata commanded.

"Yes," he said through clenched teeth. "It is true."

His heart twisted with self-loathing as she turned away. "What will you do with him now?" she asked.

"I will take him back to prison. This time we will insure that he does not escape before his Journey begins. Once it is over and his mind destroyed, he will be quite docile."

Jewel gave a nod. "Good. Now can I go home?"

* * * *

"Of course," Shata replied.

Jewel took a step toward the door. Shata followed. The alien woman's confident swagger was beyond irritating.

Shata turned away and reached for the portal's control panel.

Jewel took a deep breath. It was now or never.

She launched herself at the blond bitch's knees. Shata fell backward, arms flailing. Jewel was on top of her in a flash.

Damn, no balls to kick--what next?

Go for the eyes.

She clawed at the alien's face. Shata bit Jewel's hand. Jewel yelped and went for Shata's throat.

They rolled across the deck and crashed into the bulkhead. The impact sent a jolt through Shata's body. Jewel scrambled away, then launched herself forward as Shata's hand reached for the pocket of her suit coat.

Shata's weapon skittered across the floor. It looked more like Fisher Price than Smith & Wesson, but it had scared the shit out of Dar so Jewel guessed the little silver gun packed quite a wallop. The thing bounced to rest near one of the puny males that Dar had tied up and left in a corner.

Jewel dove for it, launching herself across the ship's bridge like an Olympic swimmer diving off the starting block. She landed on one of the alien males, who moaned when her full weight impacted with his stomach.

"Sorry, buddy," she muttered. Her fingers closed on the alien gun. She rolled, came up on her feet, and pointed the barrel at Shata.

"Don't come any closer or I'll shoot." *Oh great.* Now she sounded like a character in some spaghetti western. Her gaze flicked to Dar. He hadn't moved from his crouch on the floor, but the expression in his eyes was murderous.

Shata stalked her slowly, like some sleek jungle cat. "Shoot? A fine plan. Just be sure you know which way to hold the blaster before you pull the trigger."

Which way...? Jewel flicked a covert glance down at the gun. The trigger mechanism was fairly obvious, but the front and rear sections were nearly identical.

Great. Just frigging great.

Shata moved closer, a smile playing about her lips. "Go ahead, Jewel. Shoot."

Was the thing backwards? There was no way to tell. Wouldn't Shata just grab it if it wasn't a threat to her? Maybe, maybe not. The bitch looked like she'd be delighted to watch Jewel kill herself.

She had about three seconds to make up her mind.

Jewel!

Dar's voice. In her head. Very, very faint, but definitely there. If Jewel hadn't already been terrified she would have freaked. She centered all her concentration of the sound.

Shata is bluffing, Jewel.

Bless the man, that was exactly what she wanted to hear.

She closed her eyes and pulled the trigger.

* * * *

"No!" Shata shrieked.

Too late, thought Dar grimly. Jewel's blast hit the Mardulan full in the chest, sending a lattice of crystals shooting across her skin. Her body stiffened, encased in frost. Within seconds, the frost hardened into a thin veneer of ice.

The ice thickened, obscuring the frozen howl on Shata's face. Then it shattered.

Shata's body shattered with it. Dar watched with curious detachment as his former owner crumbled into a heap of frozen shards on the spiker's deck.

The blaster's recoil had sent Jewel sprawling on the deck. Her eyes were screwed shut, and her hands were shaking. Every instinct in Dar's body screamed for him to go to her, but as long as the collar ringed his neck, he couldn't move an inch.

"Is she dead?" Jewel whispered.

He threw his mind past the deadening barrier of the collar and brushed Jewel's mind with his own. *Yes.*

Jewel's eyes opened. She drew in a sharp breath at the sight of what had once been Dar's owner. "Is that her?"

Yes. Then, when Jewel didn't move, *Jewel--the collar about my neck--"*

"Oh!" Carefully, as if fearing a detonation, she pried her fingers from the blaster and placed it on the ground. A heartbeat later she was beside him, tearing the restraint from his neck.

He hauled her into his arms and kissed her.

Jewel pulled away. "Can we please get out of here? That pile of ice on the floor is giving me serious heebie-jeebies."

He rose and crossed to the entry hatch. Jewel stuck to his side, her gaze averted from the fragments of Shata's melting body. Dar pressed the wall panel, and the door slid open. Once in the forest, Jewel breathed a sigh of relief.

"So. You really *are* an alien. God, I feel like an idiot." She kicked at the sand with the toe of her sneaker.

He touched her chin, nudging it upward so she would meet his gaze. "Hardly that. Are you all right?"

Jewel nodded. "Fine," she said.

Then she burst into tears.

Dar gathered her close, stroking her back until her sobs abated.

"I'm sorry," she mumbled, pulling away. "I don't know what got into me. I never cry."

"Jewel, after that display of bravery, you could cry for an entire Earth year and I would not complain."

She wiped away her tears with the back of her hand. "Thanks. But ... I have to get back to the city. My father. He's sick, and I was just leaving for the bus station when--"

Her next words were lost to Dar, obliterated by the Voice.

He sank to his knees, covering his ears with his hands, though he knew the gesture would do no good. The Voice inside his head howled, calling to the demons of his soul. They answered with obscene joy, clamoring to be set free.

Darkness crowded his vision. The shadows pressed closer. The chains binding Dar's deepest horrors snapped. He slumped to the ground.

His Dream Journey had begun.

Dimly, he felt Jewel's hands shaking his shoulders, heard her frantic shout. He wanted to answer her, but a demon approached him, grasping at his wrists and ankles, clawing at his eyes. Its foul breath caressed, tormenting him with whispers of what his life might have been.

Blackness enveloped him, darker than night, than space, darker, even, than the Rift itself.

He fought, struggling against his bonds as he had done every night on Mardula, with even less effect. Still, he would not succumb to his fate quietly. If he had only moments of sanity left, he would seize every one. He clenched his fist and swung at the demon.

It vanished, leaving him gasping.

"Dar!" Jewel's voice was frantic, but he turned away. If he listened, he would hope, and that was one luxury he could not afford.

A spark of light appeared. As he moved toward it, the shining point stretched into a thin ribbon. One end came to rest at his feet, widening into a road paved with shimmering stones.

The Dream Path.

He stepped onto it. Images rushed at him, so real they left him gasping. Tar'ana. His parents. His sister. Goreth, and a particularly fine day they had shared, exploring the caves near their childhood home. Dar floated in the vision, reliving each moment.

When it vanished, the pain of its loss sent him to his knees.

He staggered to his feet and forged on. More images came, some from his life, others from his dreams, still others from his nightmares. He endured each vision, dreading the ones he knew would come--the images and emotions of his endless days of humiliation as Shata's slave.

Cold terror nearly drove him from the Dream Path. He clung to the stones as the memories rolled over him. His demons howled. Their eyes, red and gleaming, moved close. Cold fingers tore at his heart, dug into his mind.

Dar! Jewel's voice cut through the maelstrom. *Dar! Where are you?*

His fear, already so great, increased tenfold. Jewel had linked her mind with his.

Jewel, you must go! You are in danger here.

Is this your Dream Journey, Dar?

Yes. Jewel, separate your mind from mine. Now.

You can't survive it without me, can you?

Jewel--

Tell me what to do.

No, you must- A demon hand ripped into his heart. Dar cried out.

Dar! Can you hear me? I'm not leaving you! So you might as well tell me what I need to do to get us both through this.

Go, Jewel. Now.

No. Her voice grew louder. *Are you on this silver road? I'm coming after you.*

By the Ancestors! Instead of moving away, Jewel had stepped onto the Dream Path, making their bond unbreakable. She could not escape his fate now.

Only one choice remained.

Will you sing for me, Jewel?

Sing?

Yes. As you did that night in your apartment. The Guardian's Song keeps the demons at bay.

All right.

Dar felt Jewel gather her courage. In the next heartbeat, her sweet voice pierced the foul air, driving away the stench of his despair. A measure of strength returned to Dar's limbs. He rose to his feet and continued along the path, into the most fetid memories of his captivity.

Addio, valle di piante.... Farewell, valley of tears....

The demons came in droves, hurling themselves at his throat, but the purity of Jewel's song blunted their attack, and Dar was able to keep them at bay. The effort exhausted him, however, and the Dream Path stretched on into the distance. He sensed Jewel's fatigue, mirroring his own. How long could they hold out?

A noi si schiude il ciel.... The sky opens for us....

The path twisted, driving deeper into the darkness. Up ahead, the glimmering stones dimmed and winked out. The Journey's end? Dar quickened his steps, then came to a halt when he realized what had caused the Dream Path to disappear.

A demon, larger, more ravenous than any he had yet encountered, blocked his progress. Rage contorted its face. Its body oozed with open sores. As Dar approached, it leaned forward and opened its mouth, revealing three rows of pointed teeth.

Dar rushed the thing, aiming for its soft underbelly. The demon deflected his blow with a flick of its finger.

L'alme erranti volano.... Our wandering souls fly....

Dar crashed onto his back on the cobbles, chest heaving, dread clawing at his heart. This final demon was powerful beyond his wildest imaginings.

There could be no victory.

Volano all'raggio dell'eterno dì.... Fly on the rays of eternal day....

Addio.... Farewell....

Jewel's clear soprano faltered.

The demon rose.

Chapter Nine

"Damn it, Dar. Don't give up now!"

Jewel grabbed Dar's shoulders and shook. Since his Dream Journey had begun, he'd been tearing up the woods like a man possessed. The aria from "Aida" had lent him strength, but now it looked like her singing had lost its effect. He'd collapsed on the sandy ground, chest heaving.

Jewel was exhausted--not from physical exertion, but from the effort needed to sustain the mindlink with Dar while he fought off the demons of his psyche. That bond was wavering now. She closed her eyes and reached for Dar's mind, unwilling to let him go.

I'm here, Dar.

No answer.

Dar! I'm here. Whatever you need, whatever you want from me, I'm here. Do you understand? She fought back her tears. *I love you, Dar. Did you know that? I love you.*

His eyes snapped open but remained dark, unfocused, lit by a feral light. Jewel shrank back. Had the dream demons taken over his mind?

Dar lunged for Jewel, forcing her to the ground and pinning her there with his body. She struggled, then stilled and searched for him with her mind. He was there, wild but still sane, his psyche locked in a deadly struggle with a malevolent demon of incredible power.

Jewel. I need you. I-- Dar's mouth came down on hers, hot and hungry, his tongue plunging deep. She opened to him, returning the kiss, giving all he demanded and offering more.

He tore at her clothes, shredding the thin cotton of her shirt and breaking the clasp of her bra. Lust shot through her. Her fingers wrestled frantically with the zipper of his pants. Dar dragged her shorts and panties down her legs.

He lifted her buttocks on his palms and entered her, thrusting so hard that Jewel was sure she would break in two. She clung to him, accepting his need, offering him her strength. Savage heat buffeted her, searing her heart, carrying her into the heart of the flame.

She wrapped her legs around Dar's waist and strained to get closer. He braced his arms on the ground and surged harder, his face clench in fury. Deep inside her mind, Jewel felt Dar gather the last of his strength into one final blow to the dream demon.

The attack reverberated in her womb and sent her crashing over the edge, into an explosion of insanity.

* * * *

"Jewel, wake up."

Dar leaned close, his chest tight. Jewel's pale face frightened him more than any dream demon. "Please."

He shifted on the sand and gathered her into his arms, rubbing his palms over her skin. The Dream Journey had heightened his sense of touch--his fingers tingled with the contact. His hearing and sight had sharpened as well. Every nuance of the forest came alive to him. Inside his mind, his awareness had expanded. He found the mindlink he shared with Jewel and poured his soul into it.

She shivered in his arms. The long shadows of the late afternoon cast a chill, yet Dar suspected that even if the hottest firestorm were raging, Jewel would have felt cold under his hands. She had given so much of her life force to protect him during his struggle with his final, most horrendous demon.

Would she ever be warm again?

He held her tightly, stroking her, coaxing heat into her limbs. At last, her eyelids fluttered open. Dar searched her eyes, his heart flooding with joy when Jewel's clear, sane gaze looked back at him.

"Is it over?" she asked.

The breath Dar had been holding left in a rush. "Yes. My Dream Journey is complete, because of you." He bent to kiss her.

Her head jerked up, hitting him in the nose. "Oh! I've got to get back." She leaned over and snatched her shorts from the ground. "My brother called right before that bitch showed up looking for you. My father's in the hospital. I have to get to Hershey."

"I will take you there."

Dar retrieved Jewel's blouse, then, since it was far beyond repair, gave her his T-shirt. It hung almost to her knees. She gave his scratched torso and dirty shorts a dubious look.

"I hope they let us onto the bus."

The words were faint, but unmistakable. *Dar, brother--are you there?*

Dar's head snapped up. He lunged for the Rift probe. His fingers trembled as he adjusted the volume and frequency of the transmission. *Goreth?*

His twin's voice strengthened. *Dar? By the Ancestors! Have I found you at last? Are you well?*

Yes, Goreth, to both questions. Where are you?

I am on my way to you.

Dar's heart leapt in his throat. *Truly?*

Yes, and from there we go to Mardula.

Mardula! You cannot be serious?

I have never been more serious, Dar. I've devised a plan to liberate those still held captive on Mardula. I'm in the Rift, headed there now.

How in the name of the Ancestors will you--

Not just me, Dar--there are others. Will you join us?

Jewel's voice cut off his mental conversation. "Damn it, Dar, what the hell is it with you and that abysmal noise?"

He looked up. His Guardian stood in his doorway, arms crossed, a murderous expression on her face. "Turn it off, already!"

Goreth, there is something that requires my immediate attention. When will you arrive?

Three spans, brother.

I will be ready. He gave Goreth the location of Shata's shuttle, where the hapless Mardulan males were still trussed like two *kornos* ready for the roasting spit. *I will meet you there.*

He switched off the probe and rose to his feet.

Jewel heaved a sigh of relief. "I'm ready to go to the bus station."

"I will take you to the station. But Jewel, I cannot go with you to Hershey--and I will not be here when you return."

She stilled. "Not here? I ... I don't understand."

Dar gestured toward the probe. "I do not listen to this device for pleasure, Jewel. How could you think that? It is a means to enhance my mental connection with my brother, but until now, I had been unable to reach him."

"Until now? You mean--"

"Yes. Goreth has contacted me. He will arrive in just under five Earth hours."

Her eyes grew wide. "You mean you're going home? To Tar'ana?"

"No. Not right away. Goreth leads a mission to Mardula, to rescue those still held captive there. I will join him."

Her shoulders tensed. "That sounds dangerous."

He could not spare her the truth. "No doubt."

"You might be killed. Or recaptured!"

He touched her arm. "I am confident that whatever Goreth's plan, it will not fail. I would ask you to come with me, but...."

"Oh, Dar." Jewel looked away. "My father--"

"--needs you. I know. Come. Your family is waiting. I will walk you to the bus station."

She swiped a hand across her eyes and nodded. "My bag's downstairs."

"Jewel--" He met her gaze. "Wait for me. If the Ancestors allow it, I will return."

She nodded, her eyes bright with moisture.

"And please ... do not cry."

"I won't," she promised, tears streaming down her cheeks. "You know I never cry."

Chapter Ten

"You were great, Jewel."

"Fantastic."

"*Bellissima.* Your voice is like an angel's."

Jewel punched Joey's arm and laughed. "I was in the last row of the chorus. There was no way you could have heard my voice. And even if you did, it would only mean I'd been singing too loud."

Marissa shifted her toddler to her other hip and shook her head. "No way. You were perfect."

Jewel's mother nodded her agreement.

"Aunt Jewel?"

Jewel smiled down at Claudia's four-year-old daughter. "Yes, Debbie?"

"Pop-Pop said you were the prettiest singer on the stage tonight."

"Is that so?" Jewel replied, ruffling her niece's cropped. "That's what he gets for leaving his glasses in Hershey."

"I can see just fine, Jullina, and I stand by my observation."

Jewel met her father's gaze and smiled. "Oh, Pop. I'm so glad you came."

"What, you think I would miss a chance to see my youngest daughter sing *Aida* in Italy?" He opened his arms.

She slipped her own arms around his waist and gave him a squeeze. He smelled like aftershave and chocolate, scents of Hershey and her childhood. The rest of her family crowded around, everyone talking at once.

Some things never changed, no matter how far away from home you got.

Damn. Tears again. She was really going to have to do something about that.

They wove through the narrow Roman streets to a small hotel facing the *Campo dei Fiori,* a medieval square famous for its open-air market. After another twenty minutes of conversation and hugs, Jewel's family disappeared behind the hotel door.

Jewel started across the deserted piazza, toward the tiny *pensione* she called home. She'd arrived in Rome last summer, after her father had come home from the hospital. She'd worked whatever jobs she could find while she auditioned with every opera company in the city.

She'd landed roles in a few small shows, which had been gratifying, but this spring she'd hit the big time. Or at least the chorus of the big time. All summer, she would be performing in the famous production of "Aida," staged in the ancient ruins of the Baths of Caracalla.

So here she was, living her dream. Singing on the stage. In Rome. And as icing on the cake, her family finally--*finally*--was proud of her.

So why did she feel so empty?

The *Campo* looked strangely bare at night, matching her mood. Come dawn, market carts would crowd in and vendors would hawk everything from figs to olives to chickens. The bakery would fling open its door and pour its scent into the street. Old ladies in black headscarves would haggle for apples as if their lives depended on it.

Jewel? The deep, husky voice she knew so well wrapped around her mind.

She skidded to a halt on the cobbles.

No. It couldn't be. It had been a year--she'd given up on waiting. She'd convinced herself that Dar had returned to his homeworld and forgotten her. Better that than torture herself with images of his death or imprisonment.

"Jewel." The voice was closer now, right behind her, and with it came a surge of emotion so potent she nearly fell over.

"Dar? Is that you?" She turned around.

And took a step back. Because standing in the moonlight barely twenty feet away were *two* Dars. And neither of them was wearing anything more substantial than khaki shorts and sandals.

She caught her breath. One sexy, half-naked alien man was hard enough to deal with. Two were entirely out of the question.

"Jewel." Dar number one closed the space between them and caught her in his arms. He bent his head and kissed her, hard and long.

A bubble of laughter rose up in Jewel's throat. She threw her arms around his neck. This, *this* was what she'd been missing. And now he was back.

A discreet cough sounded behind her back. She pulled away, suddenly remembering that Dar hadn't come alone. But who...?

"Dar. Do *not* tell me that man is your clone. Just don't. I wouldn't be able to take it."

Dar laughed and turned her to face his companion. "Then I will not. Jewel, I present my brother, Goreth."

"Your brother?" She blinked. "Your twin brother?"

Dar nodded.

"You never told me Goreth was your *twin*."

Goreth caught her hand and pressed it to his lips. "I am honored to meet my brother's Guardian at last."

Jewel twisted in Dar's arms and looked up at him. "I was afraid you would never come back."

"The mission to liberate the slaves on Mardula took much longer than we anticipated."

"But it was successful?"

"Yes. The Mardulan women sowed the seeds of their own defeat."

"I don't understand?"

"When a man of Tar'ana defeats his dream demons, his psychic power expands and joins with that of all other Journeyers," Goreth explained. "It forms what we call a mindweb. This shield protected Tar'ana from outsiders for centuries--until the Mardulan ice blasters shattered it."

Jewel shivered. "So what stopped the Mardulans from turning you all to snowcones when you showed up on their doorstep?"

Dar gave a tight smile. "The power of the mindweb is proportional to the power of the defeated demons. Tar'ana had been peaceful for so many generations that the demons on the Dream Path had withered. The mindweb of the Elders became weak. But for the men who made the Dream Journey after enduring years of slavery...."

Jewel met his gaze. "Their demons were horrible. Like yours."

Dar nodded. "Yes. We gained power beyond measure. United, we broke through the Mardulan defenses."

"But now that you've left Mardula, won't the women just go after men on other planets?"

Goreth laughed. "No, it is not likely. They are much too busy."

"Busy?"

"That is why it took so long for me to get back to Earth," Dar said. "Goreth's Guardian is one of Tar'ana's most brilliant scientists. She devised a way to copy the DNA codes for virility from Goreth and me and transfer them into the cell structure of the Mardulan males. It took some time, but the results were--" He grinned.

"--successful beyond our wildest dreams," Goreth put in. "And given that Mardulan men outnumber women four to one--"

"--the women of Mardula now barely make it out of their beds, much less into space," Dar finished.

"Oh!" Jewel's face flamed red at the thought of four-on-one alien sex. "How ... *interesting* for them."

Goreth chuckled, then gave Dar a meaningful look. "I will need to move the ship soon."

"Where is it?" Jewel asked.

"I put it down inside a curious stone structure. A giant oval. It looked to be in disrepair."

Jewel gaped at him. "You're kidding. You landed your spaceship in the *Coliseum?"*

"No one saw us."

"I certainly hope not," she muttered.

Goreth turned to Dar and gave him a brotherly slap on the shoulder. "Ask her. Now."

"Ask me what?"

Dar shifted from one foot to the other. A wave of his anxiety reached her.

"Well?" she prompted.

His gaze darted toward Goreth before returning to Jewel. "Jewel, you are my Guardian. Will you be my lifemate as well?"

She stared at him. "Your *lifemate?* You mean you want to marry me?"

"Yes. I do. I love you, Jewel."

"But...." *Married?* To an alien? What would her mother think? It would be incredible, but--would Dar want her to leave Earth and live on Tar'ana? Jewel honestly didn't know if she could handle that.

She blinked rapidly, trying to forestall her tears. "Oh, Dar ... I ... I don't know what to say."

He trapped her hands in his. "Do you love me?"

She couldn't avoid his gaze. "Yes. Yes, I love you, Dar, but I'm not ready to leave Earth just yet. I--"

"I would love to show you Tar'ana, Jewel, but I am not asking you to live there. I thought to stay here, on Earth. If you will have me."

A surge of delight welled up inside Jewel and spilled out into the perfect, Roman night. Dar must have felt it even before she answered, because he smothered her reply with a kiss.

"Yes," she said when he released her. "I'll be your lifemate, Dar."

Goreth hugged her. "Welcome to the family, sister."

Jewel blinked. "You mean that's it? We're married?"

Dar nodded. "We can have whatever Earth ceremony you like, but a simple 'yes' before a witness is all that is needed to become lifemates on Tar'ana."

Jewel laughed. "Then I guess you're stuck with me."

"That will be no hardship for Dar," Goreth said with a smile. He embraced them both. "Keep in touch, brother," he said as he disappeared into the night.

"Keep in touch?" Jewel nearly choked. "Oh, no--not with that Rift probe thing, I hope. Because in case you haven't noticed, Yoko and I do *not* get along."

Dar laughed. "No, Jewel. The Dream Journey strengthened the mindlink I share with Goreth. I will no longer need the probe to enhance the transmission."

"Thank you, God," Jewel breathed.

A short time later, at the *pensione*, Dar pulled Jewel into his arms.

Her hands explored his incredible pecs and rock-hard abs, then snaked around and squeezed his sexy butt.

She could hardly believe he was hers for good. She was definitely the luckiest woman in the universe.

"Ah, Jewel, my heart. I will love you for the rest of my life," Dar whispered.

"That's so great." She slipped her fingers into the waistband of his shorts. "Um ... Dar?"

"Yes?"

"If it's not too much trouble, can you start right now?"

The End

SOME ASSEMBLY REQUIRED

by
Dominique Tomas

Chapter One

No one had touched Rahzel in all the years since she left her mother and home.

* * * *

Rahzel's dream lover walked beside her through a hazy landscape of blurred greens, blues, pinks and yellows. It reminded her of a watercolor painting she had made as a child. It had been her favorite, and one of her Bunker siblings dropped it in the water, to hurt her because Rahzel scored higher in all her tests.

"Nothing is quite real yet." He smiled. "Nothing except how beautiful you are. The most beautiful woman I have seen in...."

"Centuries," she said. How did she know his thoughts? "I'm the only woman you've seen in all that time. I could be ugly as a crater on one of the moons, and you'd still think me beautiful."

How did she know that, too?

"Not true." He laughed, his big, dark eyes sparkling as if they held all the stars in the night sky. "True, in strict fact, but not true where matters of the heart rule." He raised a big, hard, warm hand and cupped her face. "Does anyone realize what a treasure it is, simply to touch, to breathe, to hear?"

She shivered, stirred from her toes to the ends of her hair. Energy flowed from him, through her, into the ground, making the air hum.

"Tell me you want me," he whispered. He drew closer and she felt his breath, warm on her face.

"Want?"

"Want." He slid his other arm around her waist and drew her against him.

Heat flooded her body, melting all her joints. Her skin tingled and burned where her leg and hip and torso pressed against him.

"Come find me, love. Hunt for me. Fight for me. I'm fighting the dragons, but you have to come out of your tower before we can be real."

Rahzel winced, frowning as the warning chimes sounded through her dream. Just a few more seconds, a few heartbeats. He had finally touched her. She had felt the warmth and hard strength of him. Just a little longer ... and this would no longer be a dream.

Ridiculous, she knew. How could dreams become reality? How could her dream lover become flesh and blood?

When would someone touch her outside of her dreams?

"Rahzel, are you In-Link?" Mikla's creaky tones replaced the chimes.

At least Mikla still had a body, and she chose to use the audio Link for all communication. Most other Mind-Divers would have jumped straight into Rahzel's head when they wanted to communicate. The last time Rahzel had tried to stay in one of her dreams and ignore a communication Link, Lynnit had caught a glimpse of her private world.

Then Rahzel had caught trouble from the Mind-Diver Council.

"My shift doesn't start for another half hour," she said aloud, and opened her eyes. It was no use trying to stay asleep and slide back into the dream.

She couldn't even remember his name now or any of his features except his enormous blue eyes. They had burned like flames, making promises that sent delicious, rare tingles all through her body. Her dream lover had *touched* her. Nobody had touched her since she left her mother's Bunker and she took her assignment in Link Station Beta-Ten-Zeta.

"There's some program contamination in the etherworld. We're to report all anomalies we experience from now on. Duty shifts are doubling up," Mikla said with a weary sigh. "You'll get the new schedule after you're done with this shift."

Rahzel shoved aside the thick layer of blankets that weighted her down with the warmth she craved from a living body and sat up. She swung her legs over the side of her bed and turned to the curved wall where the microbe filter screen sparkled and hummed. Despite the height of the tower holding her Station, she had no better view of the landscape beyond the Domes than anyone else.

Someday, she wanted to see a sunrise or sunset. Was that too much to ask?

For now, despite the exalted rank of Mind-Diver, all she could see was the misty air inside her Dome and the rounded tops of the Bunkers full of sleeping families, spread out around her in every direction. This early in the morning, she had thought the air inside the Dome would be clear, instead of the usual mist. When the sun rose, so would the microbe count and the chance of catching some newly mutated disease that the regular health-checks, bio-scans and immuno-bots hadn't registered yet. The mist came from all the decontamination sprays and other provisions. Had there ever been such a thing as clear, clean air, or was that another invention of the fictions she read in secret?

Rahzel's face burned at simply thinking of her not-quite-forbidden vice. She loved to read about the interaction between men and women; adventures and physical pleasure; beautiful clothes and wild animals and lavish feasts. And especially about that outmoded, death-defying activity called ... sex.

"There was another outbreak during night shift," Mikla said, breaking into Rahzel's thoughts. "You'll have to monitor the decontamination process through to the end before you finish your duty shift."

"Acknowledged." She waited until the triple chimes signaled Mikla had finally broken contact.

Rahzel wanted to curl up on her bed and try to retreat into her dream. She had time to waste until her duty shift began, didn't she?

Even the frustration of thinking about her dream lover, knowing she couldn't hide in her dreams until night, was better than thinking about the contaminated Bunker.

Some disease had managed to bond to that Bunker clan's DNA, evading every procedure and protocol for eradicating disease and protecting human life. Every member of the clan had to go to a testing station. They would be separated into isolation bubbles, even the smallest children. They would undergo testing. The clan might be sterilized if their DNA had mutated, making the gene-family vulnerable to disease. Rahzel was glad she was a Mind-Diver, rather than a Health-Tech. She would rather unravel data tangles and computer program errors, than watch children cry and scream themselves into catatonia or tell a woman she had lost the right to breed.

Rahzel shook herself, mentally as well as physically, and got out of bed. She physically manipulated the dials to turn on the lights in her Station and close the draperies so she wouldn't see the depressing gray scenery below her. It was probably easier to go through her morning routine using mental commands to her Station's mechanisms, but Rahzel liked doing things with her hands rather than her brain. She felt more real, more alive. It gave her pleasure to move the dial controls and feel the cool metal under her fingertips. More than three-quarters of the planet's Mind-Divers had opted for upgrading to a non-corporeal existence, but she couldn't stomach the idea of having her brain removed, to spend the rest of her conscious existence in a vat of nutrient solution, wired directly into the etherworld controlling the planet.

She wanted to live. She wanted to be flesh and blood, to be tired and dirty and enjoy showers, to be hungry and taste her food. Maybe even endure pregnancy full-term--though most of her generation opted for the womb replicators.

Rahzel let herself play with the thought of having a child here in the Station. There was plenty of room. She liked the idea of having company after years of physical solitude. Hadn't she enjoyed the younger children in her Bunker home? Still, she had to consider the difficulties of spending ten hours every day In-Link, keeping the planet's infrastructure functioning properly. Babies and small children couldn't be left to the attention of robotic nurses for days at a time while their mothers lived inside the etherworld.

And yet, she wanted a baby. Wanted to feel it come to life inside her. Wanted to hold that warm, wriggling bit of life. Because her mother had enjoyed the duty, the thought of having a child thrilled Rahzel. She had even researched childbearing when she was young.

That was when Rahzel had learned the disturbing fact that males and females once cohabited, even sharing beds and hygiene implements--even touching, bare skin to bare skin. Most of the databytes claimed sexual contact, even genital manipulation, had only been for the sake of procreation. Rahzel knew better. She had learned early how to dig deeper, to find the hidden reference Links. That was when she learned about billions of works of literature that celebrated the physical pleasure that came with the act of male impregnating female.

Her dreams of decadent luxury and having a lover started soon after she had moved into her Station, just before she hit puberty. Perhaps her rebellious thoughts came mostly from her total isolation, but what if her research had prompted a slow slide into madness, even a death wish?

She knew she should abandon her research, wipe her private data files of all the fictions. Maybe she should even ask for a mental reconditioning?

The problem was that Rahzel enjoyed her research, the images in her mind, the ghost sensations in her body. If extra vigilance to avoid discovery was the price she had to pay to avoid punishment ... so be it.

"Grains," she told the nutrition dispenser. A slot opened, depositing the pre-programmed amount into the cooking cup set under the unit. She added water, then took a few moments to decide what spices to use today.

Rahzel liked experimenting, rather than opting for the pre-cooked lump that came from the central, sterile, nutritionally correct kitchens for her Dome. Mind-Divers were known to be eccentric. Encouraging their eccentricities made them more mentally agile, able to solve the planet's problems before the general populace even realized problems existed. So, when she requested a kitchen for her personal use, she received one.

She ate her breakfast while listening to an audio report of activities in her Dome and the surrounding five Domes during night shift. All quiet. No emergencies, beyond the contamination that had required the Bunker's evacuation. The report continued playing, the Station's sensors moving the audio feed to the cleanser stall when Rahzel approached it. She peeled out of her nightshirt, dropped it into the sanitation drawer, stepped into the cleanser stall and requested hot water scented with lemon. She stepped out exactly two minutes later, dried off, finger combed her hair out of her face, and strode across her room to the Link chair.

"Reminder to Mind-Diver Rahzel." The audio system buzzed, and Rahzel wondered if there was something wrong with it, or if the program file had been contaminated by that problem Mikla mentioned. "Hair length is nearing the obstruction point. Please have hair cut before it interferes with your cranial inputs."

"Reminder acknowledged," she said, and fought not to sigh while the audio pickup could catch the sound.

She punched in her security clearance codes and brought the headset out of storage while trying not to grumble. Most people, especially Mind-Divers, shaved their heads for ease in hygiene. Living alone, she was free to grow her hair as she wanted, as long as it didn't provide a haven for disease or interfere with the cranial inputs in her scalp.

The heroine of the novel she was currently reading had hair past her waist. The hero liked to weave his fingers through her hair, bury his face in it and fill his lungs with the perfume of her scent.

Rahzel wondered what it would be like to be with a person who didn't smell of disinfectants. A man who wanted to touch her, hold her, indulge in decadent sensory enjoyment. If she grew her hair to shoulder length, maybe she could brush it and pretend it was her dream lover touching her for real.

Then there was no more time to indulge in such unnatural thoughts. In ten more seconds, her mind would no longer be private, but a tool to control, protect and purify the planet. The survival of the human race depended on the Mind-Divers, and Rahzel was proud of her part in it. She lifted the headset and carefully fitted the net of microfibers and gold-plated prongs around her head. As each prong settled into the millimeter-wide sockets of the cranial inputs implanted across her scalp, a tiny click sounded inside her mind. Each click grew louder and the physical world retreated from her senses. As the last connection slid into place, a white haze of static filled her mind. She slid back into her reclining chair, left her body behind, and streaked through the etherworld.

Chapter Two

The affected Bunker was small, only four breeding-age mothers and six children. A pipe carrying waste matter had clogged, caused a backup, and burst. The sickness wasn't from disease, but nausea brought on by the fumes. The Bunker was emptied as a precaution; the mothers and their children separated and resettled in two smaller Bunkers. After decontamination, they would be allowed to return to the Bunker.

Rahzel reported the arrangements and hurried on to oversee the next emergency before her emotions leaked into the Link. She was far too old to worry about the emotional upset of children deprived of familiar playmates and parental figures--yet, she worried anyway.

An air filtration plant serving four Domes set off alarms two hours into Rahzel's shift. She took control of the robotic repair team when the baffles and valves didn't respond in the microsecond necessary to prevent contamination from outside pollution. Working and observing through the purification monitor and three stages of the redundancy system, she personally directed the shutdown, redirection of airflow and commencement of repair procedures. Then she let the system take over for itself.

Even that stress didn't tire her enough to keep her thoughts from wandering. The problem with a slow catastrophe day was that Rahzel needed something to occupy her, or she would get into trouble.

Shreds of her dream returned, lingering at the edge of her consciousness, like a playmate who didn't listen when she was told to go away. Bits of details of her dream lover were trying to integrate in her subconscious. That sort of mental activity involved the emotions, even causing physical reaction. Rahzel didn't need those images to leak into the etherworld. She didn't want her physical reactions logged into the automatic report of her duty shift.

She pulled her thoughts back to her work, almost grateful to be absorbed a short time later by four computer communication breakdowns and loss of power in a freeze-storage area.

When Rahzel had rerouted the power flow and patched the breakdown in communications, she had to deal with the disposal of the spoiled food before it became a health hazard. Her weariness made her susceptible when her dream lover stepped into the fringes of her consciousness.

Her breath caught and something stirred in the silent depths between her hipbones.

Eyes the muted, dark blue of veins seen through fragile skin. Black hair hanging in tangled curls to his shoulders. Wide shoulders, all muscle and tough, coppery skin, like the disease-ridden barbarians who lived outside the domes and safe, subterranean chambers. He smiled with perfect teeth and a square jaw. His eyes mesmerized, threatening to pull her inside his mind and drown her.

Rahzel opened her eyes and sat up--and stopped herself before she yanked the headset off. She looked around her room. Strange, how the sleek, smooth finishes and sparse furnishings had never struck her as cold, barren and lonely until now.

As if she had seen through another's eyes.

Yet that was impossible, because no one had stepped foot inside her Station since the day she took up residence.

How sad, a voice whispered at the back of her mind. The gold wires of her cranial inputs tingled deep inside her brain. The four tiny dots of metal at her temples actually felt warm. *How very wrong.*

She opened her mouth to ask "Who's there?" but another alarm went off. Rahzel hesitated before diving back into the mental realm of the etherworld. Just before all her senses immersed again, she thought she felt warm fingertips gently brush across her cheek.

* * * *

Rahzel's dreams the next three nights were unusually vivid. She woke at least twice each night, her body vibrating with the sensation of a warm body pressed against her. A hand squeezing hers. Breath against her cheek. A voice whispering in her ear.

Yet each time she thought-commanded the lights and got out of bed to step around the screen that separated her bed from the rest of the room, no one was there. A flicker of thought showed her no one and nothing had disturbed the security protocols.

She knew better than to report such disturbances. They certainly weren't anomalies, but rather problems she had brought on herself. Rahzel didn't want to endure another lecture on proper mental attitude for a Mind-Diver. She certainly didn't want to draw attention to herself and have a dozen or so friendly, more experienced Mind-Divers pressure her once again to upgrade out of her physical existence. She would much rather be lonely, "trapped" inside her body, rather than forever existing in the etherworld. Her body was part of her identity. She couldn't imagine abandoning it, reducing herself to a lump of brain sitting in a nutrient solution for a few centuries, until even technology failed her.

The reports of chain-reaction failures with the life support systems of the Domes would have made her think twice about upgrading out of her body, if she had been so inclined. Rahzel wondered about the program contamination that had the higher echelons of the Mind-Divers so worried. She knew better than to ask to get involved. Even if her mind had proven more agile at deciphering such problems, her youth and lack of experience kept her out of the loop. She had earned enough condemnation for resorting to "gut instinct" solutions--even though her hunches always proved right. Rahzel didn't want to open herself up to more criticism. No. Better to let her superiors deal with the problem while she and the lower ranks dealt with the symptoms of the contamination.

On the fourth day, a cascade failure with six power plants and filtration stations kept Rahzel In-Link nearly three hours after her shift ended. She lay limp in her reclining chair after she emerged, soaked with sweat, muscles aching from strain. She hated the smell of herself. She hated the stiffness in all her joints. She hated the empty ache in her stomach, so deep even the thought of food made her nauseous.

"Don't be a total decon," she muttered, not caring if the security system was still on to overhear her talk to herself. The system was supposed to only watch over her physical status and alert her to intruders while she was In-Link, but who could know if the Council would use it to make sure she didn't engage in dangerous activities?

Rahzel knew she should eat, before anything else. She couldn't even muster the mental energy to command a basic cooking program to start. She would take just ten minutes to lie there and rest before she acted. That's all.

It hurt to even open her eyes. Just ten minutes. That was all she could risk. Fifteen minutes of stillness would let her fall asleep. She had to eat after all she had done today or she would be sick, and the Council would lecture her on that, too.

Just ten minutes.

A wisp of steam tickled her face, irritating and then soothing her parched skin. Rahzel inhaled sharply and sat up, choking, as her mouth suddenly flooded with saliva.

The tempting aromas of spicy soy paste, drenched in red sauce, sprinkled with salted crunchies. Her favorite meal.

It couldn't be there--but her nose insisted she did indeed smell it.

Rahzel levered herself out of the reclining chair and tottered the few steps necessary to her kitchen alcove. A black bowl steamed in the cooker box, and green numerals counted down the seconds until it was ready.

"I didn't...," she whispered.

That didn't matter to her stomach.

It hurt, sending spikes from one temple to the other, but Rahzel mustered up enough concentration and energy to check the latest orders to her station's maintenance computer. No one and nothing had given any orders, other than security, since she descended into the etherworld.

Then who had pulled the package out of storage and added water, poured on the sauce and crunchies and put it all in to cook?

Ninia had once remarked that if Rahzel kept indulging her "flights of imagination," she would eventually descend into madness. Had she perhaps stepped onto the border of madness, acting but not conscious of what she did?

"Security: report on movements and activities outside of standard duties of Mind-Diver Rahzel during the last duty shift," she ordered, speaking aloud because of the ache extending from behind her eyes, down into her stomach.

Audibly, because she couldn't focus her eyes enough to read off a screen, the security system reported she hadn't moved off her chair or commanded any housekeeping programs since she started her duty shift.

Rahzel shivered, but she wasn't afraid yet. As long as she hadn't started losing her mind, nothing else at this point mattered. Maybe she was too tired to feel anything except her aching weariness and confusion. And hunger. Unless she was hallucinating the food, she could take care of that problem.

She took the bowl of steaming food out of the heater and sat down right there on the floor with her back against the storage cabinet to eat it.

Lethargy soaked through her body with every mouthful of the hot, spiced paste. Warmth soaked through her body. She felt the heat and soothing comfort of the food ease the aches out of her arms and legs. A sigh escaped her and she smiled.

What luxury, just to be warm and fed. Strange, how she imagined things when she was so drained. Right now, she could have sworn that someone lightly stroked and kneaded all the tight, knotted muscles in her calves and ankles.

A hallucination brought on by exhaustion. The warm, long-fingered, strong hands moved higher up her legs, slid under her thighs. She felt them squeezing just enough to ease the fatigue poisons out of her tissues.

Then she heard a whisper of cloth and felt her long tunic slide up, to bunch against her hips.

Rahzel tried not to freeze. Tried not to stiffen up or hold her breath. Slowly, she opened one eye, just enough to see. Just enough to look down.

Her tunic was indeed bunched up around her hips, revealing the top of her leggings. No one touched her. No one was in the room.

Yet she still felt the hands under her thighs, squeezing just a little harder, once more. Warm, solid fingers stroked, just once--

Rahzel squeaked and leaped, staggering, to her feet.

She didn't want to admit, even in her thoughts, where those invisible fingers had touched her.

Worse, she liked the sensation. She wanted to be touched there again.

There was something definitely wrong with her. Hallucinations could be sounds or images, but not physical sensations. They were like dreams; they couldn't be smelled or tasted or felt.

Could they?

Don't worry, sweetness, a voice whispered in the center of her mind. Rahzel could have sworn she felt warm breath against her ear, stirring her sweat-dampened hair. *There's nothing wrong with you at all. You're exactly perfect.*

"Who's there?" she managed to squeeze out through a suddenly dry mouth and throat.

They treat you like a slave. You'll be my princess.

"Security! Scan. Tranquilizer mist." Rahzel took a deep breath and dove for the drawer holding her breathing mask. She slapped it over her face as a thick, silvery-lavender mist filled her living quarters.

Nothing moved. No blank spaces where an invisible body displaced the mist. No sounds of coughing or struggling. Nothing and no one moved in her room but her.

Chapter Three

Rahzel instituted a full-spectrum medical scan. She had only hallucinated the voice and touch. No one could get into her station without the security program registering an intrusion and dealing with the problem. She blamed the incident on fatigue and emotional distress from the problems she had solved during the day. One of the power stations had broken down because a rebellious contingent had interfered with the distribution of power and materials. She had delved a little too deeply into the data stream to learn about the fools who would endanger everyone's welfare. Getting personal, seeing the disruptive elements in society as people, would only cause her trouble in her duties. Hadn't the senior members of the Council warned her of that more than once?

She wrote up the incident and logged it, condensing her experience down to "fatigue-induced hallucination of an intruder." Nothing would get her to admit she had imagined personal, physical contact. Nothing and no one would get her to admit that she had enjoyed the too-personal touches. That could get her into more trouble than she had the energy to deal with.

* * * *

The next day was uneventful to the point of boring. Rahzel wondered what reaction her report had prompted and called up the logs. She was surprised to see no reprimands registered by her supervisors. Instead, her report was cross-referenced with dozens of other reports. Before she had read through ten, Rahzel found a pattern. Other Mind-Divers were experiencing hallucinations of intruders in their Stations as well.

By the time her duty shift ended, she had backtracked all the cross-references. Following one of her hunches, she checked the timetable for when the hallucinations began to appear and compared with anomalies in the planetary infrastructure and problems in the etherworld.

Most disturbing--to her, personally--she discovered that her extremely vivid visitations with her dream lover coincided with power surges throughout the entire system. She couldn't be sure of the exact moment, because she knew better than to leave any record of those dreams. Still, Rahzel was sure there was more than a coincidence.

She didn't sleep In-Link, so how could the power surges affect her?

The anomalies with the life support infrastructure and other breakdowns, and the hallucinations, all seemed to commence with the arrival of an enormous datablock. It had appeared in the system fifteen duty shifts ago, after a massive power surge that was traced back to a satellite downloading non-assimilation data to the planetary central datacore. The automatic buffers had immediately dealt with the unfamiliar coding by trying to chop the intruder into smaller, manageable bytes, and then move the fragments to smaller storage that would consume less power.

All efforts to separate the datablock into smaller units had failed. It had a cohesive element to it that the Planetary Council wanted analyzed and duplicated to apply to the life-support systems planet wide.

Since it couldn't be subdivided for study, a team of six top-level Mind-Divers attacked the datablock at one time, each taking different quadrants and trying to work their way through to meet in the middle.

Hallucinations followed, after nanoseconds of exposure to the outer protective power shell of the datablock. No one had been able to penetrate beyond the coding that several Mind-Divers theorized enabled the datablock to siphon energy from the planetary core.

Hallucinations? Like hers? Could someone else be hallucinating physical contact and feared reporting it? That was something to think about. For a long time.

When Rahzel's duty shift ended, she disengaged from the Link and pulled out of the etherworld and stared out the shimmering microbe-screen. Sunset spread across the Bunker roofs filling the landscape in every direction below her Station.

Others had hallucinated. More experienced Mind-Divers had been disturbed enough, perhaps, to impede their solution to the mystery. Why? They were better disciplined. Stronger.

* * * *

"Find me, Princess," her dream lover whispered.

"Where are you?" Rahzel pushed at the shadows that surrounded her, thick enough to brush across her palms like icy, wet veils.

"Here. As close as your heart. I'm fighting the dragons. When will you come out and fight them?" He chuckled.

A hand touched her arm, stroking down from shoulder to wrist, the contact light and warm. Rahzel gasped, feeling something familiar in that touch, that hand.

"It's all lies, you know. You won't die if you go outside and look at the sunshine, the moonlight, smell the flowers." His voice dropped to a whisper. "Make love."

Warm breath brushed across her cheek. Moist, warm lips touched her ear.

Rahzel muffled a squeak of shock and sat bolt upright in bed. She pressed her hand over her ear.

It was only sweat. It had to be nothing but sweat that made her ear damp.

She could have sworn someone ... licked her.

* * * *

"Rahzel." Somehow, Mikla's voice greeting her when she stepped out of the shower an hour later wasn't a surprise. "You've begun investigating the datablock."

"Is it the reason for the current emergency?" Rahzel had to raise her voice to be heard over the jets of hot air coming from the dryer poised just above the cleanser stall door.

"It is. Do you have any theories?"

"One." Rahzel reached for her tunic and pulled it over her head while she gathered her thoughts.

Mikla never showed any emotions except disapproval. The lack of emotion in her voice right now had to be a good sign. Rahzel wondered if her inordinate curiosity and "prying habits" had finally pleased her superiors.

"The hallucinations reported by the Mind-Divers involved in exploring the datablock have all been physical in nature. The Mind-Divers have all been upgraded to a disembodied state. Retaining my physical state might provide a buffer against the hallucinations."

Silence.

Rahzel pulled on her leggings, her slippers, took her nightshirt out of the sanitation drawer and hung it up while she waited. Had she gone too far in subtly proposing she be allowed to explore the datablock?

Physical hallucinations when the sufferer had no body had to be even more disturbing than what she had experienced. As the only Mind-Diver who didn't disdain her body, Rahzel knew she possessed an advantage over the others. The puzzle of the datablock and how it affected the etherworld and planetary infrastructure and yet resisted all study and dissection fascinated her. She wanted to be given this assignment more than she had wanted anything in years.

More than she had wanted to go home to her mother's Bunker when the Mind-Diver Council first drafted her for training and duty. That said a great deal.

"You will have complete access to the datablock, all records connected to it, and freedom from all duty shifts until further notice." Mikla paused. "We're counting on you."

Those four little words took Rahzel's breath away. Instead of cautioning her not to make a mistake that could harm the Domes ... that had to be an expression of confidence. More confidence than her superiors had shown in her in years.

"I'll do my best," she said and waited until the connection closed before she let herself breathe.

Then she grinned. She wrapped her arms tight around herself and sank down onto the edge of her reclining chair, and sighed, the sound turning into breathy laughter. She had never tasted triumph before in her life, and it tasted sweet.

She found it hard to suppress a smirk and a feeling of great satisfaction and vindication. Many of her peers had expressed sympathy to her over the years, because her duty to breed had kept her from upgrading her physical existence. Rahzel had sometimes physically bitten her tongue and thought of other things when they expressed their sympathy, because she enjoyed her body. She enjoyed the exercises she undertook. She enjoyed tasting food and smelling flowers. She enjoyed the disturbing sensations in her body when she read fictions and vicariously lived the experiences of the heroines.

Because she had a body, took good care of it, enjoyed what her body did for her and didn't "suffer" until she could be upgraded, she had a chance of succeeding where the others had failed.

She vowed to make them sorry they had ever condescended to her. She would make all the higher-ranked Mind-Divers wish they had retained their bodies.

* * * *

"What sort of ghost sensations?" Rahzel asked.

To respect the privacy of the Mind-Divers who had been involved in dissecting the datablock, she used vocal communication, rather than going into the Link. She hoped they appreciated her delicacy. Using her vocal chords was more effort, when she was used to all mental communication for days at a time, than to simply submerge into the Link and contact someone. Those who had upgraded merely had to activate a speaker program that synthesized their former physical voices.

"I thought I saw someone in my cubicle." Dorienne's voice shuddered, giving Rahzel an image of a spidery, mouse-haired woman hunching in on herself.

Dorienne had been upgraded for thirty-eighty years now. Her cubicle was barely larger than Rahzel's bed; a storage cabinet holding her nutrient solution and the three levels of supplementary power sources in case the main system failed.

"In your cubicle? How could anyone fit in there?"

"Strange...." The woman sighed, her voice sounding like a gentle breath of wind. Rahzel did admire the quality of the voice synthesizers that retained so much of the original body's characteristics. "I could have sworn I was back in my Station, and someone stood just at the edge of my vision. Trying to get my attention, so to speak. You have no idea how disturbing it is to think you're being invaded, when you've had blessed, sweet isolation for decades."

"I experienced something similar already," she offered. Rahzel wasn't about to admit that she hadn't grown to the point where her isolation was either blessed or sweet.

All the others she contacted had the same experiences. Whispered voices. The impression of a hand on a non-existent shoulder or arm or hand. One Mind-Diver reported feeling someone tousle her thick, curly hair--and she had shaved her head for twenty years before she upgraded. Others reported thinking they saw someone standing at the door of rooms that they hadn't inhabited in decades.

Only Rahzel had felt someone massaging her legs. And that entirely too intimate touch. She was the only one who had personal remarks addressed to her.

What could it all mean?

Chapter Four

"Sensory overload?" Rahzel mused aloud. After two days of examining the reports, thinking of nothing else, she even dreamed of the datablock. "All that alien energy, stored in such a unique pattern, it could have activated neurons that haven't fired since upgrading."

She thought about her theory for nearly half an hour, scribbling notes with her stylus on her datascreen. Finally she nodded, closed her eyes, and mentally inscribed her theory into her research notes, using more scholarly and precise language. She seemed to spend every waking hour wearing her headset now, cranial inputs connected and ready to let her descend into the etherworld at a moment's notice, make notes, or go In-Link to request information or assistance. It was a heady feeling to have so much freedom. Rahzel tried not to use it, just so it wouldn't hurt so badly when it was finally taken away.

Alien energy. Her mind latched onto that concept and spun off all the implications. Dangerous for the planet and etherworld, or the support and protection they needed?

Energy takes many forms, sweetness, a now-familiar imaginary Voice said.

By this time, Rahzel no longer jumped when she heard the Voice. Especially when she thought she felt a warm breath brush against her ear. She told herself that when she withdrew from contact with the datablock and the alien energy stopped flowing through the Link, stopped causing problems in the etherworld, the sensations would stop.

That struck her as unutterably sad.

"I should name you," she said aloud. "Children's imaginary friends always have names."

La'rus.

"Why would I think of a name like that?" She laughed nervously.

But why be nervous? If she carried on conversations with herself, imagining a male voice in her ear, what was so odd about the name she apparently thought up without realizing it?

It's my name. The Voice laughed. *It's about time you asked. Thank you.*

The sensation of warm lips touched her hand. Rahzel flinched. The sensation moved to her neck.

Just another hallucination, she told herself firmly. *I'm overly tired. It's time to relax. Maybe I should--*

By all means. The Voice sounded more male by the second. *Read one of those lovely books. I want to know what you like, so we can celebrate properly.*

"Celebrate?" She flinched at hearing her voice.

If she was going to start speaking to herself, she needed something to cover the sound. If anyone on the Council decided to check up on her without asking for a report, all they had to do was access the security program, turn on a camera or an audio pickup--and hear her talking to herself. Rahzel didn't want this assignment taken away. Not until she solved it.

How long had it been since she listened to--

Music! Wonderful. I do hope we have the same taste, sweetness. The Voice sighed, the sound low so that it rumbled and set off a chain reaction of humming low in her belly. *I can't wait to taste* you, *in particular.*

She leaped up from her chair. The sensation of breath against her ear, of something softly stroking through her hair, dissipated. She even thought she heard a disappointed sigh. Hands shaking, she manually turned on the audio entertainment program.

"Celebrate what?" she asked. Better that question than dwell on the last thing her personal hallucination had mentioned.

Our union. My rebirth. Ah, lovely music. Pipes of some kind, yes? And stringed instruments. I should take some time to learn what they're called. We shall certainly.... He chuckled, sending more disturbing, pleasant, strangely sad, yearning vibrations through her. *We shall make lovely music together. Soon. I promise you.*

* * * *

Rahzel's dream lover walked beside her through a hazy landscape, all blurred greens and blues, pinks and yellows. It reminded her of a childhood watercolor painting that had been ruined when one of her Bunker siblings dropped it in the water. The other girl had been jealous because Rahzel scored higher in all her tests. Such jealousy had been foolish, really, because Rahzel had been watched from that moment on, and taken away for Mind-Diver training only a few years later.

"Nothing is quite real yet," he said, smiling. "Nothing except how beautiful you are. The most beautiful woman I have seen in...."

"Centuries," she said. How did she know he thought that, and that he didn't want to admit it? "I'm the only woman you've seen in all that time. I could be ugly as a crater on one of the seven moons, and you'd still think me beautiful."

How did she know that, too?

"Not true." He laughed, his big, muted blue eyes sparkling as if they held all the stars in the night sky. "True, in strict fact, but not true where matters of the heart rule." He raised a long-fingered, warm hand and cupped her face. "Does anyone realize what a treasure it is, simply to touch, to breathe, to hear?"

She shivered, stirred from her toes to the ends of her hair. Energy flowed from him, through her, into the ground, making the air hum.

"Tell me you want me," he whispered. He drew closer and she felt his breath, warm and flavored with cinnamon on her face.

"Want?" Rahzel trembled, realizing this moment was familiar, as if she had lived it a dozen times. Any moment now, it would end. She didn't want it to end. She wanted to feel his hands on her bare skin, taste his mouth in tender, warm kisses, be gathered up in his arms.

"Want." He slid his other arm around her waist and drew her against him.

Heat flooded her body, melting all her joints. Her skin tingled and burned where her leg and hip and torso pressed against him.

She was naked.

"Beautiful," he whispered, and his smile widened until she thought she would fall into it. "Mine. You are mine, aren't you, sweetness?"

Rahzel woke up, pressing her hands over her mouth to stifle the shriek, half frustration and half terror, which she felt waiting to be born. It choked her, but she kept silent. Her heart raced and sweat slicked her sleeping clothes to her skin.

Her leg and hip, her ribs and breast burned and tingled. The sensation of a hand pressed against her hip startled her, so she swung her legs over the side of the bed, needing to move to erase the feeling.

She couldn't move. A weight held her down.

Weight--in the form of an invisible hand. Two hands pressed on her legs, keeping her from moving.

"No!" She yanked free with all her strength of mind and body.

I'm sorry! The Voice followed her as she stumbled across the room to the cleanser stall.

She peeled off her sweaty clothes that stank of fear. It made sharp, sickening contrast to the warm, musky perfume that had filled her nostrils in those few microseconds between waking and terror.

Sweetness, I'm sorry. I would never hurt you. I adore you.

Rahzel spoke to the Station's robotic controls. She hadn't done that since she had strained her mental control on a massive repair project, and the medical computer had prohibited her from any use of the Link for ten duty shifts. She called up a music program. Loud. Throbbing drums and crashing discords from strings and brass.

It drowned out the pleading, apologizing, weeping Voice.

* * * *

"The hallucinations are affecting me more strenuously than reported by the team." Rahzel was rather proud of her self-control. Her voice didn't tremble.

She was relieved, and yet she also grew curious as to the reasons why Mikla preferred audio communication these days, instead of through the Link. Audio suited her, because she didn't have to expend precious energy hiding her inner turmoil or keeping it from floating near the surface of her public mind.

"You've also spent more time exploring the datablock," Mikla said. She answered so quickly, Rahzel wondered if her supervisor had anticipated her report and prepared an answer.

Curiosity prompted a quick check. Her theory proved correct: Mikla had been peripherally involved with the attempt to dissect the datablock. She wondered if her supervisor still suffered reverberations from the contact and resultant hallucinations.

Or had the experience, disturbing as it was, changed the much older woman? Was it changing all the Mind-Divers who came into contact with the datablock?

"The more time I spend, the deeper I try to penetrate through the anomalous energy layer, the worse it will get?" She stifled a groan and a curse. Rahzel suspected she would have known that detail or guessed it, if she hadn't been indulging in fictions to soothe her itching nerves.

"Do you suffer the hallucinations while you are actually working? All your physical monitoring reports show optimum health levels. No stress or distress. Normal breathing and heart rate and temperature."

"No, I don't ... but my Link will automatically shut down if I go beyond the maximum time limit."

"If you go beyond the recommended maximum, you will wear yourself out, physically and mentally. Sleep will come sooner, and you can use the Modulator to keep the hallucinations from entering your dreams," Mikla offered.

"If the Health Monitor doesn't interfere, yes. I'd like to spend more time, so I can get this over with more quickly. Longer periods of contact could be more beneficial. Keeping up the momentum of discovery, instead of having to retrace my steps each session," she hurried to add.

Rahzel didn't need to be scolded about haste causing mistakes.

"The Council will take care of re-programming your Health Monitor guidelines. Also," Mikla continued, before Rahzel could react to that unexpected leniency, "it has been suggested that you *explore* the hallucinations, instead of resisting them. It could be an attempt to communicate. Some alien intelligence could have placed a message into the datablock, and this is the only means it has found to contact us, until you decode it."

"Yes. Of course." Rahzel pressed her lips flat in a frown, knowing that facial expressions affected the voice.

Internally, she spun with glee. She wished she knew how to dance, so she could celebrate this triumph.

Dance with me, sweetness, the Voice whispered, when she withdrew from the Link and sat back to evaluate her latest batch of measurements of the datablock.

She wasn't surprised at the request. The Voice came from her subconscious or unconscious mind, responding to her thoughts.

Why do you doubt me? The Voice sounded hurt.

How could an imaginary personality have hurt feelings?

Because I thought of dancing not two seconds ago, Rahzel responded. She smiled at her silliness. This hallucination had become a friend and companion, and a welcome one at that. *Maybe I'm going mad from this isolation. All the tests when they tapped me for training didn't uncover flaws and weaknesses that are now coming to the surface.*

You're not going mad. You're emerging *from madness. You're been living in a prison all your life.* The Voice chuckled.

For half a heartbeat, an image of Rahzel's dream lover flickered into her mind. His dark blue eyes flashed bright like lightning.

I've been living in a prison too, truth to tell. We'll free each other, sweetness. I'll be your genie in a bottle. Free me--

Genie?

Don't you know what a genie is? Your education isn't as extensive as I thought.

What is a genie--why would it be in a bottle?

He, usually. Relax and do some research. Tell me what a genie is, and I'll give you a wish. Free me, and I'll give you two more. Give me my wish ... and I'll lay the entire universe at your feet.

* * * *

"Genie." Rahzel frowned, the tip of her spoon caught between her lips. She forgot about her breakfast as she digested the information filling her head from the Link.

The fiction references alone were nearly overwhelming. Even dividing them into folklore, longer fictional constructs and a treasure trove of forbidden visual media, Rahzel knew it would take weeks of free time to investigate. Perhaps she could label it as research and avoid reprisal for spending time and energy on frivolous things, if anyone caught her exploring off-limits cultural areas. It would be relaxing.

She called up one image and displayed it through the holographic program. A man with a shaved head, gold rings in his ears, massive shoulders and rippling chest muscles floated in the middle of her room. Slanted eyes and coppery skin gleamed. A tiny, pointed black beard looked silly and yet sinister on his long face. He scowled at something just beyond her shoulder. Rahzel fought the urge to turn and look. She knew there was no one in her Station room with her, hallucinations and the Voice notwithstanding.

What amused her was that this remarkable specimen of primitive male was nothing but a twisting column of smoke from the waist down. Nothing but his beard proved he was male.

How infuriating that must have been, the Voice murmured. Laughter trickled through Rahzel, wiping away the headache that sleep hadn't soothed. *No wonder so many genies were in a bad mood when their masters called for them.*

Do you want to be like him? Rahzel challenged. She snorted, muffling laughter. It would not do to be caught laughing all by herself. Even if other Mind-Divers had suffered hallucinations, she didn't want to be locked up, denied the Link--and the datablock taken away--for giving in to delusory behavior.

That emasculated monstrosity? Hardly.

He's better company than you. She flicked a thought at the holographic projector controls. The genie's image blinked, raised an arm, took a step toward her.

How did you--ah, yes, I see now. How clever. Is there enough energy control there to physically interact?

"Physically interact?" she whispered, startled yet again that her hallucination had come up with something that had not been in her mind. She knew she had never even read the word, *genie*, let alone studied it until this moment. And now her hallucination wanted to play with the hologram so it could interact with her.

In the decades since the self-defensive isolation practices had been established, many people had attempted to give holographic projections some solidity, so people could have physical contact with each other without the inherent health risks. The energy drain was too prohibitive, and the concentration of lasers too dangerous. Safety prohibitions kept people from performing private modifications in their own quarters.

Virtual reality suits were still the only option for obtaining physical sensation, and they had fallen out of favor long ago. The total encapsulation required had inherent health risks, and they were prohibitively expensive. Few beyond the elite classes could afford private suits, and it was nearly impossible to totally sterilize the suits for multi-person use, without damaging the microfibers that made sensory interaction possible.

Ah, yes, I see. The Voice sounded positively gleeful. Rahzel had no idea what it saw. She had been too busy thinking, rather than diving through more information. *This requires more energy than those idiots would spare to keep their own mothers alive ... but we're the masters of energy, aren't we?*

"I don't know--" Rahzel stopped herself. Bad enough she carried on conversations in her head. Speaking aloud seemed like giving in. She would not become slave to her hallucinations. *I don't know what you're talking about. Leave me alone, please.*

Not yet, sweetness. You can get to work soon. In fact, I want you to get to work ... but let's have some fun first, shall we?

The holograph of the genie flickered. The column of smoke shifted, morphing into legs as muscular as the arms and chest. They took on color, bronzed and lightly dusted with black hair.

Other anatomically correct details appeared.

Chapter Five

Rahzel blinked, then turned away, blushing. She had no idea that sort of vulgarity was inside her head.

Not you, sweetness. The Voice laughed, mocking her.

Despite turning her back to the holograph, she could still see the anatomical exactness that had filled in where smoke had been. She knew the differences between male and female, just as she knew the biological necessity for impregnating the female, to continue the species. She simply never thought the male organ was so ... big.

No wonder females had to be coaxed, coerced, sometimes brutally forced to submit to mating.

Males must have mutated horribly in the past. It's a miracle the human race survived at all.

Mutated? The Voice laughed. *My dear girl, I'll have you know that is a physique guaranteed to satisfy even the most discriminating woman.*

It won't fit! Rahzel barely kept from screaming aloud, trying to drown out the mocking aggrieved tones in her head. *It's too big. I know how a woman is built.*

Too big?

Silence.

She waited for a reaction from the voice--then wondered if she had finally gone completely mad. How could she be arguing with herself over something so inconsequential? She forced herself to open her eyes again and turned around to face her fears. Strangely, she felt disappointment to find the genie wore red trousers.

When we're finished here, my sweetness, I dare you to tell me this is inconsequential.

The genie holograph moved. It stopped shimmering and grew opaque. Rahzel stared at it, feeling a flicker of apprehension tighten in her belly. She sent a tendril of thought to the holograph controls to turn off the display mechanisms.

If anything, the illusion of solidity grew stronger. The genie smiled. Hair grew, crowning that formerly bald head with glistening black curls, like polished onyx. The tiny beard and earrings vanished.

The eyes changed, growing wider, deeper, the black changing to a dark, soft blue. That smirking smile softened. Yet somehow she felt even more endangered by the lack of threat.

Hunger. Need. That's what shone through the mutated genie that walked toward her, holding out his arms.

Dance with me, the Voice whispered.

The genie's mouth moved in synchronization with the voice in her head. He held out his hands. Rahzel put out her hands, unthinking.

She gasped and flinched and darted backwards two steps. Her skin tingled where it touched the holographic projection. For a moment there, she could have actually believed she touched ... not flesh and blood, but something solid. Something pulsing with energy.

"The energy output is increased. These are lasers of a sort," she muttered. "That's why it feels almost real. I could have burned myself."

She never would have ordered the projectors to do something like that. The lasers *couldn't* do that without extensive physical reconfiguration, and she certainly lacked those skills. So how did it happen?

The power needs to be phased differently. Sorry about that. The Voice sounded almost cheerful. Like one of Rahzel's video teachers, who enjoyed challenges and problems almost more than the solution.

"This is ridiculous. Holo, off," Rahzel snapped.

For a heartbeat, she thought the audio controls would refuse to respond. She reached with her mind for the overrides. Usually, she could Link without her headset to control anything within her Station. Today, even that simple task seemed beyond her. Had she strained herself? Rahzel gritted her teeth and pushed harder with her mind, refusing to accept insubordination from a mere machine.

The genie opened his mouth as if to speak. Sadness glimmered in those eyes. He shrugged and blinked out of existence.

Yes, sweetness. Go to work. We'll meet soon. Though ... not soon enough.

The Voice sighed. Rahzel thought she felt warm, gentle breath against her cheek, and a gentle brushing across the ends of her hair at the base of her neck. She shivered, liking and yet disturbed by the sensation.

When she solved the mystery of the datablock, the hallucinations would fade and then stop permanently. She found she didn't look forward to that occurrence as much as she should.

* * * *

Rahzel wished the genie was real, when she finally emerged from hours of work in the etherworld and ended her attempt to find a seam in the protective energy wall around the datablock. She wished there was someone to pick her up and carry her across the room to her bed. Someone to put her in the cleanser stall and rub the aches out of her limbs, pressure-soothe the base of her neck and her temples, make her dinner, and hold her until she fell asleep. She was tired of smothering under blankets, just to approximate the feeling of being held. She wanted the warmth that came from another body, not her reflected and collected warmth. She wanted touch.

She wanted the hallucinations to be real.

"La'rus?" she whispered.

Rahzel took a quick, shallow breath and held it, waiting for the Voice to respond.

Silence filled her room, so thick it muffled the ever-present soft humming buzz of all the equipment that served her. No sound of the cleanser stall automatically spilling water and steam, waiting for her pleasure. No whirring of the heater unit as her dinner cooked all by itself. No sensation of large, strong, warm, caressing hands easing the aches out of her body.

If she didn't want to wake up stiff and cramped and smelling like a sewer pipe had burst, Rahzel knew she had to get up and take care of herself. Not even her most potent dreams of her lover could do that for her.

Food, for the time being, was more important than being dry and clean and smelling like a human being instead of a filthy machine. She had to manually program the controls because her mind was so threadbare and achy.

Too tired to fall asleep, she yanked a chair over to the reading screen and reviewed a written report of what the team had tried to do to aid their explorations of the datablock. Rahzel had found that differences often showed up in the written reports, bits of information that were lost when information downloaded directly from a mind into the etherworld.

Slouched in her chair, holding her bowl on her lap, resting one elbow on the edge of the console and her cheek pressed against her hand, she read. Amazingly, it wasn't all boring repetition. Maybe because she loved to read rather than get the personal impressions and flash-feed of audio-visual-thought that came with the download.

"Huh." She went back and read that last part again--another advantage that printed words had over searching the databytes in the etherworld.

The reaction of the energy readings came more strongly, more rapidly--and hallucinations were stronger--when the teams worked on many individual sections of the datablock simultaneously, rather than everyone concentrating on one section at a time. Rahzel had taken a cursory glance through the overview of the information on the datablock, and had wondered how to prompt those interesting, alien patterns of energy.

She sat back in her chair, half-closed her eyes, and finished eating as she thought about that. She barely tasted what was in her bowl while her mind raced and played with a dozen different theories. When

Rahzel stepped into the cleanser stall, she spared it only the fringes of her consciousness while she focused all her thoughts on the fascinating new problem.

When she finally fell asleep.... *She dreamed of splitting her conscious mind into a thousand pieces, a thousand shooting stars in a myriad rainbow of colors. The datablock became a world wrapped in a spider's web of multicolored strands. Each strand was a different phase of energy patterns. Each star from her mind penetrated the juncture point of the strands.*

"Come to me!" The genie reared up in the starry blackness of space beyond the datablock world.

He opened his arms and they filled the universe. His smile made her tremble, full of pain and hope. His dark blue eyes swallowed all the stars, and as Rahzel watched, she felt herself drawn into his eyes. She fell forever.

When she woke, she lay curled up on the very edge of her bed. Despite being covered by only the thinnest blanket, she felt warm.

She felt as if a large, warm body had curled around her and held her.

Rahzel didn't want to move, didn't want to wake fully. She lay still, content to rest in the fleeting shreds of her dream.

"No," she moaned, as her mind awakened fully and latched onto the puzzle that had followed her into her sleep.

It shoved the dreaming part of her to the background. The fleeting memories of a warm, full mouth moving across her face, her neck, faded. She no longer felt the large, callused hands on her arms, her belly, holding her close.

Just at the edges of her consciousness, she thought she heard someone whisper. Rahzel couldn't hear the words.

Damp warmth closed around her nipple.

She sat up, flailing--or did she reach for the retreating lover? Even as she jerked to full wakefulness, Rahzel couldn't be sure what she had wanted.

No one was in the Station with her. As always.

Rahzel started to scream, but the sound caught in her throat.

She was naked.

Chapter Six

Work was the only antidote to drive away the strange, conflicting feelings that remained after her dream faded. Rahzel barely spared herself the time to get something to eat and jump into the cleanser stall. A tiny part of her loathed washing, as if it would erase the memory sensations. She was ashamed to look at her naked body and dressed with her eyes closed.

Still, every time she thought about that last, farewell impression from her dream, both nipples tingled. Why? Did she like it, or didn't she?

Her relatively clear mind confirmed the ideas she had taken into sleep with her last night: when many sections of the datablock were explored at the same time, more energy patterns awoke and became stronger. The datablock seemed to grow and change configuration and gain energy, without taking anything from the surrounding containment field that tried--and failed more rapidly over time--to keep it separate from the etherworld. The energy itself seemed to create a baffle field, blocking clear sensor readings.

"They were never meant to be taken in separate units," Rahzel whispered.

Strange, how she needed to physically hear a voice. Even if it was her own.

The sum of the whole is greater than all its parts, the Voice whispered at the back of her mind. *Ready to go treasure-hunting, sweetness?*

She chose not to answer. Rahzel wondered what she thought she was doing, trying to block her thoughts away from the Voice's access. It was part of her--of course it would know what had happened in her dreams last night, how she had awakened in the morning. Yet she still tried, as if ... as if the Voice were a real person. But that was impossible. Even the disembodied members of the Mind-Diver Council still needed some residing place, some anchor for the electro-chemical processes that supported their consciousness.

Rahzel shoved aside that thought and made a report of her new theory. She made a written report, so the non-Mind-Diver members of the Sciences Council could see what she intended.

She could very well kill herself, if her plan didn't work. Rahzel wanted somebody to be able to follow what she had done, in the hopes that they could figure out what she had done wrong.

What makes you think you'll do anything wrong? the Voice asked. Somehow, he didn't sound as cheerful as Rahzel would have preferred.

Where was that irritating yet pleasant teasing? Could the Voice possibly be worried about this new step?

Not worried, sweetness.

An impression of a sigh flowed across her cheek, warm and soothing, and the sensation that if she took one step backwards she would be enveloped in strong arms. She could almost hear a heart beating in a muscled chest pressed against her back. Her own heart picked up pace in response.

Impatient. Weary. A thousand feelings and thoughts that have grown too heavy for me. Hurry with your work. I'll be waiting when you're finished.

"I'm not getting to work just yet," Rahzel muttered.

Her plan required full immersion in the datablock. That required multiple permissions to go past protective overrides in the Link, the power sources for the Stations, health safeguards and other areas governed by outside authorities.

If she succeeded in her plan, she would rise so far above the authorities on this planet, they would never be able to say no to her again.

You were meant to be free, to rule, sweetness, the Voice whispered. He sounded far away and weary, and that made her feel sad for some inexplicable reason. *You'll be my queen. They're all fools, but it's not too late to shake some sense into them. We'll do that together. But first, you'll have to find me, won't you?*

Rahzel shivered, hearing an echo of those first disturbing dreams that had started this mess.

No. It wasn't a mess. For the first time in years, maybe since she had left her mother's Bunker, she was happy. She was moving through life, not drifting. Making her own choices, not letting everyone else dictate to her.

This was living as it was meant to be.

Even if she died soon, she wouldn't have wasted her life.

If only....

Dreams will come true, sweetness. I promise you. If I draw one breath after all this time, and it's my last, I promise it will be spent on you.

* * * *

Rahzel sent out her requests for permission. She formulated the general outline of her proposal and plan of action, and made that available for any authority that cared to truly investigate. Then, there was nothing to do but relax and wait.

Correction. She would gather her strength. She would prepare mentally and physically. She would catch up on all the little self-indulgent activities that she had let slide, neglected, while she investigated the datablock.

Her hair had grown. She had never seen it this long, covering her ears, brushing the collar of her coverall, hanging low enough to touch her eyebrows. Wisdom said to cut it--but why? Who would care? Her hair was fine enough to never get in the way of the cranial inputs dotting her head. She could use something to push it aside when it got long enough to be bothersome. Why not grow her hair long? Her favorite heroines had long hair. Wasn't what she attempted with the datablock heroic? Why couldn't she look like a heroine?

The trouble was, she didn't know what she looked like.

Easily enough fixed.

"Holo--create image of Mind-Diver Rahzel. Three-dimensional. Full color. Life-size."

As she waited for the image to form, Rahzel felt a pressure growing in her throat. Just before it released, she realized it was a giggle. She hadn't giggled since childhood.

She clearly remembered chasing her siblings around the central room of their mother's Bunker. Laughing. Spattering each other with precious water. Giggling and tumbling down in a corner filled with cushions and wrestling. Playing with her mother in the evening, pretending she didn't want to go to bed. Being tickled.

Rahzel swallowed the giggle. She was no longer a child. She no longer had the right to be frivolous.

Wasn't it frivolous, though, creating a life-size image of herself so she could know what she looked like? What could she do about her appearance, anyway? Short of wasting precious resources and medical supplies better spent elsewhere, what could she do? Why make herself unhappy?

You won't be unhappy, the Voice whispered, before Rahzel pushed it out of her consciousness. *I am most pleased.*

The holographic figure sparkled into being, hanging at knee-height above the floor.

A mental nudge sent the image of herself slowly revolving, so Rahzel could get the full view.

"Arrogance," she muttered, even as she smiled.

The years had been kind. Her breasts and bottom didn't sag. Her thighs and arms were still lean. No flaps of flesh to jiggle and wag when she moved, despite her sedentary existence. Her hair looked dark at her scalp, and lightened as it got longer. Rahzel thought a command, and a strip of gray material joined the image, pushing her hair back from her face, back from her ears--and covered the four golden dots of the cranial inputs above her temples. That was a nice touch she hadn't anticipated.

Feeling vain and rebellious, she changed the color of the cloth band to pale blue, to match her eyes.

Then she made her hair longer. To her shoulders. Past her shoulders, over the slight curves of her breasts.

Feeling ridiculous, she made her breasts larger. A grin and then a giggle followed as she made her breasts larger than melons, then shrunk them until they were flat, then brought them back to their normal size.

Her frown faded when she realized she waited for a comment from the Voice.

Rahzel made her hair longer, past her waist, thicker, and curly so it hung in glistening, dark gold corkscrews.

"I look like an idiot," she muttered, and put her hair back the way it was in reality.

Why not play with her clothes while she was at it? A quick visual check of her progress screen showed three authorities reviewed her requests and two had already approved. She had plenty of time to relax and play.

Rahzel changed the color of her coverall from faded dun to lavender. Did it change the shade of her eyes, or was it just her imagination? She tried other colors; crimson and emerald, saffron and gold, royal purple and cobalt blue. Somehow, nothing truly pleased her.

Not the colors, sweetness, the Voice whispered. He laughed. *You did miss me, after all, didn't you? Not to worry--we'll be together soon enough.*

How can I miss what really isn't there? she retorted.

You should get rid of something that's not necessary. A rumbling chuckle that Rahzel could only describe as "wicked" followed. *Get rid of what you won't miss.*

A shriek of pure surprise caught in her throat. Her holographic image went naked. A blush covered her face. Rahzel tried to look away ... but somehow, she couldn't.

Perfect. Warmth flowed down her arm, as if a hand gently brushed along her sleeve. *Look. There's nothing to be ashamed of. Beauty comes in many forms. Only fools hide from Nature's beauty. Only fools refuse to enjoy the simple joys and pleasures and make everything into danger. They preach against excesses and irresponsibility, but even caution can be done in excess. Moderation, sweetness. Everything in its own time and place. I promise you, when the time comes, we will feast and no one will dare condemn us.*

That warmth curved around her face. Pressure brushed her lips. It felt like a finger, slowly caressing her bottom lip. The simplicity and sensuality in that touch made her tremble and melt, deep inside where she had always been numb. Until her dreams began.

Forgive me. You aren't ready yet. Here--do you prefer seeing yourself this way?

This isn't real, Rahzel responded. *This is a dream. I'm not hallucinating, I'm dreaming.*

But she had never dreamed of anything or anyone in her simple, chill, efficient, bland Station room. So why did she dream it now?

Unless she wasn't dreaming?

But if she wasn't dreaming, then was she going mad?

Or was it--

You approve?

Rahzel tore herself out of her ever-inward spiraling thoughts. She gasped, but this time in pure pleasure.

She wore a crown of white roses on her head. More roses twined with her hair, which hung in long, gleaming waves over her shoulders. She wore a gown of gold and blue, such as she had read of in the fictions. The gown was low cut, revealing a hint of shadows between her breasts. It cupped her breasts--which did seem slightly larger than usual--then flowed down to nearly sweep the floor, with many gauzy layers of blue and gold and white petticoats peeking out. Her sleeves had long, trailing cuffs that nearly touched the floor. White satin slippers gleaming with green and blue jewels decorated her feet.

"I'm a princess," she whispered. Then she laughed.

Perhaps madness could be enjoyable.

A magical princess, a prisoner in a dreary tower. When you set me free, you will make me king and you will be my queen. Come to me, my princess, my priestess who holds the elixir of life. Come to me.

"Where are you?" Rahzel closed her eyes.

You know where I am.

"No, I don't."

She waited, but the Voice didn't answer.

"I am going mad," she whispered, and dared the security monitors to listen and report her to the Council.

Still, no response.

She turned off the holograph and wished it was a painting, so she could tear it down from the wall and rip it to shreds.

Chapter Seven

When Rahzel woke from a restless nap, she remembered no dreams, but she was drenched in sweat. Her heart raced. A musky perfume that came from her body filled the air. She trembled, afraid to look under the covers and see she was naked again. She had gone to bed clothed, but who could guarantee she hadn't awakened in the night, disrobed, and crawled back under the covers? How could anyone approaching madness be sure of their actions?

Finally, she couldn't stay in bed any longer. Eyes closed, Rahzel shoved back the covers. Cool air brushed her sweaty face. She struggled upright and staggered toward the cleanser stall, one hand out, moving blindly. She stubbed her bare foot against the corner of the cabinet in her kitchen alcove.

A curse rang through the room.

Rahzel gasped and her eyes flew open and she almost missed the corner of the countertop when she reached for it.

Had that come from her?

She forgot her shock when she looked down, expecting to see blood on the floor--and saw she wore her nightshirt, as usual. Sweat plastered it to her body.

What had she dreamed to have her body react that way, and why couldn't she remember? More importantly, why did she suspect she should be disappointed that she couldn't remember?

* * * *

The moment for plunging into the datablock came quietly. Slowly. Creeping up on her with more reluctance than Rahzel felt toward the experiment.

She wasn't surprised when all authorities granted permission with no questions, no reservations, no qualifiers logged into the system. Somehow, she didn't think anyone would disapprove or object. Someone wanted to know what was contained in the datablock, and how to open it and understand all its secrets--not the least of which, its cohesive qualities and self-contained power core. If it would cost them a Mind-Diver and put a hole in the tight network that kept the planet's infrastructure functioning, no one seemed worried.

Maybe Mind-Divers weren't as hard to find and train as she had been led to believe. Or maybe she was considered a problem that was expendable.

Not that she cared. She was going mad, after all.

And if she wasn't going mad ... then what?

Could La'rus be real?

Had someone gone beyond the highest dreams of disembodied Mind-Divers and found true intellectual existence, free of the physical plane?

Rahzel thought about that as she ate her final meal and went through her physical examination, for the records.

If La'rus was real, intelligence without physical form, then why had he been tormenting her with illusions of *touch* all this time? Why had he haunted the other Mind-Divers with hallucinations? Why did he seem so preoccupied with physical things, when he had ascended beyond such ... earthy concerns?

Be careful what you wish for.

Rahzel couldn't decide if that was her own thought, a memory, or the Voice--La'rus?--spoke deep inside her head.

She settled into her reclining chair and fitted the headset into place with a feeling of relief. Soon, she would have her answers.

Or, her struggles--and her life--would all be over.

The last cranial input connected. Rahzel closed her eyes and envisioned herself streaming into the computer, ten thousand points of light and data, self-aware and able to move where she chose instead of going where programmers commanded. She felt herself falling, deep inside her own mind. With one last glance toward the controls that would monitor her body's health and safety while she explored the etherworld, Rahzel closed her eyes--and flew.

The datablock appeared instantly before her, glowing softly in dozens of colors, and dozens of shades of those colors. It was indeed a world of overlapping spider's webs, as she had dreamed. Had she guessed it, had she somehow foreseen this, or was this only a projection of her imagination?

That didn't matter. Doubts and hesitation now would only harm her. Rahzel concentrated on what her mind told her existed. The myriad small parts of her spread apart, forming a cloud that enveloped the datablock.

She dove.

This was like flying through mist.

Where was the resistance, the layers of obstruction the other Mind-Divers found? The multiple juncture points flared and enfolded her myriad points of consciousness with ease. Warmth. A joyous expansion of power. She felt welcomed, as she had never felt welcomed anywhere.

"That's because you belong here," a familiar voice said, emerging from the maelstrom of colors, flashes of gold and silver like far-off novas. "Wherever I am, that's where you belong."

Where--she started to ask.

Her mind froze as all her illusory senses screamed and she fell. Plummeted. Tore through the mental atmosphere while it raked at her, trying to stop her downward plunge.

Rahzel screamed at the same moment all movement stopped. She was herself again, one cohesive unit.

The nothingness of the ether vanished, replaced with an emerald field that stretched out forever in all directions. A silver and blue stream rambled and bubbled through the middle of the field, creating ponds where swans serenely sailed.

"Never fear again. I caught you. I'll always catch you. I'll never let you fall," La'rus rumbled in her ear.

Rahzel felt his breath. No illusion or hallucination, this time. It brushed her long hair aside, tickling and warm and scented with something spicy and clean.

She felt strong arms under her. She leaned against a warm, bare chest slightly sprinkled with coarse curling hairs. Rahzel blinked and turned her head and gazed up into the face of the genie as it had been altered in the hologram. Deep, dark, muted blue eyes and thick, sharply arched eyebrows and a mane of curling, thick, gleaming black hair. One mass of curls fell across his forehead. A faint shadow of beard darkened his cheeks.

"Time to wake up, Princess. Sweetness," La'rus whispered. He bent his head and his lips parted.

The squeak of fright caught in her throat, muffled by La'rus' mouth pressed firmly, inescapably against hers. Rahzel held her breath. She held still, and tried to convince herself this was yet another hallucination.

But hallucinations never tasted and felt and smelled so intensely. They didn't have a pulse, throbbing against her mouth. They didn't have warmth and texture. They didn't hold her up. They weren't solid arms under her knees and around her shoulders, holding her against a solid, muscular chest. They didn't have mouths and tongues that invaded her mouth and paralyzed her with shock and curiosity. Who knew a human mouth could taste of pungent spice and fresh air?

Rahzel screamed and pushed at his shoulders and kicked. Knocking herself free, she fell to the ground and scrambled away, crawling on all fours because she couldn't find make her shaking legs push her upright. The grass tickled her bare legs and hands. It was damp with dew. The most delicious, sweet, clean scent filled her head. She huddled in on herself, trying to hide behind her dew-spattered arms.

She was naked.

La'rus laughed. He dropped to his knees and reached for her. The laughter died when she screamed again.

"Sweetness--"

"Stop it!" She wrapped her arms tighter around herself, until she thought she would tear her arms from their sockets. "My name is Rahzel."

There were dozens of things she should have said to him, but they caught in her throat. Questions and furious demands battled for precedence, and it took all her strength not to scream again.

Screaming wouldn't do her any good. She had gone mad. For all she knew, she was screaming already, helpless in her chair in her Station. How long would it take for someone to hear and to do something about it?

"You're not mad, sweetness." The man flushed and nodded. "Rahzel. This is just as real as the world where you were a prisoner and I was little more than a ghost. A hallucination," he added, with a faint flicker of a smile. "Dying to touch you, to feast on you."

She shuddered, imagining La'rus tearing her to pieces, drinking her blood and devouring her shredded flesh.

"A feast of pleasure, princess. A feast of unity and joy and recompense for all we have suffered." His gaze slid over her. She sensed he could see every speck of her naked flesh, despite her efforts to hide behind her arms. "Just as I feast on your beauty."

"You have no right," she snarled.

"Whatever you wish, will be. Will you allow me to take care of you?"

Before she was even aware a tiny part of her wanted to agree, Rahzel felt a caress of cool smoothness across her skin. She managed not to shriek this time as she leaped to her feet. She wore the gown her image had worn in the holograph.

"Feel better?" La'rus gestured for her to sit.

When she hesitated, he waved his hand and chairs as delicate as flower stems appeared. He got to his feet with a grace she had only seen in wild beasts stalking their prey. But instead of leaping on her as she feared, he sat down in one of the chairs and gestured for her to take the other one.

"Are we inside the datablock, or are we on another world?"

"Inside, outside, it doesn't really matter. This is the only world I have known for what you consider centuries." He closed his eyes and tipped his head back, so the rays of sunshine seemed to coat his face with honey-thick golden brilliance. "As pleasant as it is, I think I would kill to leave it." He opened his eyes and his smile went crooked, mischievous, yet with a touch of menace that made her legs weak. Rahzel sat down quickly before her legs folded. "It's about time you got here, my sweetness."

"I'm not your property." She bit her lip, terrified more bitter words would escape her. This wasn't the meeting she had envisioned in all her sweet dreams.

"No, you're not. You're my partner. My equal. My completion. The soul that gives me life again."

"How is this happening? Are we really in a world, or is this just in our minds?"

"Reality has always been constrained by the power of our minds. You can see and hear, taste and smell and feel in this place. Anything you have ever dreamed of doing, you can do here. Explore and be whatever you want, unlimited possibilities. But can you imagine, two things aren't possible here?"

He waited. Rahzel held her breath, unable to think, wanting an answer, strangely desperate to give it to him.

"The impossible," he finally said. "Nothing is beyond me here, except finding something I can't do. And companionship. A partner through all life has to offer. Until I found you, when our minds touched."

"You touched the minds of other Mind-Divers before me."

"Flat. Dead, though they think they're still alive. Not beautiful and strong and pure. So very pure," he added, dropping to a whisper.

"Did you deliberately come down into the etherworld, or were you caught?"

"Why do you want to ask all your scientific, duty-bound questions, when we could be enjoying ourselves? It's time to celebrate."

"I don't know you!" Rahzel flinched, surprised and ashamed at the harsh tone of her voice. When had she ever addressed anyone that way, even as a child?

Yet a tiny corner of her mind and soul was perversely pleased at her lack of good manners and self-control.

"Not even now, after all the lovely nights we spent together, exploring your every dream? Sweetness, don't you remember all the times you woke, aching for something that evaded you? Think for a moment. Feel. Remember the hunger deep within you, in your soul as well as your body. You weren't made for the sterile, cold, lonely cage they put you into. It's killing you. I am here to give you life, just as you will give me life once again!"

La'rus leaped from his chair, the force of his movements shoving it aside. It vanished as it tumbled to the ground. He caught hold of her hand and pulled her to her feet and into his arms. Rahzel clung to him, completely off balance.

The heat of his body tore through her clothes. She could feel every line and curve of hard muscle. The need to melt into him, to merge physically with him took her breath away. Then La'rus cupped her chin in his hard-callused, hot hand and tipped her head up to meet him. His mouth captured hers again. His lips stroked across hers, insistent pressure that eased her mouth open. His teeth nipped at her bottom lip, then his tongue invaded, hot and salty and insistent, stroking across her tongue and sending a tidal wave of weakness through her.

Was this how she would die? With her soul sucked out of her body?

"Little fool," La'rus whispered. "Didn't anyone ever teach you you're supposed to kiss back when a man starts to make love to you?"

"Kiss?" Rahzel blinked rapidly, trying to regain her scattered wits. "So that's what kissing is?"

La'rus burst out laughing. He sank down to the ground, drawing her with him so she ended up cradled on his lap. He rocked, laughing until tears ran down his cheeks. Rahzel found she rather liked being held, even though it had an element of helplessness to it. As La'rus' laughter began to slow and he caught his breath, he gently cupped her face between his big hands and kissed her cheeks, her forehead, the tip of her nose, before coming to rest against her mouth again.

His lips trembled against hers. Rahzel sensed the restrained hunger that hummed deep inside him, that somehow made his tenderness a threat she welcomed.

Slowly, as she learned to mimic him and then to respond on her own, the intensity and depth of the kisses grew. Rahzel could hardly think for the rapid pulse pounding deafeningly loud in her ears. She clutched at him, to the point of digging her neatly trimmed nails into his flesh. The need to get closer, to somehow sink through his skin, took her breath away. When she realized that she had begun to invade his mouth, she wanted to laugh. She couldn't recognize herself.

That momentary thought shattered with a moan as La'rus' hand closed gently around her bare breast.

Chapter Eight

The first five pearl buttons were undone, allowing La'rus just enough room to expose her breasts. How and when he unfastened those buttons, Rahzel neither remembered nor cared. The pulsing need to sink into him and merge with his flesh and bones, the fiber of him, to flow through his veins, drove away every other consideration.

Besides, she liked the humming that filled her skin when his hand gently kneaded her flesh. Then his mouth closed over her nipple, warm and damp. She remembered that morning she had leaped from her bed in shock, and she laughed.

"You like that, eh?" La'rus raised his head. His smile was fierce. His eyes held flames.

Rahzel didn't have the breath to respond. She nodded and lifted her hand to curve around his neck and draw his head back down.

His teeth closed around the tender flesh. She gasped, arching her back, and a pleasant ache settled in between her legs. La'rus rubbed his fingertips against the exact spot, through the multiple gauzy layers of her dress, as if he knew what he had done to her. He turned his head and suckled on her other breast. Another nip. The ache inside rose higher.

"Please ... stop. I think I'm going to die," she whispered, her voice staggering up and down the scale.

"No." La'rus raised his head and their gazes locked. "You won't die. We'll finally start living, you and I."

"What are you doing to me?" Her thoughts began to settle, no longer distracted by the totally new sensations jolting through her body.

Rahzel tried to sit up, and La'rus helped her. He drew her up close against his chest, so her head rested on his shoulder. She liked that position, along with his arms wrapped securely around her. It had been her entire lifetime since someone had held her.

"Nothing that shouldn't have been done years ago." He pressed a kiss against her forehead. She sighed, pleased by the humming that shot through her body at the simple brushing of his lips across her skin.

Lips. Tongues. Physical contact. Dampness. Bites. Licking. Saliva. Body fluids.

"We're going to die!" Rahzel twisted in his arms, surprising La'rus enough she wriggled halfway to freedom before he tightened his grip.

"We're not going to die." He grunted when her elbow caught him in the gut.

"Yes we are! Do you realize what a health risk sexual contact creates? That's what you were planning on doing, weren't you? Rutting like two stupid animals in heat."

"For humans, it's called making love." His tender, amused expression faded. The lines of his jaw grew harder.

"Sex. Insertion of male genitals into female genitals for the purpose of procreation. It's unsanitary. Why do you think laboratory fertilization was created? So the human race wouldn't be wiped out by disease!" With another jab of her elbow, Rahzel shoved herself free of his arms. She rolled off his lap, onto the sweet, dewy grass.

La'rus snarled and lunged, straddling her in an instant, his knees on either side of her thighs, his hands on either side of her shoulders.

Rahzel closed her eyes, knowing she couldn't stop him from destroying her life.

"I'm not going to rape you," La'rus whispered. "Don't you realize yet, nothing can happen here that you don't allow?"

"Then why are you holding me prisoner?" She opened one eye.

"You're not a prisoner. I'm trying to get you to listen to me. Sweetness, this is a place we've created together. All your dreams, the things you read about and wished to see, fueled by my loneliness, my years of waiting and preparing and saving my strength. Why would I kill you, when you are the very center of my life? Without you, I am nothing."

"Sex will kill us."

"It won't be our *real* bodies." He laughed when she opened her other eye and her mouth dropped open.

"But it feels so real...."

"Our souls, our spirits, our minds--however you want to label the plane where we meet. We create this place, it is our inner reality. Whatever we do here is real in all dimensions and aspects but one. We feel it. Every sense is involved. But right now, your real body is still safely tucked into your chair. Your body shows no reaction at all to what's going on here." His grin widened. "Not yet, anyway."

Rahzel blushed, not even sure what she blushed for. Then another thought rose through the confusion that was half physical overload from things she had never felt before.

"All those anomalies and malfunctions in the planetary infrastructure--you caused them. You've been learning how to get into everything, run everything, manipulate what everyone sees and hears and what they can and can't do. You control all the computers, all the servos, the maintenance and security--"

"Your food dispensers and monitors and everything that serves you. Yes. How else was I to take care of you when you insisted on wearing yourself to a frazzle? To a shadow of your lovely self," he finished on a whisper.

She closed her eyes when he began to lower his head. Maybe it was stupid, foolhardy, even deathly reckless, but she wanted him to kiss her. She wanted to feel his hands on her bare skin again. If this wasn't real--no matter how real it felt--she could know what all the heroines in the fictions felt and wanted and were willing to risk their lives for. This was better than any virtual reality suit, and no stink of sweat, no sticky suit to peel off. No burning of disinfectant in her skin afterward to penalize her for a little bit of illusory contact.

Real, but not real.

Rahzel sighed and opened her mouth a little wider and nipped at La'rus' bottom lip. Just experimenting. His yelp of surprise, then his pleased laughter sent a sense of power through her.

"Dreams, anything we want, can come true here?" she asked, her voice ragged, when his insistent mouth moved down to her breasts again.

"Anything you...." La'rus raised his head and stared into her eyes. His smile widened, then he started chuckling. "Oh, my darling, you have been a naughty girl, haven't you? Reading all those delicious, forbidden books. If the authorities knew they were stored in the archives, where innocent little girls could find them, they would have wiped them out long ago."

"But can I have it? Here?" she insisted.

"Close your eyes and paint the picture in your mind." He gently brushed his fingertips down her eyelids, making her eyes close.

Rahzel recalled all her favorite scenes from the fictions she had read and loved all the lonely years in her Station.

She felt the grass ripple and solidify under her. The sweetly scented breeze changed, taking on a perfume that she had never smelled before. Rich, warm, filled with a thousand scents. The ground grew soft. She felt herself rise up in the air, then sink down, into what she imagined clouds were like--back when the planet still had clouds.

"Wake, my sweet dreamer," La'rus whispered. He rolled off her and took her hand and helped her sit up.

Rahzel could only stare for the first few moments. The blaze of color and richness of texture and the variety stunned her. She wondered if the breathless, dizzy, heart-racing feeling was what people felt when they were drunk. She liked it. Was there wine, perhaps, among all the things she had wished for?

"Wine and pheasant, ices and the richest sweets you could ever dream of tasting, fresh fruits and steaming breads and pastries in a thousand varieties." La'rus chuckled and gestured out beyond them. "We could stay here for ten years and never sample everything you created. You ought to be ashamed, demanding everything at once." He waved one finger reprovingly in her face, but his grin belied his scolding tone.

She didn't care, lost in the wonders that surrounded her on all sides. It was a feast such as she had seen in paintings and read about in books.

Golden dishes and crystal goblets. Dozens of crystal decanters of liquids in colors ranging from amber to blood red to a red so dark it was black.

Frosted cakes and braided breads with glistening glazes and colored sugars. Roasted turkeys and whole piglets, bowls of fruits in colors and shapes she had only imagined because she couldn't find pictures.

All of it, spread across tables covered in snowy white cloths, interspersed with sheer scarlet and green and azure cloths. More than a dozen tables, arranged in a semi-circle around the bed where she and La'rus sat and stared.

The bed sat high off the lushly carpeted floor, wide enough for ten people to sleep without touching. Rahzel bounced experimentally and sank into the thick blankets, layers of them in a rainbow of colors, softer than the silken dress she wore. A blue canopy painted with white, fluffy clouds arched over her head, hung with sheer draperies in gold and crimson and purple, tied with golden cords. At least twenty tasseled pillows embroidered with fantastical pictures piled up against the gilded headboard.

"Satisfied, sweetness?" La'rus asked. He bounced a little on the bed and a delighted chuckle exploded from him. "Quite the hedonist, aren't you?"

"A lifetime of dreams...."

"Make my dreams come true?"

When she nodded, he moved slowly, taking her into his arms. He didn't kiss her, but slowly unfastened her dress, one pearl button at a time, spreading it open, then sliding it down and off her. Then he removed the sheer, lacy underdress, the layers of flouncy, wispy petticoats. Rahzel could hardly breathe, watching him, stunned by the intensity of his expression, the delicacy and care in his large, warm hands. Finally, when she wore nothing but a filmy pair of pale blue briefs that were little more than decoration, La'rus gently pressed on her shoulders and guided her down into the thick blankets. Rahzel sank into them. She bit her lip against a giggle as she imagined sinking down completely out of sight. Out of reach.

The fictions had been skimpy on the details when it came to this portion of what was variously labeled "pleasuring" and "lovemaking" or other ambiguous terms. La'rus obviously knew what to do. She would have to trust him to lead the way.

Lead the way he did. He knelt over her, straddling her at her knees. That crooked, knowing smile tightened and his eyes filled with fire. With one finger, he toyed with the thread-thin top of her briefs, sliding under it, stroking her belly and following the line across. Rahzel shivered, feeling that simple, gentle stroke down to that aching place deep inside that suddenly flared to pulsing life.

His finger slid a little further under the band. Two fingers now, stroking, pressing. Rahzel dug her fingertips into the thick blankets, forcing herself to hold still. La'rus' gaze held her prisoner.

Four fingers now. Dipping in to catch in the curls between her thighs. Rahzel gasped and closed her eyes. He laughed and leaned over her to gently kiss her lips, her chin, marking a warm line down her throat. His thumb circled her navel, then his hand dipped down, combing through the strangely damp curls between her legs. Then one finger. Inside.

Chapter Nine

"La'rus!" Her eyes flew open and she stared at him, shocked cold.

He met her gaze, all laughter gone, his eyes blacker than the stars with intensity. And he slid his finger deeper inside her. Rahzel whimpered, but she couldn't lift her hands to push him away.

She couldn't close her eyes. Couldn't turn her head away.

"It's all right, sweetness," he whispered. A growl hovered at the back of his voice.

La'rus sat back, resting on his heels. He tugged down the briefs, below her knees. The trail of his fingertips left streaks of burning down her skin. Then he tugged, hard, and the thread-thin band snapped with a tiny shrieking sound.

"Don't," was all she could squeeze out through vocal chords so tight they were ready to shred her throat.

She suspected what he was about to do.

Then she knew, when he got up, kneeling, and yanked down his trousers.

This was worse than when he teased her with the holograph of the genie. Rahzel choked on her scream at the sheer size of him. Even as she stared, it grew darker, engorged with blood and moved, lifting like a beast that scented its prey.

He was going to shove it up inside her. He was going to rip her open. She would bleed to death.

Despite the surprising pleasure of bare skin touching bare skin, this was indecent. Barbaric. Bestial.

No wonder males had been wiped out of existence decades ago. They weren't needed anymore, now that genetics could be controlled and programmed for traits. Science and civilization had destroyed the necessity for women to submit to pain and abuse and indecency in order for the species to continue.

"Men still exist," he whispered, and stretched out alongside her. La'rus wrapped his arm around her and turned her onto her side to face him. He twined their legs together and tucked her head under his chin.

Rahzel felt all her paralyzed muscles relax. Pain from tension she hadn't been conscious of leaked out of her body. She whimpered and closed her eyes and went limp against him. This part, the warmth and touching, she liked. Why couldn't it stay this way?

"There are still males outside, beyond the Domes," La'rus continued. "Real men and real women, who know that there has to be a balance, pleasure paid for with some pain, joy paid for with grief. Satisfaction earned with hard work. Nothing truly worth having is free. The Domes have taken away the risk, but they've taken away the color and light and spice of life."

He drew her up closer against him. She flinched at the heat of his skin and the hard length pressing against her hip.

"Men have quite a few uses beyond killing monsters and acting as beasts of burden. As I will show you. Don't you trust me, sweetness?"

"Considering that you haven't been honest with me--"

"And what would have been your reaction, if I told you that I wasn't a hallucination, but a lost soul, seeking salvation in your arms?" One eyebrow quirked up. Laughter gleamed again in those deep, muted blue eyes.

"All right." She felt her own mouth starting to curve into a smile. His touch, the lightest stroking down her spine, had a soporific effect. All her limbs felt heavy. Yet that empty, pulsing ache deep inside grew stronger. "I would have considered it another phase of my madness."

"And if you had believed me? If you knew that an alien mind grew strong enough to control the etherworld and had come to reside in your mind through the Link?" He stopped her response with a kiss, just as she opened her mouth.

She moaned, the sound turning into a sigh, and responded eagerly to his kisses, battling with her tongue, with her teeth, suckling gently as she had learned from him.

It felt so very right when he gently lowered her onto her back and he stretched out on top of her. She liked the weight of him, making them both sink deep into the blankets.

"If you knew?" he repeated. "What would you have done?"

"I don't--La'rus, please." She closed her eyes, lost in the sweet certainty they would melt into each other.

She knew between one heartbeat and the next that this was how she wanted to live and die. Merged totally with him. Lost forever, never separated. He frightened her. She could never understand him. But she had never felt so alive. Nothing had prepared her for the pleasure, the floating, buzzing, aching sweetness that could come from simply touching.

"Tell me," La'rus insisted. He moved slightly off of her kneeling between her legs, braced on his arms on either side of her head, yet still close enough the weight of him warmed her and stole her ability to think.

"I...." She sighed and forced her eyes open. "If I didn't turn myself in for complete madness, I would have ... called for someone to drive you away."

"We'll never be separated, Rahzel, my sweetness, my princess. Promise me that. Never parted, ever again. One mind, one soul, one heart, one flesh." He groaned and took her mouth in a bruising kiss. "Most especially, one flesh. Promise me."

"Promise," she whispered on a breath.

"Say you want me. With you forever. Joined."

"Want you ... forever ... La'rus, please, kiss me!"

He never took his mouth off hers while his hands roamed over her until she thought he knew every particle of her skin. Despite what she had seen of him totally naked, she let him spread her legs, shuddered in shocked eagerness when he slid a finger inside her again. Then two fingers, stroking and teasing and leaving just as she thought she approached ... something that made her want to weep, breathless with hungry frustration.

La'rus guided her hands over him, laughing, making her mouth vibrate, tickling when she shied away from touching that hot, hard part of him that terrified her.

Curiosity soon pushed aside her fear. She liked how La'rus twitched and moaned when she stroked him with her fingertips. The smoothness and heat and the pulse under the soft skin fascinated her, yet she still trembled and went cold when she thought of something so thick and long shoved up inside her.

Women simply weren't made to endure such treatment.

Yet why did the heroines of all those fictions she loved want the heroes to remove their clothes and tumble them down into beds as grand as the one where she lay under La'rus? Could it all be a lie? Maybe all those stories had been written by men, to trick women into allowing this?

Perhaps the judgmental members of the Mind-Diver Council were right, and her curiosity and imagination had led her into trouble and danger. But was it so wrong to be here with La'rus? It wasn't real, after all. They couldn't catch some horrid, mutated disease from each other and die in pain, with their flesh liquefying off their bones. Would they?

"Such thoughts, princess." La'rus nipped at her earlobe, then laughed when she squeaked and arched her back against him. "Not conducive to pleasure at all."

"Why do you know everything I'm thinking, but I don't know anything inside you?"

"I want you inside me, my love. I want us so tightly joined not even death can separate us. Do you trust me to make it so?" He drew back just enough that she could see the seriousness in his face.

It only took a moment of thought, and very little thought at that, for Rahzel to make her decision. She nodded.

Sooner or later, she reasoned, she would have to return to her Station, to her body. If she couldn't stay here with La'rus, where touching was a gift instead of a danger, then the next best thing was to be fully joined with him, mind to mind and soul to soul.

"Say it. Tell me to make it so. You inside me, and me inside you."

He lowered more of his weight onto her, and the pressure sent delicious ripples through her, stealing her breath. She closed her eyes, aching for the feel of his hands smoothing across her skin, struggling to balance her fear of the unknown and this strange needing that tore her apart and remade her--all while she felt totally helpless. And glad of it.

"You inside me--me inside you," she said, feeling as shattered as her voice sounded. "Please, La'rus."

"My love," he coaxed.

"My--love."

She could do nothing but kiss him, cling to him and let him do what he pleased. From the rebellious shadows at the back of her mind came the certainty that this was worth dying for. Rahzel closed her eyes and held on to La'rus and smiled, even as his mouth and hands wrung whimpers from her.

Then, he grew still. His weight lifted off her. His hands gripping her hips tightened, threatening bruises. His breath thundered raggedly in the vast room.

"My queen. My love."

Her eyelids felt as heavy as if her entire Station held them closed. Rahzel looked between her lashes as La'rus leaned over her. She smiled, feeling his hands move under her thighs--just like he had touched her when she thought he was only a hallucination. A gasping laugh escaped her as he lifted her hips.

He was covered with stars.

Her heavy, sweet lethargy began to dissipate in curiosity. Rahzel opened her eyes wider.

Yes, La'rus was covered with stars. They streamed off the ends of his hair, swirled around his eyes, clung to the crisp hairs on his arms, glimmered all over his skin in the damp from his loving exertions. She smiled, following the play of streaking lights. La'rus' mouth twisted in a grimace of effort. He bared his teeth in a snarl. He spread her legs, lifting her up to meet him.

Fire streaked and swirled all around his hard, erect male weapon. Fire streaked up over his flesh to meet the stars. Rahzel inhaled to scream. She tried to brace her arms under herself, to pull free of his grip. La'rus' fingers dug into her thighs, holding her still.

He plunged in, nearly falling down on top of her.

Rahzel froze, her scream caught in her chest.

The scream died.

No pain.

The stars completely enfolded La'rus. They swirled across his skin, falling down on her, blinding her. She inhaled stars. They burst into life inside her, filling her blood.

Now, love! he roared exultantly inside her mind and heart.

She felt La'rus wrap himself around her and they climbed, soaring to join the stars. He moved inside her, moved up inside her, filling her until she was nothing but fragile skin and the soaring, sparkling sense of flight.

The heavens exploded around them. She began to fall.

Rahzel screamed, terrified of hitting the ground. Furious that the flight had ended so soon. Breathless with a sorrow she couldn't understand.

"Sshh, love, it's all right," La'rus whispered, and his arms were around her again. Holding her tight against him.

She felt his chest heaving with ragged breaths, felt his heart thundering through the thin wall of flesh and bones, pounding into her own suddenly too-frail body, dominating her pulse. Their bodies were glued together with sweat that smelled of musk and exhaustion and a sweetness she could only ascribe to overwhelming pleasure.

Chapter Ten

La'rus wouldn't let her dress when he brought a wide platter of food back to the bed. Rahzel laughed when he said he wanted to feast on her while they feasted on the luxuries she had provided.

For the first time in her life, she tasted wine and pomegranates, roasted turkey and all the old-fashioned sweets her mother had described to her.

He told her how he played pranks on the other Mind-Divers, testing them, trying to find the spirit and mind that had called him down from the stars. She laughed at one of his stories and spilled wine on herself. La'rus stopped her when she reached for a cloth to wipe the drops off her breast. He took the emerald-encrusted goblet from her hand and slid his arm around her waist to draw her close.

Rahzel thought she would melt, all her bones dissolving, something deep in her belly churning to the point of explosion, when he slowly licked the wine from her breast. She fumbled for the platter of food to push it out of the way, then wrapped her arms around him.

La'rus surprised her by stretching out on his back and drawing her down on top of him. Rahzel laughed as she took him deep inside her and the stars swirled around them again. She cried out in disappointment, not terror, when the falling began. La'rus held her close as the blackness of exhaustion swallowed them, taking them as deep into the bowels of the planet as the heights they had risen among the stars.

This time, it seemed she lay for hours in a mind-empty stupor, arms and legs limply wrapped around La'rus. It was enough to feel his heart raggedly thudding against her hollow bones.

* * * *

Their feast passed in quiet. Rahzel snuggled into La'rus' lap, holding the plate they shared. He stole kisses in between bites, brushed against her cheek, into her hair, down the length of her neck. No sparks and bursts of fire came from those touches, and Rahzel wondered if perhaps the explosive passion had already begun to fade.

"Blame yourself," La'rus rumbled. He curved one arm around her waist while lifting the goblet to his lips with his free hand. "You're a demanding lover, draining everything out of me."

Rahzel laughed. It was true. With her bottom pressed snugly into his lap, she could tell his arousal--wasn't. She tried to muffle her laughter. Hadn't her voracious reading taught her that men were inordinately proud of their stamina, and insulted if it was ever called into question?

"Soon enough, princess. I'll prove just how much stamina I have. After centuries without a body, without any company, a man gets rusty."

"Centuries of waiting should give you plenty of ... endurance," she murmured, catching an image from his mind that made her feel hot and restless.

"Wicked woman." He drained the goblet with one last swallow and tossed it toward the end of the bed. It hit with a muffled thump and rolled twice across the undulating valleys of the blankets. "Eaten enough?"

"More than is probably good for me."

"Here, nothing is bad for you. Remember that, love." He picked her up, his hands easily gripping her waist, and slid her off his lap. "Let's explore."

"But this is your world. It's all from your mind, so you know it all."

"This is your world. Your planet. The way it was and the way it shall someday be." La'rus slid off the bed, turned around once and was instantly clothed.

He wore thick-soled, dark brown boots that reached past his calves, with sheaths for knives, a gun, and other equipment only hinted at by metallic silver gleams. His pants were mottled green and brown and black. His shirt, dull green, with a long, multi-pocketed vest in the same mottled hues.

"Soldier gear," he explained. "Join me?"

It took a moment of thought to decide what she wanted to wear, how she wanted to look. In two heartbeats, she wore a slimmer version of his costume, complete with a billed cap and her hair hanging in a long braid past her waist. La'rus laughed and gave the braid a tug, then bowed grandly and held out his hand. When she gave her hand into his, their elegant bedroom and feast vanished, replaced by a vista of gold and silver-gray stone, mottled with mud and moss in ten different shades of green.

At the edge of the plateau, the sun peered over the edge as it began to rise. Rahzel caught her breath, wondering at the scarlet, purple, gold and rose glory of colors spilling and running across the landscape. She hadn't seen such colors from the sun except in pictures.

They walked for what felt like days, going from desert to mountain to forest, river plain to jungle to arctic vista. Birds and insects hovered around them, pausing to allow easy viewing, even coming to rest on their hands for examination. Furred and fanged creatures watched them from the shadows, sometimes emerging to run a head or flank against their legs, to allow a caress along their rough-textured backs, and then disappearing into the darkness again.

On a grassy plain, Rahzel stood for hours, lost in awe as horses in every possible shade and color raced and circled and pranced. Their manes flew, tossed by the wind and foam flecked their sides. Her favorite toy, as a child, had been a rocking horse and she had spent many happy hours riding and dreaming. Her wildest dreams couldn't approach the untamed, rough-hewn beauty of the creatures surrounding her.

La'rus didn't offer to bring one close for her to ride or touch, and Rahzel didn't ask. She sensed it would have been a violation of the horses' nature to be forced to submit--even if they were nothing but illusions.

"You say this used to be my world?" she whispered, when they left the horses behind and started climbing a winding, grassy path to a peak where the sun seemed to have caught and come to rest.

"It was and will be. My world, now," La'rus added after a pause of a few heartbeats. "Your world, if you have the courage to claim it. They'll hate you when you tear apart their lies. Can you do it, princess? For me? Will you give up everything to be with me?" He stopped her, both hands tight around her waist.

Abruptly, they were at the top of the peak, with the entire wild, brutal, achingly beautiful world spread out below them. The fires began to rise in his eyes again.

"I gave up everything I was, everything I owned, to endure through time and find this place. To find you. Someday I'll show you all the minds I touched and discarded. Weak and fearful and flawed. Only you had what I needed and wanted. Only you needed me, or even hoped for someone like me. Only you can give me your world, to remake. Will you?"

"As long as we're here--" She shook her head, sensing he spoke of things far beyond this idyllic place of the mind. "I'll have to go back, eventually. Back to my Station and my body. Someone is probably wondering what happened to me by now. I can't take you back with me."

"Oh, yes you can," he whispered. His smile flattened, grew hungry. Fierce. "You have the power I need. You gave me your heart and your soul. Now, you'll give me your world."

"La'rus."

He stopped her questions with kisses that quickly passed from hungry to scorching. He ripped her rugged outdoors clothes to shreds, bruising her arms and legs as he struggled to free her. Rahzel didn't care. She whimpered in pure frustration as she struggled with his clothes. Fury cleared her thoughts long enough to wish them both naked, and they were. Their luxurious bed didn't appear again as La'rus bore her down to the moss-covered slabs of rock. She tasted blood from the ferocity of their kisses. Her mouth or his, she didn't care.

When he spread her legs, his arousal looked as thick as her arm, blue-white with power ready to burst from him. Rahzel closed her eyes and raised her hips to meet him, eager to the point of pain.

Fire moved through her, burning like acid in torn flesh. A tiny part of her mind tried to cry out in protest, in terror. Tried to hold fast against the tidal wave that swept away all thought. She screamed as release drowned her, pure pleasure that threatened to separate soul from body and tear her apart, atom from atom. The soaring didn't stop, but continued, faster, burning, pressing her into La'rus and La'rus into her, until they were a tiny package too small for even thought or feeling.

When it came, the blackness was both relief and torment.

* * * *

Images and sensations came to her, in bits and pieces like badly transmitted bytes of data.

La'rus spoke. She recognized his voice, but made no sense of the words.

His hands, gentle on her face.

Water, sweet and cold, filling her mouth. Then warmth wrapped around her, helping her body remake itself. She shivered, unaware until then that she had been cold.

A warm and grainy smell filled her nose. Then sweetness. Taste exploded through her mouth. Warmth trickled down her throat.

Blackness intervened then, but not as deep and solid as it had been before. Rahzel surrendered to it, unutterably weary.

Warmth. Lemon-scented water on her face. Hands massaging her scalp.

"These have to go, sweetness," La'rus said. "You don't need them anymore."

Pain. Tiny pricks all through her scalp. Feeling like clumps of hair were yanked out with chiming, sharp sounds, like tight wires breaking.

Iron and salt filled the air. Blood? She couldn't be sure.

"It's all right. Sleep, love. I'll watch out for you."

More blackness, but softer. Less enduring. Not as deep, not sucking her down into stickiness that sucked at her thoughts.

Gray light filled her eyes, soft but heavy. Rahzel closed her eyes and turned her head. Her arm felt trapped, caught under something. She struggled to sit up and yank it free without opening her eyes. That plan didn't work.

Giving in, she opened her eyes.

La'rus lay next to her, sharing her bed that had always felt more than wide enough for her. Until now. Her arm was trapped between them. Beyond him lay the decorative screen painted with a rocky waterfall, which separated her bed and clothes rack from the rest of the Station.

Why in the world would I bring us here? Rahzel almost laughed, but she didn't want to wake La'rus.

Obviously he had been more exhausted by the cataclysm of their lovemaking than she had been.

The last place she would bring La'rus was here. Her entire world was a place of imprisoning precautions meant to preserve life against the vicious, constant mutation of disease. Yet, Rahzel had to wonder now if this was truly living. She was among the privileged and elite of the planet, yet she lived isolated in all but mind from everyone who lived. Her door had been sealed when she walked through it. No human being would walk through that door until she decided to disembody or she died.

Yes, this was the last place she wanted La'rus to be. The sterility of her Station cried out in protest against the luscious, vibrant, sometimes brutal, solid reality of what she and La'rus had made in their mind-world. Rahzel could well appreciate the irony that they had found something more real than physical reality. She didn't belong in her Station any more than La'rus did. Perhaps she would try to leave it, when she returned to her body? If she did, would she be able to find La'rus again? How could she go into the etherworld and access the datablock again if she left her Station? The moment she rebelled against the Mind-Diver Council, she would lose all access. She could be imprisoned in a Bunker with no technical amenities at all. How could La'rus find her there, even with his control over the planetary infrastructure, if she was blocked from all access to the etherworld?

She hated her life, she realized in that moment of conflict. The more her mind woke up and she thought about it, the more appropriate it seemed to be here in this illusory replica of her Station. She would make love to La'rus here, on her lonely bed, in defiance of all the restrictions the Mind-Diver Council had ever laid on her. True, it wouldn't be for real, it wouldn't be on her actual bed, in her sacrosanct Station, but it would be enough. A start. A gesture that would become reality eventually.

Perhaps when she returned to her body, separated from La'rus in all but thoughts, she would find some way to put her defiance into concrete action.

She slept again and woke cradled in La'rus' arms. He carried her across the room to her cleanser stall. He chuckled when she startled and tried to sit up.

"We're still here." Despite her earlier thoughts, Rahzel was disappointed. She much preferred their decadent, luxurious bedroom. At the very least, for the food. It felt wrong to be here, sliding to the floor and stepping into the cold ceramic stall. It felt wrong to be naked in her Station.

Yet, how could she be in any other state, while La'rus looked at her with such hunger burning in his eyes and his mouth taking on that crooked, mischievous grin?

"Finally awake, are you?" He gave her a tiny nudge backwards.

Icy water streamed out from the ceiling and sides of the stall. Rahzel yelped. He reached for the suds wand and grasped her shoulder, turning her. The water warmed, scented like the dark green, conical trees that had filled some of the forests they explored. He scrubbed her back with the brush tip of the wand, down her legs, teasing by directing the water up between her legs. When she turned to escape, he slid the wand into her hand and turned his back on her.

Half the pleasure of the experience, she decided, was the utterly strange newness. Rahzel couldn't remember helping to bathe any of the babies in the Bunker, when she was a child. Touching another body, scrubbing rolling, tanned muscles, watching the suds streak down his flesh made her feel tender and protective toward La'rus. Another new feeling. This proximity, without the passion, gave her a chance to study and appreciate how he was put together.

"That's enough," La'rus rumbled, when she let the wand slide from her hands and leaned against his back.

Rahzel laughed and pressed her face into his sleek spine and kissed the warm water from his skin. She wrapped her arms around his waist, barely able to span all the solid muscle. She felt tiny compared to him.

Strange. It was almost as if their proportions had changed. Was this another trick of his? He had told her this world was hers to command, yet she couldn't seem to tell the scenery to change or even rework their relative sizes.

"Temptress." La'rus captured her hands and guided them down his belly, to the thick hair around his groin. She caught her breath at the first feel of the slick, hot hardness that trembled under her fingertips. His pulse leaped, responding to the first blind caress.

"Hurry," she whispered, and pulled her hands free.

La'rus turned, pinning her against the wall, lifting her so her feet dangled. Then he wrapped her legs around his waist, all the while devouring her mouth with kisses.

La'rus didn't pause in the hot jets of air when he stepped out of the cleanser stall, carrying her. He skidded twice, crossing the tile floor on wet feet, leaving a trail of water all the way to her bed. They tumbled down, tangled in each other.

Every sense felt doubly sharp. His hands were rough, hot, almost clumsy with eagerness as he caressed her. Her breasts tingled and ached as he kneaded, then suckled, then bit. Rahzel didn't care, as that sweet, aching hunger churned deep inside. She laughed, turning to a groan when he teased, sliding first one finger, then two inside her, while his thumb pressed hard and circled the hyper-sensitive spot just above.

La'rus sat up, drawing her up onto his lap, her legs wrapping around his ribs. He lifted her up and held her there, laughing, while she wriggled and resorted to pounding ineffectually on his shoulders. The tip of his manhood rubbed against her bottom, teasing her.

"Brute! Beast!" Yet she couldn't help laughing when he growled and bared his teeth, laughter sparkling all the while in his eyes.

He slowly lowered her, sliding down his chest, his head tilted up so their mouths met. Rahzel wound her arms around his neck and welcomed his hard kiss, the demanding thrusts of his tongue, sweeping through her mouth to possess all of it. She sighed, anticipating the rush to the stars as he lowered her onto him and all that glorious hard, hot, swollen male flesh slid up and inside her.

It hurt.

Her tender flesh tore. Rahzel tried to gather her legs under herself, to slow down. Her heart raced in terror she didn't understand. All her movements forced her down on him harder, faster.

She screamed, smelling blood in the air and acid pain-tinged sweat and tears before she even realized she had begun to cry.

La'rus smothered the sound, his mouth pressed hard against hers. His large, hard hands dug into the soft flesh of her hips, holding her tight against him. She bit him, bearing down hard on his lip until he roared and twisted his head away and leaned back.

"Make it stop!" Rahzel tried to fight him. He caught her tiny wrists in his hands and held her against him, then under him as they fell onto the bed.

"Can't." He spat drops of blood and glared down at her. The passion still burned in his eyes. His hips rose--she inhaled in relief, thankful to have the rod of near-molten iron withdrawn. His hips fell, driving into her again.

"It won't change! What's wrong?" She hiccupped, startled to realize that second thrust didn't hurt quite so much.

"Nothing is wrong." His expression tightened. A groan escaped him. He shuddered and cursed. More thrusts, each one less painful. La'rus' grip loosened. "Silly princess ... this time it's *real*. Didn't you realize that? Do you think I'd make love to you in this ice-pit if I had the choice of all the worlds?"

"Real?" Rahzel subsided, ignoring the ache. La'rus thrust into her again, with less force. She felt the rushing in his blood, like floodwaters, begin to slacken.

She burst into tears.

Chapter Eleven

Rahzel knew she had gone mad, because she had never been one to cry, even when they took her from her mother's Bunker by force.

"Yes, love, now you remember," La'rus whispered. He withdrew, rolled off her, and turned onto his side. He drew her up tight against him and held her, wrapping the tangled blankets around them both while she wept.

She wept until her eyes were swollen almost shut and her throat ached and her head wanted to explode and her stomach had tied itself into knots. La'rus held her, rubbing her back, keeping her warm when she would surely have frozen from the cold welling up deep inside. He comforted her, and she thought in that moment she hated him.

Finally, she couldn't cry anymore. La'rus guided her stumbling steps to the cleanser stall and she washed again, lingering in the hot water. He didn't join her. She was grateful, yet she ached. She couldn't stand to touch the suds wand, so she scrubbed herself with her bare hands. Her stomach turned over as she saw the streaks of her own blood on her thighs, felt the aching of her torn flesh every time she moved injudiciously.

He helped her dress in her favorite jumpsuit of pale blue; something she had considered frivolous because it was of finer material than her usual clothes. Raking her fingers through her damp hair to sweep it into place, she stopped, aghast.

"You removed my cranial inputs!" As clearly as if she could see it happening, Rahzel knew those pinpricks she had felt were real. The tiny sockets and the gold, hair-fine wires that went down into her brain--gone. "You stole the Link from me! The etherworld!"

"You still have them." La'rus perched on the end of her bed and watched her. He had found trousers somewhere and went bare-chested and barefoot, and looked even more dangerous than when he had been naked.

"Without my inputs?"

"We've been living inside the etherworld. We've made it part of us. There's nothing beyond us now. Reach with your mind, and you'll see it's true."

Quickly, before doubts could block her, Rahzel closed her eyes and thought of what she wanted. Her mind flashed through dozens of connection points within the Link, gathering the information at a speed that dizzied her. In a matter of moments, she understood everything that had happened, even the reasons for what La'rus had done.

The long, luxurious days of decadence and sensuality had all been an illusion. She knew that, of course, but knowing that she had only been

In-Link fourteen hours stole her balance. When she and La'rus had made love, she had destroyed the barriers that kept him from regaining physical form. The mathematical formulas and twisted rules of physics were beyond her, but she had made it possible for him to draw on the energy of the universe to create a body for himself. He had turned energy into matter and she had helped form that matter into living flesh.

Flesh to flesh. They had had sex. Unprotected sex, with no germicide and spermicide. No contraceptives. Nothing to prevent contact with body fluids. He had spilled her blood and torn her flesh. Her blood had touched his bare flesh.

"We're not going to die," La'rus said. He sounded weary, yet Rahzel knew fury waited just below the surface.

It didn't please or amuse her to realize that she could see into him just as easily as he could see into her.

"You're healthy, free from disease. My body, as you have observed, is brand new. It has never left this sterilized little cage you let them put you in to, so how could I be exposed to any disease?" He gestured around the Station room. "I didn't rape you, sweetness. You welcomed me, practically begged me to take you."

"You hurt me."

"You were still a virgin! It won't hurt the next time."

"There won't be a next time. You used me," she hurried to add when his eyes widened and his mouth dropped open.

Rahzel knew she had hurt him and she was glad. Yet she ached, too. She didn't like the disparate feelings that warred inside her. La'rus had done that to her, too.

"You agreed. You bound yourself to me, just as I bound myself to you. I never forced you to do anything."

"You tricked me! I didn't understand. I thought it was all ... an illusion." Her voice wavered, threatening more sobs. Rahzel didn't want that, any more than she wanted to argue with him. "Can't we go back?" she whispered. "Back to where we were happy and no one could stop us? They'll come for you soon. They'll punish both of us. Destroy us. Take away the etherworld. We'll never see each other again."

"They don't know I'm here." His smile was flat, but at least it was a smile. "We've both been inside too deep. Every ether-port and Link access on this planet will listen to us. Every machine will obey us, when they won't even acknowledge the existence of anyone else. The authorities don't know I'm here, any more than they knew the changes going on in your body while we made love--in there and out here. If I tell all the listening ears and watching eyes and vicious tattletales to ignore us, they will."

"How long will that work? Eventually, someone will demand a report from me. What do I tell them?" She sank down to the floor with her back against a cabinet.

"By the time anyone comes to look, we'll be gone."

She shook her head, staring at him but not seeing him. His plans sprang into her mind, an image that stunned her.

"We'll die if we go outside the Domes," she whispered.

"They had you believing you'd die if you had sex, but that hasn't happened, has it? They told you there were no more males, but here I am. They told you there was no more need for males, but if you'd ever bother to check, you'd see birth rates have dropped steadily and the mutations have risen twice as fast, since the first generation sealed the Domes."

"That's not true. The Bunkers clans are given the right to have more children every year."

"*Given* the right, princess. Having a right and exercising it are two different things. They've lied to you, and to twenty generations before you. The lie has gone on so long, everyone believes it. Everyone is a dupe, and they don't have the brains to look at the facts right under their noses and see the truth!" La'rus got up to pace. His presence filled her Station until she thought she might suffocate, squeezed down into her tiny spot on the floor.

Yet somehow, she felt more alive than she had felt in years. Since they took her from her mother's Bunker.

Watching him scowl and pace with his gaze turned inward, Rahzel thought about his words. She touched the spots where her cranial inputs had been. Where she had expected tenderness and holes in her skull from the removal of the gold sockets, she felt nothing but silky short hair and whole flesh. No wounds. No scars. No scabs.

Tentatively, she reached to Link. It took only a moment of concentration, deciding what she wanted. The etherworld's datablocks yielded their information as easily as she took a breath. She asked for information to prove him wrong, probed into places and asked for statistics and charts of figures. Reports that had taken days to process now came in nanoseconds.

She saw how the Planetary Council's minions had sorted through the data, inputting calculations and trimming information. Always presenting a picture that supported the beliefs of the ancestors who first sealed the Domes.

Rahzel saw that those who altered the information didn't know what they were doing. As La'rus had said, they were dupes just as much as those they lied to and manipulated. They did what their ancestors had done, following orders and patterns they didn't even understand.

Tears spilled down her cheeks as the truth flowed through her mind. She watched La'rus pace and mutter and deep inside her mind, she saw her world crumble.

Bunkers weren't evacuated, the occupants relocated because of disease. There were fewer viable children born every decade. No one was sterilized because of disease that damaged their genetics. Inbreeding and mutation had sterilized them already.

The world outside the Domes had been poisoned, but centuries of lying fallow and ignored had allowed Nature to heal itself. Life flourished, lush, abundant and healthy everywhere but inside the Domes.

Barbarians didn't live outside the Domes, waiting to savage innocents. They were simple people who had abandoned technology and lived by the sweat of their brows. They had small villages and farms. The highest form of technology was water-powered mills and a few steamships. All their science concentrated on their doctors, and those were few because their outdoor lives and unprocessed food protected them from disease.

People died younger outside than they did inside the Domes, but Rahzel wondered if those inside the Domes had ever really lived.

"Why did they wipe out all males?" she whispered.

"Mostly, they really did believe sex caused disease and death. It was another good way of maintaining the peace and controlling the gene pool. Control a woman's ability to have children, you get very docile women. And for a while, screening all genetic material did keep the human race viable. But you can clone and play at being gods only for so long before Nature gets angry and starts fighting back." La'rus settled down next to her, leaning against the counter.

"Like I told you, there still are males alive on this world. Besides me." He managed a nearly normal smile, but lacked that mischievous glint. "All those people outside the Domes. How do you think they breed without science? They do things the way Nature intended them." He held out his hand to her. "And they enjoy themselves, no matter what all those misguided, mistaken, frigid old harridans told you."

Rahzel just looked at his hand. She remembered how she felt when he touched her. She remembered the strength in his arms, carrying her. She knew now how he had taken care of her when she was helpless and half out of her mind from the shock of that final merging with him. The merging that had created his body. She knew that if she gave her hand to him, she would be giving her life into his keeping.

Leave the Domes? Could she?

"We'll have to. Imagine the reaction of those thousands of women at learning a male has come into the Domes. For every one who sees me as the stuff of nightmares, there will be one who has been just as curious about sex as you were. I've never been the harem type, sweetness. I'll be king of this world, and there's room for only one queen at my side."

"Harem." The answer came instantly, almost before she sent the query to her newly enhanced information source. Rahzel's face warmed.

La'rus, making love to a different woman every night? Never touching the same woman twice?

Not if *she* had anything to do with it.

Somehow, it was easier imagining five thousand women clamoring to kill the dragon that had emerged in their midst, rather than five thousand clamoring to spend one night with him. La'rus belonged to her. Not because he had chosen her, forced himself on her, tricked her and seduced her--

"You seduced me," La'rus whispered as he caught hold of her hand. He raised it to his lips and kissed each fingertip, all the while meeting her gaze. "We chose each other. Yes, I tricked you. Would you have traded what we've known already, for the truth right from the start, and all your fears?"

"Rahzel!" Mikla's voice buzzed through the Station. "Rahzel, bio-sensors say you're there and awake, but we've lost all signs of you in the Link. Respond immediately."

"I don't want to," she said, and knew the audio pickups wouldn't carry her voice to her supervisor unless she so wished.

Thanks to La'rus, all the monitors and life-support systems and every other piece of machinery on the planet would obey her. If she had given him physical being, he had given her intimacy with the etherworld that only came from existing for centuries as a pure energy and intelligence.

"If you don't respond, we must assume contamination has taken place. We must assume you are physically or mentally unable to respond. Protocols will be enacted and your Station breached. Respond or we will be forced to act," Mikla continued.

"Nobody ever forces them. They choose what they do. Don't ever let someone make you feel guilty over something they choose to do." La'rus stood and dragged her to her feet with him. "Come, love. It's time to go. Choose me."

"Isn't it too late for that?" she had to ask. Something between a sob and a bitter chuckle caught in her throat.

"It's never too late. You can still choose this tiny, cold, sterile little world over me. Respond to them. Turn me in. Have me butchered as a carrier of disease."

She knew he was no such thing. La'rus had as perfect control over his body and all its functions as his control over the etherworld. Just as she had now. Just as they would have, in a muted way, over the bodies of others, just by touching and accessing their biological systems. Like a diagnostic unit accessed other computers to fix them.

"The outer world needs healers and teachers, doesn't it?" she asked, and tightened her grip on his hand.

La'rus laughed, but not for long, as she flung her arms around his neck and smothered the sound with kisses.

* * * *

An hour later, the security team finally arrived. Repeated attempts to enact security protocols had proven futile. Orders went out and were lost in an electronic maelstrom. No tranquilizer gas filled Rahzel's Station. The power feed and air circulation systems stayed working, despite every attempt to shut them down. When the security team in their gas masks and decontamination suits arrived to unseal Rahzel's door, they found it open. The Station was empty, though the monitors said the occupant of the room was still there.

In the ensuing years, messages infiltrated the Link, telling of the outside world. Invitations to come out and join the simple, free life. Tales of animals and mountains, storms and other things that most inhabitants of the Domes thought only existed in history. Nothing the Planetary Council did could stop the invading information from reaching every Bunker and Mind-Diver Station.

Especially perturbing were the messages from those extinct creatures, men, looking for brides, mates, mothers and lovers.

Women went looking for the sources of those stories and never returned. The authorities tried to tell everyone the women had died, but no one believed them.

* * * *

Rahzel and La'rus became healers and teachers and had many children. In the generations that followed them, their story became a fable just as popular as the fictions Mother Rahzel used to love.

Finally, they faded into the legend of the Maiden in the Tower and the Man Who Fell From the Stars.

The End

THE LOVELAND CURSE

By
Jane Toombs

Shortly after she roared past Gerlach on her father's old Harley, Zenna Ruthven saw the towering form of the Burning Man silhouetted against the early evening sky. Not on fire yet, still waiting. Northern Nevada's Black Rock Desert stretched out to either side of the road, miles of flat land where little grew, with bleak rock hills in the distance. The most desolate part of the state, according to those who decided such things.

This was the last night of the event, festival, orgy, choose one or all. After true darkness fell, the crowd would burn him, dancing around the flaming pyre, many either drunk or stoned out of their minds, some naked, some in bizarre costumes. She smiled. Here, tonight, might be the only place in the world where she wouldn't be noticed. Or if she was, no one would be surprised. Or care. Anyway, wasn't a desert the proper place for someone like her?

Olga, about the only friend who hadn't deserted her after that horrible surprise ten years ago, had tried to talk her out of going. So it was risky, so what? Leaving town overnight held risks for almost anyone from Loveland. Zenna didn't care. If she wanted to celebrate Labor Day by mingling with the other Burning Man aficionados, that was her business. It wasn't as though she'd betray anyone.

As she came closer to the site, her eyes widened at the milling mob kicking up desert dust as they interacted. All types and ages of vehicles, all types and ages of people. Thousands more than she had anticipated. But what better place to lose herself than in a massive crowd celebrating this bizarre ceremony? The only worry she admitted to was how to keep the Harley safe.

She throttled down and eased off the road into the desert proper, weaving between people until she finally saw a vast herd of bikes tethered to a long metal pole supported by many, many crossbars. Noting the Hell's Angels insignia on most of them, she nodded. Hers would be safe here. The worn dragon insignia her mother had given her father for his bike would fit right in. As she chained her bike to the pole, Zenna ran her hand over the dragon. Should she have made the connection? Shrugging, she picked up her backpack, turned away and plunged into the crowd.

Tents, campers and makeshift shelters littered the ground. A helicopter whirled overhead--no doubt a news crew videotaping what they regarded as the weirdoes below. A man hailed her.

"You alone, babe?"

She glanced at him and shook her head, but he followed her, a big guy with a beer gut. "My old man's one of the Angels," she lied. "He packs iron."

The guy veered off. Zenna sighed. She'd come here to get laid, hadn't she? Yeah, but she got to choose and he wasn't even close to the one. Not much time before dark, though, and the moon was just past full, so she'd best do some quick looking.

She found herself distracted by the many weird characters in the immense crowd--what a zoo. She'd known from the articles she'd read and from seeing the Burning Man on TV last year that it would be like this, but experiencing the festival in person was still more frenzied than she'd expected. Would she be able to find anyone who appealed to her?

No faltering now, girl, she told herself. You're here, do what you came to do. There must be someone here at Black Rock, among more men than you've ever before seen in your life. The problem was she wasn't at all accustomed to crowds.

A half hour later she'd rejected at least fifty possibles. Some were okay on looks, but too stoned or drunk to suit her. Others she might have considered were with women already. Nothing was really wrong with many she passed, but they just weren't right. Was she being too picky? No fun still being a virgin at twenty-seven because of what she was. No man in Loveland would touch her, which is why she'd gotten desperate enough to try the Burning Man. She was trapped for life in Loveland--who knew, this might be her only chance to find out what it was like to have a man. At least once.

The chopper seemed to be settling down. As near as she could tell in the fading light, it seemed to land toward the dark hills, some distance away from the camp area.

She'd have to keep an eye out for the news crew. No way was she going to be on camera either now or later.

Tunneling through the mob made her increasingly uneasy. There were far more people here than the entire population of tiny Loveland, she decided as she fought her way toward the edge of the crowd. Eventually it thinned out enough so she wasn't jostled on all sides, but, just as she'd begun to relax a little, Zenna felt someone watching her. An older man, his graying hair in braids. Looked to be Indian. Native American to be politically correct. Paiute probably, this being their stomping grounds in the old days. His interest in her didn't seem sexual though.

"You do not belong here," he said.

She stopped and stared at him. "Why not? You're here."

"I came to meet the stranger."

Zenna swept her hand to indicate the entire scene. "You picked the right spot. I never saw so many strangers in one place in my life."

"They belong here as much as anywhere on this earth."

"And I don't?" What a strange conversation. Time to break it off and continue her search.

"You belong, but not in this place. The stranger--" The old man paused as though listening, never taking his gaze from her.

Feeling he'd pinned her to the spot, Zenna found herself listening, too. For what? She shook her head, preparing to leave. "I won't keep you from--"

"Ah," the old man said, "now I see. You were in the dream, after all. Like me, you're here to meet the stranger."

She could hardly deny her purpose in coming to the Burning Man was to meet a stranger, but this old guy was weirding her out. What dream? She didn't want to know. "Maybe I'll see you around later," she said and started to turn away.

He reached out and grabbed her wrist, his grip surprisingly strong. "I mean you no harm, but you must wait. He's coming near, the stranger. Wait and meet him."

Although at the far edge of the crowd, they were far from alone. Stragglers continued to pass them, aiming at getting closer to the effigy before the fire was lit. She tugged at her arm and he let her go.

Before she could move further or speak, he said, "Do you dream?"

Zenna blinked. Sure she dreamed, dreamed that when she looked at herself on those certain moonlit nights she was not what she saw.

As though she'd spoken the words, he said, "I have true dreams."

She knew what that meant. He fancied himself a shaman. Could even be one for all she knew. At another time she might have been interested. But she had no time to waste.

"Whether for good or ill, you will meet the stranger," he added.

Shaking her head again, she started to veer away and almost ran into a tall, tanned man with golden eyes. Everything else about him was the same appealing shade of tan: skin, hair and clothes. Even the cape he wore--a cape, of all things--was tan. He glanced at her, but then focused on the Paiute.

"You are Sleeping Fox?" he asked. "They told me at Pyramid Lake you'd be here."

The old man nodded. "You are called Curtis Helms."

"You know me, then?"

In answer, Sleeping Fox fished a cell phone from his jeans.

Curtis smiled, revealing white, somewhat pointed teeth.

The better to eat you with, my dear? Nonsense. Her own teeth were somewhat pointed. Why am I standing here gaping at the man? Zenna asked herself. Yet she knew. She might never have dreamed of Curtis Helms as the Paiute had, but he was *it*, cape or not. Her chosen one--for tonight at least.

She cleared her throat. "I'm Zenna," she told him. "Sleeping Fox dreamed we would meet. I didn't believe him, but he seems to be right."

The cape swirled as Curtis turned to take a good look at her. She hoped he wasn't into voluptuous blue-eyed blondes, because she was slender, with dark hair and hazel eyes.

"Zenna," he said, holding out his hand.

She placed her hand in his, expecting him to shake it. Instead, he continued to hold hers, warming it--and more.

"She's been waiting for you," Sleeping Fox said. "You and I will talk later by your helicopter. I go there now." Without waiting for any answer, the old man trotted off into the desert.

The helicopter belonged to the stranger?

"Waiting for me," Curtis repeated as though to himself. He smiled at her. "I've rarely been so fortunate."

Zenna realized now that he had a slight accent, one she couldn't place. His words seemed to mean he liked how she looked, but where did they go from here? She'd never seduced a man in her life.

"If that's true," Curtis went on, "you're not here as a participant in this ritual."

"Um, well, I would like to watch the effigy burn tonight." She couldn't trust herself to be with him after darkness completely cloaked the earth and the moon rose.

"We have time before that happens. Time to become acquainted."

She could only nod. Here he was. This was no time to back off.

Still holding her hand, he led her away from the crowd, pausing only to lift a blanket from an improvised clothesline strung between two campers. She drew in her breath.

"I'll return the blanket," he told her. "Thievery isn't my line."

Finding her voice, she asked, "What is your line?"

"At the moment, you. I find it best to focus on the moment."

Now that it appeared she was going to realize *her* moment, the one she'd longed for, doubts sprang up like sand fleas, nipping at her. What was she doing with this utter stranger?

He squeezed her hand. "This Black Rock Desert appeals to me almost as much as you do."

"Most people find Black Rock barren and desolate."

"Which you are not," he said. "But I can tell you're nervous. Don't be."

Not a chance in hell she was going to blurt out that it was her first time. Okay, she'd stop jittering inside. This might be her one and only chance to find out what it was like to be with a man. He was the one she'd picked, and she wasn't going to be sorry she'd made the choice. This man in tan *was* the right one.

"Do you know Sleeping Fox?" he asked.

"I met him shortly before I met you. He told me a-a stranger was coming and I should stay and meet him. I didn't want to or mean to, but...."

"Zenna," he said, and she noticed he said her name differently than most, with a slight stress on the Z. It charmed her. "I won't take more than you wish to give."

As he led her to an isolated spot between two boulders, some distance away from the crowd, she kept turning the words over in her mind. How much did she wish to give? Shouldn't it be all if you expected good sex? It crossed her mind he could be anything--a serial killer for all she knew. Yet Sleeping Fox had more or less sent her off with him. Was it possible they worked together, preying on women?

She couldn't bring herself to believe that. So, okay, was she in any more danger from this man than any other stranger at the Burning Man? If she started worrying about his character, she might as well have stayed in Loveland where her purpose would never be fulfilled.

He spread the blanket on the ground and gestured for her to be seated. She forced herself not to hesitate. Instead of seating himself, he knelt at her feet and started to remove her biker boots.

"You don't have to--" she began.

"Allow me."

So she did. He then took off her socks and began massaging her feet. His hands were magic, no denying that. At least he wasn't just going to jump her bones with no preliminaries. That was a plus. Also, he'd taken charge, making her relieved she wouldn't have to fumble around trying to be the aggressor when she hadn't a clue how. She relaxed under his expert touch, refusing to let herself wonder what was to come. She intended to enjoy every moment, just as he'd suggested.

Her jeans came off next, his hands continuing their gentle strokes up each leg, no farther than the knees at first. Her anticipation mounted. How wonderful to feel a man's touch. This man's touch. By the time he ventured higher, stopping just short of touching her bikinis, she caught her breath, aroused without even one kiss.

After removing her T-shirt and bra, he caressed her breasts, sending her further up, her mind in chaos, her body throbbing for completion. And still his hands slid over her, promising everything. She'd waited twenty-seven years for that promise. Any moment now her wish would be granted. Her eyes drooped shut as she gave herself up to unadulterated pleasure.

His hands continued to work their magic, finding places where she'd never even touched herself. She sensed an inner wave beginning, one that would lift her higher than she'd ever been before. With more to follow.

"You've closed your eyes," he murmured.

Languidly, she opened them, startled to find darkness outside as well as behind her closed lids. Over his shoulder she saw the moon. And felt the first wrench.

Terror slithered through her. She pulled free, scooped up her clothes, jumped up and ran, aware his touch had made her forget what she needed to always remember. She'd stayed too long, now she must lose herself in the darkness. And find a safe place to hide while it happened.

By the moon's thin silver light, she spotted a good-sized rock that she thought she could move. Stopping, she gave it a heave. The rock tilted up and she shoved her clothes underneath, letting it ease back down, then stripped off her bikinis and dropped them nearby for a marker before taking off again.

The change was almost complete by the time she located a boulder large enough to crouch behind. When she stood again, she stared toward the effigy, now aflame. The Burning Man. No longer did she have the courage to venture near, not as she was now, not even to catch a last glimpse of Curtis. There were far too many people. And she was weirder than any of them. Her sigh came out in a hiss.

She'd never see him again. Her entire reason for being here was no longer valid. If she were able to mount the Harley and ride back to Loveland right now, she'd be off like a shot. Since that was impossible, she'd have to stay where she was until moonset.

* * * *

Back in Loveland, Zenna moped around her small house, the one her father had left her when he died. Better to have stayed home and never learned what a man's touch could do. Because now she longed to feel the stranger's hands on her again. Although she dreamed of him, the dreams fell short of the reality. She'd told Olga about seeing the effigy burn and the crazy crowd, but not a word about Curtis--or even Sleeping Fox.

A week passed and the next one rolled around. Then the next. The town had never seemed so small. Same old, same old for the rest of her life, she figured. Now that she'd met Curtis, she wanted only him, so chances were good she'd be a virgin librarian until she died.

Heading for her job, she was a block away from the library when she heard the unmistakable clacking sound of helicopter blades. Even as her heart began to pound, she shook her head. Choppers weren't unknown in Nevada skies. But she looked up anyway, just in time to see the craft turning in a circle over the town. They had no official airport, but there was a level dirt field a ways beyond the north edge of Loveland where a copter could land if necessary.

Without realizing what she meant to do, Zenna found herself running toward that field. Not him, it couldn't be him. Even if he looked for her, he had no way to find where she lived. Though she could see the craft meant to land, she forced herself to stop, fearing she wouldn't be able to stand disappointment. But then, noticing others heading for the field, she hurried on. No harm in making sure.

Brian Sora, Olga's husband and the town cop, caught up with her. "Last thing we need is another stranger showing up here," he muttered as he jogged past her.

Like her father had been twenty years ago when he brought her here. They'd let him stay after he told the town doctor why he'd come. Her mother had been one of the fortunate ones they called Nulls, who'd escaped Loveland when she was thirty. If it didn't happen by the time you were twenty, it never did, so no one cared that she went. After all, she hadn't become one of them, even though her parents had been. And those raised in Loveland, even the Nulls, kept its secret.

On the outside, Zenna's mother married a normal man, planning never to have children. But at forty-two, she became pregnant unexpectedly and the pregnancy triggered a partial change, which her husband helped her conceal. After she died seven years later, Zenna's father fulfilled his wife's deathbed promise to bring their little girl to Loveland. Because who could know what might happen?

As far as Zenna was concerned, what did happen was worse than anything her father could have expected. Luckily he'd died the year before. But then again, he might have had an inkling. If only he'd told her more about her mother.

By the time she reached the edge of the field, the copter had settled onto the dirt, blowing sand in the draft from the blades as they wound down. When they stilled, a man climbed out. Because a small crowd was gathering around the craft, she couldn't see for certain who the man was. Yet somehow she knew. Against all odds he'd found her. She pushed her way closer, near enough to see he still wore his tan cape, near enough to hear him talking to Brian.

"...studying Paiute legends for a project I'm doing for the government." Curtis' voice, beyond all doubt, slight accent and all.

"I was told this area was a sacred spot for them. If no one objects, I'll set up camp near the chopper for the short time I'll be here." Curtis looked past Brian and saw her, but his expression didn't change. Surely he recognized her? A moment later she realized it was best for both of them that no one in town knew they'd ever met before. Best and safest--for him.

"A short time," Brian repeated, with emphasis on the short.

"Possibly a week. Is there any place in town I might find references to Paiute legends?"

"Library." Brian's voice was gruff. He glanced around and spotted her. "Zenna, come over here." Turning back to Curtis, he added, "She's the librarian."

Actually she had no degree, but the former librarian, even then an old woman, had trained her before she died. Zenna pushed through to stand beside Brian.

"You'd be the one to help Curtis, here," he said. "Man's in a hurry, so the more help you can give him the better."

What Brian meant was he wanted the stranger out of town as soon as possible. Definitely before the next full moon. As he introduced her to Curtis, she showed no sign they'd ever met before. Nor did Curtis.

Was he actually studying Paiute legends for the government? Could be, since Sleeping Fox had been waiting for him at the Burning Man. And she did know this secluded little valley, tucked between two barren hills, had been held sacred by the Paiutes. Probably because of the spring. Water was rare in the area. So he might not have come here to find her. Why on earth would he? Even if he had known she came from Loveland, which was clearly impossible.

"Don't mean to sound unwelcoming," Brian said, his gruffness belying the words. "Thing is, we like to be left alone."

"I'll take care not to bother any of you except Ms. Ruthven," Curtis promised. "And I'll do my best to be no trouble to her. As I said, I'm set up for camping."

"May as well take the man right up to the library and get him started on what you got there," Brian said to Zenna as the crowd started to drift away. "He don't want to waste time hanging around here any longer than he has to."

"Let me secure the copter, Ms. Ruthven, and I'll be right with you," Curtis told her.

She watched him, realizing as she got a good look at the helicopter, that it was different from any she'd ever seen. Which meant nothing, since such aircraft weren't exactly common around Loveland. By the time he finished, the two of them were alone.

"Lead on, Zenna the Fair," he said.

"I thought I was Ms. Ruthven. You didn't know I lived in Loveland, did you?"

"Sleeping Fox figured you must. Had something to do with his dream. He also told me his grandfather warned that Loveland was a bad spirit place. Apparently his people shunned it long before his grandfather was born, but he hedged about why. Does your library have anything that can shed light on that?"

"So you really are here to study Paiute legends," she said as they walked toward town.

He smiled. "Let's just say I have a dual purpose in visiting Loveland. Where did it get the name?"

"The founder of the town was named Loveland."

"Humans do take pleasure in naming places after themselves. I'm interested in the site. And in you."

She stumbled, quickly regaining her balance.

"I didn't mean to frighten you at Black Rock," he added.

"I--it wasn't you, not exactly." She stole a glance at him, noting again the perfection of his features. Combined with a body to die for--no wonder she'd chosen him. Except for those unusual golden eyes, again he was all tan: skin, clothes, hair. And that cape.

Before she thought, she blurted out, "Do you wear contacts?"

He blinked. "Why do you ask?"

"Your eye color."

"This is my eye color, but I do wear contacts for other reasons." He seemed amused, as well he might. Being with him scattered her wits, making her sound like a ninny, which she went right on being.

"I don't think I've ever seen a man wearing a cape before. It sort of reminds me of those old vampire movies. Dracula always wore a cape."

"Yes, but I seem to recall from my studies of the vampire legends that his was black. Do you believe in vampires?"

About to deny it, she held. No one would believe Loveland's secret, so were vampires any more bizarre? "Who knows?"

"I assure you vampirism is not a problem of mine."

"I didn't mean--that is--well, I rather like the cape."

"Good. Because my cape and I are inseparable."

Actually she thought it made him look rather dashing. And not even remotely like Dracula.

At the library, Zenna gathered all the material she had on the Paiutes and laid it on one of the tables for him. He made no move to look at any of it.

"You wear no wedding ring," he said.

"I'm not married."

"Good. Neither am I. Tonight, then."

"Tonight?"

"I believe the saying is 'your place or mine?'"

"Oh, but you can't--that is, I mean you promised to stay in your camp."

"I'm not there now."

"I mean at night."

"Your local law enforcer made it quite clear he didn't like me being here--day or night. Why?"

Zenna moved her shoulders uneasily. "We've never liked strangers coming to Loveland. It's a--a peculiarity of ours. We keep to ourselves and don't welcome strangers."

"Since that means I'd best keep to camp, then it has to be my place. Unless you don't want to be with me."

Couldn't he tell she was practically drooling over him? The moon wouldn't be close enough to full to be troublesome for a few more days, so it'd be safe enough to visit him, but.... "They'll wonder," she said lamely. "They won't like it."

"Do you care what your townspeople think?"

How was she going to explain that she cared what might happen to him, not to her? Strangers had disappeared from Loveland before.

Heaven only knows she wanted him to finish what he'd started at the Burning Man.

"If I decide to come, I will," she said finally.

"Clandestinely, I gather."

She nodded. For his safety there could be no other way.

He leaned over and kissed her, just a brush of lips, but heat rushed through Zenna. When she could think straight, she looked quickly around, sighing with relief to find they were still alone in the library--her trainee hadn't arrived yet.

"I imagine your local constabulary would be happier if I took what you've given me to my camp rather than contaminating your library to study it. As I told you before, I'm not a thief. I did return that blanket, so you needn't worry about what belongs to the library."

She flushed, reminded of what they'd done on that blanket, at the same time anticipating more. Tonight. If she went to him. But how could she stay away?

Some of the material she'd set out for him was reference, but he was right about Brian not wanting him in town, so she decided to waive the rule and let him take everything for now: papers, booklets, books. And her as well tonight?

He gathered it all together, taking her silence as agreement. Before he left, he said, "Remember--you get to set the rules, just like at Black Rock."

* * * *

He strode away from the library, ignoring curious, and sometimes hostile, glances from the people he passed. Since Zenna was unable to conceal her feelings from him, he rather expected to see her at his camp tonight. Or by tomorrow night, anyway. He'd been careful not to involve himself with any females on this trip--too risky. But once the old Paiute had told him about Loveland and said that had to be where Zenna came from, nothing could have kept him away.

She was different in a way he couldn't define. He'd pushed Sleeping Fox to find out why the shaman connected Zenna with Loveland, but got no satisfactory answer. Apparently a shaman's true dream had helped Sleeping Fox make the connection, but he gave no particulars.

"You are strange, she is strange," Black Fox had said. "If there is to be anything between the two of you, then it must be one forged by you both."

Wise old man. Also one who kept his own council, luckily. Curtis hated unpleasantness.

Some children had gathered to stare at the helicopter. None of them stood near it, and they all scattered when they saw him. Not that they could have gotten close, he'd seen to that. He stashed the library papers temporarily inside the copter, retrieved his camping equipment and set it up within the protection. While he waited for the dark curtain of night to obliterate light, he studied what Zenna had given him. The indigenous people of North America had legends that varied interestingly from those he'd picked up in Europe and he was looking forward to learning more about the Paiute taboo of this area.

Later he napped, waking when he heard coyotes singing to one another at dusk. A lonely sound, reminding him he had no one to sing to. Even if she came....

He rose, stepped out of the tent and waited.

Much later, when stars danced in the desert night sky, he sensed her approaching and smiled as he lowered the protection and went to meet her.

"I decided you'd be hungry," she told him as he led her, basket over her arm, into the tent. "Brian made it pretty clear he didn't want you in town, and I figured you might not have much in the way of supplies, so I brought you supper."

He was charmed by her excuse. Also glad of the fresh food. Dried supplies were nourishing, but that's about all he could say in their favor.

"Will you join me?" he asked.

"No, I've already eaten, thanks."

She was nervous; the way she'd been at first at Black Rock. "I have an after-dinner cordial we can share later, then," he said.

"Well, I really shouldn't stay, but--"

"But to make me happy, you might?"

Without answering, she glanced around. "Nice tent. Very roomy. I don't think I've ever seen one quite like it before. What's that humming I hear?"

"Generator." Which was true in a way. He'd renewed the protection.

"Oh, of course."

"Is that an actual fur rug on the floor?"

"Synthetic. But just as soft and caressing."

He watched her flush. Another indication she still wanted him. Whether it was a good idea or not, the feeling was definitely mutual. Zenna fascinated him in a way no female had before.

He ate quickly, but carefully, stowing the remaining food before producing the cordial and two small glasses. After pouring it, he dimmed the lights. Later, he'd turn them off completely.

"Real glass, not plastic," she said. "I'm impressed." She tasted the colorless cordial and smiled. "Delicious. I can't think what it tastes like. Sort of reminiscent of raspberry, but different. Not like any I've ever had before."

No, it wouldn't be. It would also relax her so she'd be able to feel what she wanted and act on it.

"Have you looked at what I let you take from the library?" she asked when she finished the cordial.

He nodded. "Read it all and took notes. You can put the material in your basket to return to the library so Loveland won't have to deal with me in the morning."

"You're leaving already?" She sounded alarmed. Good.

"No. I'll be scouting around the area on foot for a few days." He took her hand, turning it over to examine the palm. "Did anyone ever read this?" he asked.

"Don't tell me you're an expert in palmistry."

In answer he lifted her hand and took one of her fingers into his mouth. She drew in her breath.

He tasted each finger in turn, his sharp teeth nipping her thumb just hard enough to make her gasp. Then he held her hand against his heart, aware she'd be able to feel its faint throb within his chest. At the same time, he placed his free hand between her breasts, slightly to the left so he could feel her heart beat in turn.

She offered him a wavering smile. "Two hearts that beat as one?"

He admired her try at flippancy when she must realize he could tell how rapidly her heart was beating. Zenna was a female to admire. And savor.

"Shall we test the manufacturer's claim that their product can't be told from the real thing?" he asked, nodding at the rug covering the tent's ground cloth. Without waiting for an agreement, he took her hand from his chest, eased her up from the camp chair, moved away from the small table, and lowered them both to the rug.

Not giving her a chance to sit up, he gathered her close and kissed her. Not as deeply as he wanted, but that would be a risk. Some things couldn't be hidden. Her immediate response warmed him, even as it told him she wasn't an experienced lover. Unusual in the United States in a mature woman. Could it be possible he was to be her first? He found himself breathing faster, instantly ready.

Ready or not, he wasn't going to make their coming together into the slam, bam, thank you, ma'am joke he'd heard when he first arrived in this country. That had never been his way and certainly not with a relative innocent, no matter how high she drove him.

Was it her scent? With no overlay of perfume other than the clean smell of soap, her essence teased his senses. Subtle, arousing, almost familiar and yet elusive. He reveled in the smell as he enjoyed her taste. Was this female going to make him lose his head completely? If her skin hadn't been so smooth, he knew he'd be, as they said here, a goner.

* * * *

Zenna thought his raspy breathing showed he must be as aroused as she was. When they were still girls, she and Olga had discussed kissing. Even then Olga and Brian had been going together, sure because of their parentage that they'd be compatible later, when it mattered. So Olga knew more about kissing that Zenna, who had uncertain parentage.

"Sometimes Bri opens his mouth," Olga had confided.

"Ugh."

"No, it's really sexy. Just wait and see."

Finally Zenna's chance to find out was here, but so far Curtis had kept his mouth closed. Not that she was complaining. If he kissed any sexier she'd melt into a puddle of eagerness. She was close enough to that as it was. Her entire self pulsed with need.

Time and place ceased to have any meaning. The caress of his mouth and his hands became the only reality. She savored the intimate sensual pleasure of skin against skin, wanting more and more. Wanting all of him.

She knew she'd never forget his smell, no aftershave or other fragrance contaminating his scent. It reminded her of the desert in the spring. Not sage, exactly, or any other clearly defined smell--just uniquely his, infinitely arousing.

He stroked her in places secret to her, where no man had ever touched her before. She fragmented, feeling as though she'd shattered into shards of exquisite sensation so powerful she'd never come together again. How could there be more? Yet there was. His hardness thrust into her, something inside gave with a tiny shock of pain and then the pulsing deep within her started anew as she rose to meet each thrust, wanting, taking and giving at the same time.

She gave a great cry of release and heard him call her name. Somehow she knew that meant he'd gone over the crest too. After a timeless moment, they lay spent in each other's embrace. He turned on his side, bringing her with him, still holding her.

So now she knew what being with a man was like. This man. Curtis. How could it ever be so fantastic with anyone else?

"Zenna," he murmured. How she loved the way he stressed the Z.

"Mm?"

"Your first time. I'm honored you chose me."

She smiled, sighing. What a sweet thing to say. She'd chosen well, picked a man she would never forget. A man to remember with pleasure.

"Why did you change your mind at Black Rock?" he asked.

She didn't want to lie to him. "I can't tell you why I had to leave so suddenly, but the reason had nothing to do with you."

Somewhat to her surprise, he accepted what she said without comment or any more questions.

After a time he said, "But I found you again anyway."

Yes, he had. On purpose. Or at least finding her again had been part of his purpose. She snuggled close. A first for her, discovering a man who wanted her. At least the way she was now.

Being in his arms felt so right. As though she belonged there. Belonged with him. If only it could always be like this, be so perfect.

A worm of apprehension crawled into her mind. She'd been so besotted by desire she couldn't recall whether or not he'd used protection. She had none because it had never been necessary--Loveland men wouldn't dare touch her. No way could she afford to get pregnant.

Easing away from him, she asked, "Um, did you--I mean, I didn't notice whether you used a condom?"

"If you're worried about getting with child, there's no need to. And I have no diseases."

Relieved, she nestled closer again.

"But those are questions I'd advise you to ask ahead of time in any future encounters with a man."

Since there wouldn't be any once he left, she didn't reply.

"Why did you choose me?" he asked.

"Because of Sleeping Fox." No, that wasn't the real truth. The shaman had made her wait to meet him, that's all. "Partly anyway, but mostly it was because I knew you were the right one the moment I saw you. Don't ask me to explain why."

"Of your kind, Zenna, you're unique."

"Of my kind?" She tensed. Did he suspect?

"Womankind."

She relaxed. How could he suspect? Tonight was safe with the waxing moon not near full, but she mustn't stay too long. She lived alone, but if she wasn't home all night, someone might notice and realize where she'd gone.

Zenna sat up. "I have to leave. No one must know I'm with you."

"Because I'm a stranger?"

"The inhabitants of Loveland don't have anything to do with strangers. Ever."

He turned up the lamp as she got to her feet and began to dress. He was naked, she noted, except for the cape, which made her smile.

"Yet you've had quite a lot to do with this stranger," he said.

"Didn't you say I was unique?" She gathered up the library material and placed it in her basket.

"Tomorrow night we can discuss what the Paiutes believed about the Loveland area," he said.

Zenna stiffened. She'd read about that, so she knew. Reminding herself Loveland was safe because he wouldn't treat what the Paiutes believed as truth, but myth, she forced a smile and said, "We'll see."

"I meant afterwards."

After they made love again. Already she wanted to. But how many times could she come to his camp without someone noticing?

* * * *

The next morning, Olga cornered her in the library. "I hear the stranger was in here yesterday. What's he like?"

Zenna chose her words carefully. "All right, I suppose. He's studying legends and myths from various peoples, in various countries."

"Yeah, that's what Bri said. He thinks it's kind of odd, though, that the guy chose Loveland."

"Curtis is currently researching Paiute myths. Loveland used to be one of their sacred places."

Olga raised her eyebrows. "You call him by his first name?"

"Oh, come on. Who doesn't these days?"

"Considering he's a stranger, it sounds sort of too friendly. Is he going to come to the library again?"

"I don't think so. He took notes while he was here."

"Then he's ready to leave? Bri'll be glad about that."

"He mentioned something about looking around the area, so I don't know how soon he'll leave."

"But there's nothing to see."

Zenna shrugged. "Then he'll find that out, won't he?"

"Well, he'll have to get out of here before it gets too close to the full moon. Otherwise...," Olga let her words trail off.

Though chilled at the reminder, Zenna kept her expression neutral. "Let's not borrow trouble."

"You know his being here upsets Bri. And you know Bri."

After Olga left, Zenna decided she had to warn Curtis. Even as a child, Brian had always been one to act first and think later. He might not harm Curtis, but the possibility was there. She couldn't bear to think of anything like that happening so she'd told herself she wasn't going to risk returning to Curtis' camp again when it could put him in danger, never mind how much she wanted to. Now she had to. Or maybe the truth was she'd found an excuse to go. She could hardly wait until dark.

* * * *

Because of the bond he sensed forming between them, he'd been sure she'd visit him again tonight. Odd that such a bond could exist, even in tenuous form, since everything he'd been taught told him otherwise. Perhaps it wasn't wise to stay. Yet his curiosity was one of the reasons he'd been chosen. All his life he'd wanted to know the why of things. The why and the how. He couldn't leave until his curiosity about Zenna was satisfied. Amused at his own pomposity, he admitted that wasn't the only reason. Or the only satisfaction.

When he sensed her approach, he damped the protection, raising it again after she stepped inside the tent. Again she brought food.

"Plying me with edibles will get you everywhere," he said.

She smiled, but he could feel her tenseness. "Did you find any artifacts of interest on your walkabout?" she asked, setting down the basket.

"No artifacts. Did you expect me to find some?"

She shook her head. "Now that you realize there's nothing to interest you in the area, you must be planning to leave."

"Your words, not mine."

He watched her, aware she struggled to find the right words, words to warn him, he knew.

"We're not--that is, Loveland prefers to be left alone."

"I believe your lawman made that clear shortly after I landed."

She caught her lower lip between her teeth. Rather sharp teeth, he noted with interest. "You really should heed him."

"Or?"

After a moment she said, "Brian will make sure you leave, one way or another."

"But not tonight." It wasn't a question. If she was worried about tonight she'd be much more agitated.

"Well...." She drew the word out.

"So we shall dine at our leisure and then see where fancy leads us?"

This pulled a smile from her, and she began setting the food from the basket onto his small table.

"I rather thought there'd be references to this spot in the material from your library," he said as they began to eat.

She glanced at him. "References to what?"

"To the Paiute legend that paints this area as one of bad spirits."

"There were so many massacres in Nevada in the past."

"I'm aware of the enmity between tribe and tribe and between Indians and the invading Europeans. The legend, though, comes from before there were people, when animals who spoke had the run of the place."

"Mythic creation stories. Every culture has them."

"I'm more aware of that than most."

She flushed. "Sorry, I didn't think. Of course you must know all that since it's your specialty."

"It troubles you to speak of these things. So--zut." He flung out his hands. "Away with them. Instead, I'll tell you how happy I am to see you. You've been in my thoughts all day."

Which was true. Wrong though he knew it to be, he spent far too much time thinking about her, fantasizing about touching her, burying himself within her. If only he could be himself. But that was not possible. Fortunately, the rest was.

He smiled at her. "May I offer you a glass of cordial?"

She slanted him a sultry look. "Thank you, but I believe we'll do just fine without it."

And then she was in his arms.

He no longer cared that her skin was smooth, nor that she was, in some ways, not quite complete. All that faded away when he felt the heat of her body and the surge of eager passion she projected. His own urgency rose to meet hers. The first time they'd joined together he'd believed his need deceived him into glorifying the union. Now he knew better. Zenna was different in some way from all the other females he'd met on this expedition. They meshed in a way inexplicable to him.

But he didn't care--not when her scent surrounded him, potent and irresistible. He craved her taste, her touch, her cries of pleasure, the soft, heated wetness that awaited him. They could never mate properly, but joining with her was far more than a substitute. All thought fled and he gave himself up to the enjoyment of thrusting inside her, to the erotic journey they traveled together.

Afterward, he held her next to him in the dark, prolonging the moment of parting.

Some time later, she said, "I wish you could stay here, but even if you could, you can't."

He disentangled her meaning. His obligations did prevent him from staying. In any case, the Loveland lawman wouldn't allow it. He wasn't quite sure why. Not unless legend was truth. Sometimes a myth did prove to be a half-truth, or the truth concealed within a cocoon of fable. He had yet to uncover any legend, in any land, that was the straight, unembellished truth. Though legends often provided a way to get at what was true.

She eased away from him. "I must go. It really isn't safe for me to come here."

He retrieved his cape and settled it over his shoulders, then turned up the lamp. "Because I'm a stranger and Loveland doesn't accept or trust strangers?"

"We can't. Please don't ask me why."

"I'm not leaving for a few more days."

She flung her arms around his neck, and he tasted the desperation in her kiss. When he would have taken it further, she eased from him, rose, and began to dress. "You've learned all you can about the Paiute myth so there's no reason for you to stay any longer."

"Are you telling me goodbye?"

"I have to." Tears clogged her voice.

She hurried from the tent so fast he barely had time to lift the barrier.

* * * *

Zenna didn't come the next night. Because of the bond that wasn't supposed to be there, he knew she was all right, though he could sense a growing fear. For him, not for herself.

To ease her mind, he should leave. Yet he didn't, determined to wait it out, to see what would happen. To discover what truth was buried within the legend.

The second night he watched the moon, approaching full, rise into the dark Nevada sky, a beautiful moon in its way. Through his bond with Zenna he also sensed the rise of danger. But she didn't come to him.

As a result of two restless nights, he was napping when darkness began to settle over Loveland on the third night. By the time he roused enough to sense her presence, he had no time to shut off the protection before she blundered into it. He lowered the barrier and rushed out, finding her sprawled, stunned, on the ground. He carried her inside, raised the barrier and laid her on his cot. A quick jab of antidote brought her around, but she was too groggy to make sense.

"Bears," she muttered. "Bears are coming tonight."

There were no bears in this part of Nevada. He thought of the Paiute legend. How, in the long ago before there were people, the animals could speak. They all lived in accord until some of the animals deliberately killed one of their own, angering Coyote, who wiped them away, all except a few who eluded him. Then some of the newly made people, looking for water, found the spring where these few speaking animals hid out and slaughtered them so they didn't have to share the water. Though angry, Coyote didn't punish all the newly made people, only those at the spring, decreeing that, thereafter, those people who drank the water from the spring would become animals part of the time.

The spring at Loveland? What was the truth within the myth?

Moonlight shone through the partly open tent flap, a ray touching Zenna's face. She moaned and twisted, crying, "No!"

Before his eyes she flung off her clothes, her smooth skin changing, altering into a pattern of scales. A tail grew from a body no longer human. He gaped in awed surprise.

* * * *

The moon was too close to full to resist. Zenna couldn't prevent her change, even though she knew Curtis was watching, even though the last thing in the world she wanted was to have her secret revealed to him. Helpless, she waited for his amazed expression to turn to fear, to disgust as he stared at the large lizard-like beast she'd become.

Instead, she was shocked by his laughter. He ducked out of sight behind a cloth hanging. Giving her a chance to escape? No, she needed to stay with him, to do what she could to protect him from the fury of Brian and the others who'd be shifting to bears tonight. She forced herself up from the cot, standing upright, dreading having to face Curtis again.

She watched apprehensively as he emerged from behind the curtain. In her lizard form her jaw couldn't drop, but she was shocked down to the very end of her tail when she saw him. Saw a lizard man! Was it possible?

How beautiful you are. His words weren't spoken aloud, but in her mind.

Never, in her shifted form, had she thought to have anyone say those words. As for him, he was gorgeous, golden tan all over his sleek, scaled, streamlined body.

Moments later he embraced her. Not as a human would, which intensified her desire and need. Who would dream that the wrapping of tails together could be so erotic? His scales felt so right under her claw-like hands, and when his tongue, long, thin and forked, touched her face, she trembled with anticipation.

Greatly daring, she tasted him, enjoying, for the first time, how sensitive her own forked tongue could be. His flavor flamed through her, igniting a fire only he could quench. His sage scent was stronger, more arousing than any male scent had a right to be. No wonder she'd been drawn to him at the Burning Man. This hidden part of her must have sensed his secret.

When he drew away from her, she made a hiss of protest, her only speech as a lizard.

The bears come. His words in her mind, repeating her earlier ones.

She found she could answer mind to mind. *They won't harm a shifter. Stand with me in the tent opening so they can see what you are.*

He hesitated, then flicked a switch. They walked to the flap, he threw it all the way back and they stood together just outside the tent. The four bears charging toward them halted, staring.

She did her best to project her triumph. *You see? There is someone for me, after all.*

The lead bear growled. The one next to him nudged him sharply. He shook her off, but then looked at her, nodded, turned and gestured to the others. All retreated toward the town. When they were out of sight, her lizard man drew her back inside the tent, flicked the switch again and pulled her down with him to the soft rug, curling his tail intimately around hers.

In her years of lonely desperation, she had sometimes fantasized meeting a lover who shifted into a creature like her, but had never been able to quite imagine what male equipment a lizard man might have. Their couplings in their unshifted bodies had been in the dark and he'd kept her so bemused with his lovemaking that she hadn't thought to touch him. But now the lantern remained lit, and she drew in her breath at his potent male beauty.

May I suppose you like what you see? His words danced in her mind, showing his amusement.

Finding herself bolder in her lizard state, she shifted her gaze to his golden eyes and managed to wink at him.

If I could, I wouldn't change a single scale on your lovely body. His thought melted her heart. It was beyond belief that she'd found a lover who'd accept her altered form, much less thought it beautiful.

His clawed fingers stroked her scales as his tongue caressed her face. With a quick dart of her tongue, she touched his, the contact sending an urgent message of need along her nerves. She'd never felt so consumed with wanting. Yet when she reached for what she wanted, he moved so she couldn't touch that part of him. His tongue, tasting her all the way down, found her readiness and explored inside. Since she could neither moan nor cry out, she made do with tiny, gasping hisses.

Now, she projected. *Now, now, now!*

She was cresting when he entered her, driven up farther by his hot thrusting. When the explosion came it was beyond anything she'd so far experienced with her human body. He was not through, and he took her up again into a second burst of pleasure so acute she very nearly passed out.

Afterwards, laying next to him, tails still linked, she slipped into a deep sleep.

Before morning he made love to her again, dazzling her anew. She was once again drowsing when he told her, *Tomorrow night the desert is ours. We will hunt together.*

She carried a picture of them, shifted, skimming the desert together under the moon, into her dreams. But the dreams disturbed her, rousing her as dawn slithered across the sky. Never before had she hunted as a lizard. Or as a human, for that matter. She'd heard the howls during full-moon nights of those who changed into wolves and knew they hunted, but it had never occurred to her that lizards hunted too.

With the moon down she was her human self again. Curtis must be, too. She turned to look at him. Sometime during the night he'd shut off the lantern, but the tent was light enough to show her she was wrong. He was asleep, still a lizard. Maybe it took him longer to shift back. Or maybe he had to wake up first. Though her human eyes did find his scaled form beautiful, would she want to make love with him as they both were now? She in human form, him in lizard? Could they, even? Uneasy at the thought, she inched away from him and rose.

As quietly as she could, she gathered her clothes but, as she started to dress, she paused. Although it shouldn't make any difference if Curtis woke before he shifted back, somehow she didn't want him to watch her dress while he was in his lizard form. So she ducked into the curtained-off section of the tent to pull on her clothes. Not much light penetrated behind the curtain and, in the dimness, she didn't at first pay attention to what hung suspended from a rod. But as she raised her head from buckling her belt, she started, thinking she'd come face to face with Curtis. He must have changed back. Almost instantly she saw she was wrong.

Zenna stared at the--the--what was it? A naked replica? She reached out her hand to touch it, shuddered and drew back. What she saw was like the outer shell of Curtis, even down to the male organs. She retreated further, trying to make sense of what she looked at, apprehension darkening her mind.

She didn't want to know, didn't want to be here. Emerging from behind the tent flap, she glanced at the rug and saw Curtis stirring, but not really Curtis. What purported to be Curtis was hanging up behind the curtain. Not human, the creature rising from the rug. He really did have a tail. Was that why the cape--to conceal his tail or the lump it would make in the human body disguise?

Zenna ran for the tent opening. He flung himself toward her, not touching her. A glance showed her he was reaching for a switch. What for? Whatever the purpose, she was free, running from the tent, from the helicopter, from the lizard man.

At home, she locked herself in and sank down on the couch, too out of breath to even cry. The tears didn't come until she heard the clack, clack of helicopter blades that told her he was leaving Loveland. Leaving her. As she sobbed, she tried to tell herself it was good riddance. The thought only made her cry harder.

* * * *

Olga didn't visit for four days, not until the moon was well past full. "Why did that guy named Curtis leave?" she asked. "I saw with my own eyes that he'd shifted into a lizard, just like you--a one in a million chance. Didn't he like you? Or you him?"

Zenna couldn't tell her the truth, couldn't bring herself to betray the alien. For that's what he must be, no matter what the odds against it. "He was through with his research here. It was time for him to move on."

"And he just left you like that?"

Zenna shrugged.

"Bri's upset about the guy taking off before he could talk to him," Olga said. "How much did you tell him? Does he know enough not to talk about Loveland to anyone?"

"I didn't tell him anything."

"Well, he saw us as bears, and he must know there aren't any in this part of Nevada."

"He's not from here. How could he know?" As she said the words, Zenna controlled a shiver. Where *was* he from if not from Earth?

Olga shook her head, frowning. "Bri's gonna come to see you. You shouldn't've let the guy know about you. I bet he fucked you when you were both that way, didn't he? Shifting makes for horny."

Zenna knew Olga could see her flush so she didn't deny it. Nor did she confirm it.

"Be that way then," Olga huffed. "I thought maybe you'd want to share, since God knows that probably was your first fuck."

"There's no reason for Bri to talk to me," Zenna said. "I can't tell him any more than I've told you."

"Can't--or won't?" With that parting shot Olga flounced off.

Brian came by that evening and got right to the point. "You let that guy go off without giving me a chance to talk to him, see if he meant to keep his mouth shut."

"I doubt he'll ever say anything to anyone," Zenna snapped. Why would he when he had more to hide than Loveland did? But she wasn't going to tell Brian why that was.

"Yeah, but you don't know. So here's how I see it. You got us into this, you're gonna get us out."

Zenna stared at him. "What can I do? I don't have a clue where he is."

"He's been going around talking to Paiutes. Chances are he's still somewhere in Nevada. You get on your old man's bike and go look for him. We don't want you back here till you find him--and kill him."

She couldn't believe what she'd heard. "*Kill* him? What kind of--?"

"We came for him that night, came to get rid of him. It's your fault we didn't. "Shouldn't've turned back. But Olga's always felt sorry for you, and there you were with another lizard at last. She'd've given me hell if we'd rushed him then. So the blame lies with you and you got to be the cure. Either way you're gonna leave town. You can go after the bastard and kill him or never come back to Loveland."

"But how can I?"

Brian shrugged his massive shoulders. "Easy. You just take that bone-handled hunting knife that belonged to your pa, get on his bike and go looking."

"I won't survive outside of Loveland."

"Hey, tough shit. Your ma did. I give you two days to settle up any affairs you got pending. If you're not gone on the third day, you'll get an escort out of town."

After he left, Zenna slumped on her bed, head in her hands. If by some fluke she found the lizard man, how could she possibly kill him? Even if he was an alien?

By morning, she realized she had no choice but to leave. After she paid all her bills, put in her resignation from the library, telling the trainee it was all hers now, stopped her mail and drew money from the bank. She packed, using her father's old duffel bag. She weighed the bone-handled knife in her hands for long minutes before sliding it back into its sheath and threading the leather sheath onto her belt. Would she try to kill the lizard man? Hadn't he lied to her by omission? Lured her into believing he was a shifter like she was? Made love--no, Olga's word was the right one--fucked her under false pretenses? She had every right to hate him.

She gassed up the Harley, dropped the key to her house off with Olga, and roared out of Loveland.

* * * *

Zith circled the copter over Nevada's Lake Mead. Southern Nevada was nothing like the northern part. Here the barren desert suddenly blossomed into Las Vegas, the fun destination for this country. Vegas had its own myths, but they were come-lately ones, not those rooted in the past. It was time for him to go on to California and research native legends there before heading for the northwest. Somehow, though, his heart was no longer in his work.

No one in Vegas had found him the least unusual. Unlike the northern part of the state. Before he'd left Pyramid Lake, he'd felt Sleeping Fox sensed something strange about him, but he didn't believe the old man could possibly suspect the truth. He liked the old shaman and felt it was reciprocated.

But someone in Nevada did suspect what he was. Zenna had left her scent behind the curtain, so he knew she'd discovered his disguise. He also knew, given the secret Loveland concealed, that she'd never tell anyone about what she'd seen. If he'd roused a few minutes earlier, he could have tried to explain, but as it was, he'd barely had time to shut off the protection that might have killed her as she rushed from the tent. After that, his only choice was to leave.

So here he was, finished with what Nevada had to offer, yet wasting time circling Lake Mead. There was no excuse to go back to where Sleeping Fox lived. The rez the shaman called it, short for reservation. Zith knew, from his research, how badly the indigenous peoples of the Americas had been treated by the later comers. Yet Sleeping Fox bore no hatred. Like Zith's own people, he'd learned that hatred sickened the heart and soured the soul. Which didn't mean the shaman accepted the wrongs. He continued to fight for Indian rights.

Though he enjoyed the old shaman's company, Zith knew full well his urge to revisit Sleeping Fox had nothing to do with that. He was hanging around Nevada because of Zenna. She was the hidden truth behind his reluctance to go to California. Time to remember why he'd been sent on this mission.

He pulled the copter out of the circling pattern and pointed it toward California's Central Valley and Sees Far, the Miwok medicine man Sleeping Fox had arranged for him to meet.

* * * *

Having gotten a late start, Zenna knew she wouldn't reach Pyramid Lake, where she believed Sleeping Fox lived, until after dark. He was her only possible contact for Curtis. She winced as she thought the name. Curtis. Another lie, she was sure. No alien would be called Curtis. She hoped Sleeping Fox might know where he was or where he'd been heading next, but she might not be able to find the old man if she arrived too late at night. The map had showed her how to get there, but she didn't know the area. Didn't even know if the shaman lived on the reservation. Maybe she should find a motel along the way. Not that there were any on this sparsely populated route.

The map told her Reno was only about ten miles from the lake, and she'd never been there. Even though her journey wasn't for the bright lights of casinos, wasn't for any kind of pleasure, Reno was a city with many places to stay. Zenna smiled grimly. Since everything about this trip was a real gamble, maybe Reno was the appropriate place to hole up for the night. Why not?

Could she carry out Brian's order? She'd have to if she wanted to go back to Loveland. How could she survive away from there without revealing her secret sooner or later? She touched the bone handle of her father's sharp hunting knife and shuddered, then swerved sharply to miss a mule deer that leaped onto the road in front of her. As she wrestled the machine under control again, a scene from Snow White's story popped into her head: The evil queen commanding her huntsman to kill Snow White and bring the girl's heart to her. The huntsman who had, rather than harm the girl, killed and cut out the heart of a deer to bring back to the evil queen.

Zenna sighed. Anything like that was beyond her.

Did Curtis deserve to die? He *had* betrayed her.

She was too tired to think any more about what she might have to do. She badly needed a night's sleep. From far away came the faint cry of a coyote. A loner, as she was. But then another coyote answered. Lonesome as the cries sounded, the animals could find each other. While she, if she found her someone, her reason would be to kill him. But not tonight. Making a decision, she turned off onto a road that would lead her to Reno.

She chose a motel in the very heart of the city. An old one with reasonable prices. She fell into bed, seeing the flashing neon lights of a nearby casino through a gap where the window drapes didn't quit meet. Red, then green, then yellow, the changing colors adding to the unreality of where she was and why.

Exhausted, Zenna slept.

They ran together in a desert, one unlike any she'd ever seen, a desert with sands of gold. Like the eyes of the man beside her. Who wasn't a man, but a lizard. As she was. They raced the moon, tasting the wind, hunting together for whatever exotic prey flourished here, linked mind to mind.

He wanted her, she knew. Wanted her more urgently than any prey, wanted her here and now on this golden sand. The knowledge flooded her with need for him, need hot as the desert sands under the fiery sun of day. He caught her need, tangled it with his, and slowed, reaching out for her, bringing them both to a halt.

Overhead the moon's rays, golden as the sand, fell around them in a curtain of erotic light, heightening their mutual desire. He flicked his forked tongue over her thin lips, inviting her to open, to let him in. She let her tongue play with his, inviting him deeper and deeper inside. When he linked his tail with her, sweeping her off her feet, they fell together, deliciously tangled like their tongues.

Having no clothes to impede intimacy, they explored each other, stroking, probing, finding and caressing the zing spots on each other's bodies. How strong he was, all male, potent and beautiful, his scales glimmering in the moonlight. Without words he told her she was lovelier than the moon, shining brighter than any star.

He was her beloved, she was his. The world was theirs. No one could ever separate them; their karmas were linked for eternity.

His rising passion matched her. Soon they'd be joined in the vibrant intimacy of love....

A growl, low and menacing, startled them both from their erotic daze. Looking up, she saw dark beasts surrounding them. Bears. One reached a paw toward her, offering her--what? She shrank away, but the bear thrust the object into her hand, moonlight glinting on steel. A knife.

Horror flooded her mind as she understood what the knife was for.

"No!" she screamed and tried to toss away the knife. But it clung to her clawed fingers and the bear grasped her arm in his strong paws, forcing the blade of the knife toward her lover....

Zenna woke gasping, soaked with perspiration, heart hammering in her chest. She sat up and switched on the lamp next to the bed. The bear was gone, the knife was gone, the desert was gone. *He* was gone. Nothing looked familiar. Where was she?

Reno. A motel. The red numbers on the bedside clock told her it was early morning. She thrust the shards of the dream away from her. Time to get moving. As she showered, her stomach reminded her she hadn't eaten since yesterday noon. Okay, breakfast, then she'd be off.

All casinos served food, she knew, so, leaving her knife behind in her room, she walked to the one next to the motel. Inside, she wrinkled her nose at the stench of old tobacco smoke and ignored the noisy slot machines as she passed them, all demanding that she notice them and dig into her wallet. Even at this early hour a few people sat crouched over the slots. Something on the floor caught her eye. A quarter. She bent and picked it up, glancing around to see who it might belong to. No one was near by.

Zenna shrugged. It wasn't her quarter so she had nothing to lose. She fed it into the closest quarter machine, hardly watching what came up, preparing to go on to the cafe. She jumped when a loud bell rang and a red light on the top of the machine began flashing. Jackpot.

"Hey, lady, guess this is your lucky day," the cashier told her as she counted out three hundred in bills.

Sure it was.

* * * *

Sees Far looked to be as old as the giant sequoias on the hill above them, Zith thought as he hunkered down next to the Miwok.

"You watch the big trees," the shaman said. "What do they tell you?"

"They have seen more time pass than I can ever hope to."

Sees Far waved that away. "What is time? One of your own people--" He paused and gazed long at Zith. "Or maybe not yours," he said. "A man not of my people told all who listened that time was not locked up in clocks. We knew this already."

What was it with these shamans? Zith wondered. Here was another who suspected he was not what he seemed to be.

"The sequoias tell me I can never be like them," he said.

Sees Far nodded. "And yet I am like them. What I am made of, what is now called DNA, differs only slightly from theirs."

Caught out, Zith looked directly into the old man's dark eyes.

"Enough talk about such things," Sees Far told him. "Or about anything more. You say you come here to learn about my people. You may think you speak truth, yet your spirit isn't with you. It seeks someone other than me."

Shocked by his words, Zith had no answer.

"A wise man is guided by what his spirit seeks," the shaman added. "We will talk when you return." Without another word, he rose and walked toward his cabin without looking back.

The old man had seen far into him, no denying that. Zith got to his feet, well aware of who his spirit sought. A who he couldn't have. He was getting into his helicopter when his cell phone rang.

"I have dreamed, " Sleeping Fox told him. "You must come to Pyramid Lake."

* * * *

Zith set the copter down on a flat area near the lake, got out and set the guards. He hadn't told Sleeping Fox he was coming back, yet he wasn't surprised to see the old man standing on the nearby road beside his car.

"It is good you are here," the shaman said as Zith approached.

"What about your dream?"

"She comes soon."

Zith's heart leaped in his chest.

"With a knife," the old man added.

* * * *

Sunshine warmed the high desert as Zenna carried her packed belongings out to the Harley, parked beside her Reno motel. As she stowed them, she saw with dismay the back tire was low. Damn. It'd been getting close to threadbare. She should have gotten a new one long ago. Now she'd have to.

At the dealer's, Barry, the guy she talked to about the tire, tried to flirt with her--the last thing she was interested in doing. She left her bike in his care and walked outside to get away. Strolling along the shining row of new hogs, she pretended to be looking at them while her mind persisted in replaying last night's dream. She could almost feel their tails linked together as the claws on his hands rasped erotically over her scales. Stopping, she stroked the leather seat of one of the bikes, her eyes closing as she tried to imagine it was his skin she caressed....

"Fell in love with that one, have you?" Barry's voice jerked her back to reality. "Don't blame you, it's top of the line. My favorite."

"I prefer the one I have." She moved off.

He followed. "Might be a tad much for you to handle, at that." His smirk suggested that he'd like her to give a try at handling him.

"Shove off," she muttered.

"Come on, babe." He reached a hand toward her.

Even though the day was now too warm for a jacket, Zenna had kept hers on because it concealed the knife tucked in the sheath on her belt. She stepped back and eased the jacket open just enough so the sheathed knife was visible. "Don't mess with me, sucker." As she spoke, she fondled the knife handle.

He backed off. "No need to get nasty. Just trying to keep the customers happy."

She jerked her hand away from the knife as she watched him retreat inside. Touching it had made her remember the nightmare end of the dream.

The knife in her hand. The bear forcing the blade toward.... No! She wasn't going there.

By the time her bike was ready and she'd gassed up, it was afternoon. Zenna wasted more time by stopping at a sub shop to eat. As she was finishing the sandwich, she realized that she was afraid to start off for Pyramid Lake, afraid of finding the man she was looking for. Because she'd have to kill him.

Even her subconscious failed her, letting her choose the wrong road at first, so that she had to backtrack. By the time she saw the strange formations of Pyramid Lake thrusting up from the water, evening was wrapping its dusky cloak over Nevada. The darkening water gleamed in her headlight as she pulled up her bike and stopped at the side of the road. Though she'd seen pictures of the lake, nothing had prepared her for how eerie it looked in the fading light, this body of water set in the middle of nothing but rocks and dirt. There wasn't a tree or bush visible anywhere. Or a building. She was alone. There wasn't even any traffic on the road. Not surprising since it wasn't a major highway.

Here she was. All she had to do now was find Sleeping Fox. Yet she remained where she was, staring at the lake. After she found the shaman, what? Would he lead her to the man she had to kill?

How could she kill anyone? Even if he wasn't human. But she had to. She owed it to--who did she owe it to? Those of Loveland, so the secret could be kept? The inhabitants of earth so they wouldn't be taken advantage of by an alien? But was he harming humans? To herself because he'd deceived her?

She stood waiting for an answer, expecting to hear the lonesome wail of a coyote, if nothing else. No coyote sang. Maybe none were lonesome tonight, but she'd never felt more alone.

"Lonesome," she whispered, knowing she always would be.

Words infiltrated her mind. *Two are never lonesome.*

Zenna froze for a long moment, before looking around. He stood no more than a few feet in back of her, a dark form in the night, but she could tell he was in his human disguise. How dare he invade her mind? Anger driving her, she dropped her hand to the bone handle of the knife.

"Curtis, or whoever you are, I--"

"My name is Zith," he said aloud.

"Alien!" she accused.

"Am I so much more alien to humans than those who inhabit Loveland?"

Taken aback for moment she asked herself, *Was he?*

At least, though, part of her was human. Firming her resolve, she tightened her grip on the knife handle.

"If you use that knife," he said, "you'll miss my company."

"I have to kill you." She'd meant to make it a stern announcement, but to her dismay, her voice wobbled.

"You don't want to, do you?"

Her throat clogged, she forced the words out. "I have to." She freed the knife from the sheath.

Unmoving, he held out his arms to her, offering her a choice. She could lunge and ram the blade into his chest, or she could--what? Find herself wrapped in the arms of an alien who really was a lizard man?

Zenna took one step toward him, two, the knife clutched in her hand.

"Alien or not," he told her, "my heart's in the usual place."

Three steps, close enough to kill him, yet he made no move to stop her.

"Zenna," he murmured, accenting the Z. No one else had ever said her name in just that way. No one else had ever really wanted her.

She burst into sobs, dropped the knife and felt his arms close around her, breathing in his familiar sage scent. She'd chosen.

But, later, after she'd given him a ride on her Harley back to where his tent was set up next to the helicopter, inside the tent she watched with apprehension while he removed the human disguise, absently noting she'd been right about the cape. Once again the lizard man, the alien, stood before her.

His words filled her mind. *This is Zith. This is the way I am.*

She knew what he was asking. Could she accept him for what he was even when the moon wasn't full and she wasn't shifted into her own lizard form?

"I don't know." She spoke the words aloud. The truth, plain and simple.

Shall we try?

Did he mean--sex? Now? With him a lizard and her human? Zenna stared at his shining scales, then into his golden eyes.

I would never harm you.

She believed him. Besides, her curiosity was rapidly erasing apprehension. How would it feel?

Making a decision, she shrugged off her biker jacket, then pulled her T-shirt over her head. Boots, jeans, bra and bikinis discarded, she stood before him naked.

He reached a clawed hand to her and she laid her soft human hand into it. Slowly, carefully, he eased her down onto the rug, his tail wrapping around one of her legs. It felt almost as good as if she had a tail. The sensation of his scales against her skin was so exquisitely arousing that she relaxed completely, moisture gathering inside her.

His forked tongue began tasting her lips, her breasts, all along her skin. By the time he reached her thighs, she was gasping with pleasure. And then his tongue entered her, tasting, caressing, touching all the sensitive spots. She moaned and writhed, more than ready, so ready she was on the verge. She reached to touch him and held his magnificent maleness in her hand, wanting to feel it inside her, driving her over the top.

When he entered her, she cried out with the intensity of her climax, which continued without diminishing until he, too, had reached the peak.

One surprise after another when she joined with Zith, each more thrilling than any fantasy.

Holding her close, he asked, *Will you come with me? Will you be my partner on my long journey to many worlds?*

She blinked. Other worlds?

Before she could answer, he added, *I never believed it was possible to love a human female, but I do love you, my Zenna.*

"Don't forget I'm not always human," she murmured.

That, too. When at last we return to my home world I will be envied for having found such a marvel to love.

Zenna tensed. "I'll be as much of a freak on your world as I am here."

Never. My kind accept many different peoples, for we have been space travelers for longer than your human species have existed. You belong with me, I belong with you, so all will wish us joy.

"Oh, Zith, I do love you. I'll go with you anywhere, any time." Then something occurred to her. "We can't ever have children, though."

Who can tell? Now that I know you aren't a typical human, it might, after all, be possible. One of my kind has never mated with a human who can shift into lizard form.

"Good heavens, what would they be like?"

He made a sound she recognized as the way he chuckled. *Does it matter?*

On earth it might, but not where they'd be going. The future would be strange, but as long as she was with Zith, nothing else mattered. Zenna smiled and stroked her hand along him. Her life from now on was going to be far more exciting that she ever could have imagined.

"And all because I went to The Burning Man hoping to get laid."

Another chuckle. *Then ran off before I could get to that.*

"How did you know I'd be at Pyramid Lake tonight?"

Sleeping Fox had one of his true dreams, right down to the knife. The only thing he didn't foresee was what would happen once you arrived.

"You took a chance."

I left my spirit with you. What good is life without one's spirit?

He twined his tail around one of her legs again, and she sighed with pleasure. *We'll try it again to make sure.*

"Sure of what?"

To make sure we really do fit like this. She sensed the amusement in his words.

"Excuses, excuses." How free she felt with Zith. Free to be herself, to accept what she was, as she accepted him for what he was. Freed, at last, from the Loveland curse, that made her not only different from most humans, but even from those who had to live in Loveland.

Free to be happy, to love and be loved in whatever form she happened to be.

The cashier in the casino had been right. This *was* her lucky day. She'd truly hit the jackpot when she found Zith again.

The End

Printed in the United States
41317LVS00002B/295-366

9 781586 086718